# CHASING YOU

## VANIA RHEAULT

BOOKS BY VANIA RHEAULT

*On the Corner of 1700 Hamilton*

*Summer Secrets Novellas 1-3*
*Summer Secrets Novellas 4-6*

*Don't Run Away*
*Chasing You*
*Running Scared*

*Wherever He Goes*

*All of Nothing*

*The Years Between Us*

*His Frozen Heart*
*His Frozen Dreams*
*Her Frozen Memories*
*Her Frozen Promises*

*To Drake and Shy*
*I know you like it when I leave you alone to write, but I*
*pretend you miss me. I love you!*

*Chasing You*
Copyright 2017
Published by Coffee & Kisses Press

This is a work of fiction. Names, characters, places, and incidents are the product of the author's imagination or are used fictitiously. Any resemblance to actual persons, living or dead, events, or locales is entirely coincidental.

The author does not take responsibility for any weight-loss or running program advice offered herein. Please consult your primary care physician to begin your own weight-loss journey.

Cover design by Vania Rheault via canva.com
Picture purchased and used with permission from
depositphotos.com
Photo by VitalikRadko| ID: 237447738

Coffee & Kisses Press owned and operated by
Vania Rheault and David Willis
Printed in the United States of America

E-reader ISBN: 978-9977930-9-3
Paperback ISBN: 978-0-9977930-8-6

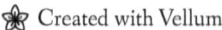 Created with Vellum

## CHAPTER ONE

Don't allow anyone to make you do anything you don't want to do—Alyssa

Sometimes someone other than yourself knows what's best for you—Brett

———

WITH THE TOE of her black high-heeled boot, Alyssa Barnes kicked her black suitcase across the hardwood floor of her loft apartment.

The plastic case skidded across the shiny wood and stopped only when it crashed into the wall painted a delicate eggshell white.

The impact rattled the pictures hanging in the hallway, and one gold frame gave way, falling from its nail to land on the floor, the glass splintering.

Perfect.

She finished the job by slamming her apartment door. She dropped her purse, pulled off her boots, and was about to fling her jacket when a knock on her door interrupted her tantrum.

Not now.

After such a disastrous trip home to Tower City, she needed time and space. What she desperately wanted was a glass of wine, her emergency stash of chocolate, and a hot bath.

She ignored it. No one knew she was home. Well, no one but Nikki, and she was the one who'd picked up Alyssa from the airport.

Brushing away slivers of glass, careful not to cut her fingertips with the shards, she studied the picture. In the photo, she was standing with Nikki in the corridor of the hotel where their friend Kayla had held her wedding reception. Nikki looked strained and sad, and Alyssa, well, she looked tired and . . . fat.

She was happy Nikki had gotten her own problems straightened out and was on her way to her own happily ever after.

She wasn't so lucky.

Grimacing, she pulled at the waist of her jeans, hating the feel of them cutting into her skin. So maybe she gained a little weight on her trip. Book tours and seminars were stressful, and the food was never in short supply. What was she going to do, turn down chocolate cake?

Yeah, right.

As she hung the picture on the nail, she noted to herself to buy a new frame. She let the suitcase remain where it lay and shuffled into the kitchen to begin phase one and two of her recovery.

The knocking came back.

Whoever was at the door was *not* going to give up.

Alyssa sighed. She wasn't going to get any peace until she sent whoever it was on their way.

Just as she was about to open the door, someone pushed it open, striking her on the forehead.

"Holy shit." She slapped her hand to her temple and doubled over in pain.

"Fuck. I am so sorry."

Alyssa's gaze jerked up at the sound of his voice, and the rage mixed with disbelief made her forget the sharp throb racing through her skull. "Get the hell out of here," she said, narrowing her eyes at her visitor.

"Aw, don't be like that." He stepped into the hallway of the loft, already looking around her living space.

*Her* living space. The space she had not permitted a man to enter.

Ever.

"Get the hell out of here," she repeated, stepping in front of him, forcing him to stop.

"Nice place you got here." He dodged around her and wandered into the living room, taking in the gleaming wood floor and the white vaulted ceiling. "What's up there?" he asked, his gaze traveling up a wooden staircase, a white handrail attached to the wall.

"My office." She followed him as he strolled, his hands shoved into the pockets of his jacket, keys jangling.

The man's size didn't intimidate her, and she glared at him when he turned his cool hazel eyes to her.

His blond hair shone in the light streaming through her balcony doors, the late afternoon sun creating a halo around his head. He was no angel, and she wished he would leave her alone and go back to hell where he came from.

She shook him off and headed to the kitchen to proceed with her plan. It didn't matter if he was the only male she'd ever let inside her apartment. She wasn't going to do anything with him.

There would be no intimate embraces, no soft kisses.

He wouldn't sleep in her bed, leaving his scent on her pillow.

She wouldn't be forced to remember him in her kitchen drinking morning-after coffee because there wouldn't be a night before.

She was done with men. Done being hurt, being humiliated. No one wanted her, and she was perfectly fine with that. Experience taught her she would rather be alone than abandoned.

Turning her back on her unwanted and ill-timed guest, she started her search.

She didn't cook; she didn't count microwaving meals and making sandwiches.

Nikki cooked, and Alyssa always enjoyed eating with her, but those meals were fewer and more far between now that Nikki was engaged. Her eyes slid to the man still milling about her living room fingering her knickknacks and book collection.

Alyssa shot down a twinge of empathy and sympathy. She remembered what he'd told her, remembered how she felt when the barb had dug underneath her skin. The thorny insult may very well still be there.

She pressed her fingers against her forehead, where a lump was forming.

Great.

Groaning, she grabbed an unopened bottle of wine and a wine glass. She easily broke the seal of the cheap pink champagne she favored and twisted off the cap. After pouring and draining a glass, she dug into the cabinets for her stash of truffles and hummed in happiness when she found a full package.

The man in her living room turned from the partial view of the park he could see through her balcony doors. "How's your head? I didn't mean . . ."

Alyssa chugged more of the champagne. "This will go a long way".

She took a swipe at her aching forehead before stuffing a melting truffle into her mouth.

"What the fuck are you doing here, anyway?"

She wanted to move on to phase three of her plan: a long hot bath. Flying made her feel filthy, and she needed to wash the travel smell out of her hair, the dirt from her skin.

When an answer wasn't forthcoming, Alyssa looked up from choosing another truffle from the box.

He shuffled his feet, his running shoes making the floorboards creak. His warm up pants matched his t-shirt which matched his warmup jacket. They all bore the logo of the Tower City Marathon.

Her gaze reached his face, and she pushed down the feeling of sadness for the man standing in her loft.

"I see you've gained a little more weight," he said instead of answering her question.

The words washed over her, freezing her to the bone.

She knew what she was, goddammit.

Alyssa's throat burned, and she swallowed the acrid taste the sweet champagne had turned on her tongue.

"Get out. Get out, right now."

Her chin trembled, and she clutched her wine glass.

He took a step forward. "I'm sorry. That's not how I meant it."

This was too much.

"Just go. Go, and don't come back." Alyssa pressed the back of her hand to her lips.

His shoulders sagged.

To make sure he left, she followed him to the door. She drained her glass as he looked back at her.

"I'm sorry."

The last swallow of champagne hit her head and loosened her tongue. "Fuck off."

He let himself into the hallway, closing the door with a soft click.

Alyssa paused for a moment.

She flung her goblet at the place he'd been just moments ago and smiled grimly as the delicate stemware broke into a million pieces.

Glass everywhere.

Shattered.

Like her heart.

---

"So how did that go?"

"Fuck off," Brett Sommers growled. He flopped into the chair behind his desk and ignored Dane Montgomery's knowing smirk.

"What happened?"

Brett shook his head in disgust. He was so goddamned stupid. What did he think he was going to accomplish waltzing into Alyssa's loft apartment and insulting her?

He didn't know what it was about her that brought out his beast, but it seemed the twice he'd seen her he couldn't keep the contempt from pouring out. "I slammed her head with her front door and then called her fat."

Dane scowled. "Nicely done. You treated her like crap

at Thanksgiving dinner, too. Why do you want her to help you write a book if you can't stand being around her?"

Exhausted, Brett ground the heels of his hands into his eyes.

Dane was right. Yet, even with the way he felt about her, he couldn't help but think Alyssa would be the perfect person to help him. If he could stop treating her like shit.

"I just think she would be an excellent case study for the book. And since she'd be writing most of it, her experience would be authentic."

"Even if you could stop trashing her, Alyssa hates running. She would never do it. And I know for damn sure she won't do it with you if she won't do it with Nikki. Give it up, you're wasting your time. The marathon is only two months away. Forget about it until it's over."

Brett scoffed. "It's never over. You know that. It's one right after the next. Now we have that goddamn women's run that's Nikki's baby, and I'd never have let her do it if I would have realized what a time suck it would be."

"You knew." Dane laughed. "Besides, wait until October when it actually comes about. It was a great idea to use this race to advertise it and grow anticipation. The flyers Nikki helped make up to stuff into the swag bags for the race are, in her words, cute and adorable. I think the women's race will be a big hit, and Nikki is going to personally man the booth at the expo to talk it up."

Brett waved a hand. He didn't care. He was tired and cranky, and going home to an empty studio apartment knowing Dane was going to his fiancée's place for a hot meal and hot sex didn't make him feel any better.

Never mind Dane worked his ass off to get where he was. He'd been fortunate hiring Nikki to manage his running shoe store, but luck only went so far. He also put in a lot of time and effort to fix mistakes he'd made in the beginning of their relationship.

Brett didn't have it in him to do that.

He used his women for sex and spit them out like pieces of gum that had lost their flavor.

Maybe that was the problem.

Maybe it'd been too long since he'd gotten laid, and he needed a little to take the edge off. But the thought of a face-less woman didn't hold any appeal, and he stood, too defeated to spend any more time at the marathon office.

"What about the race?" Dane asked surprised when he palmed his car keys.

"It's what I have you for."

"Well, what the fuck is this? Musical chairs? I hire Nikki to run my store, I take your place here to keep the race going while you do what? Go home and jack off?"

Brett heaved a sigh. "You know I appreciate what you're doing."

Dane zeroed in on Brett's face. "You alright?"

"Let's not do the pansy-assed, share our feelings crap, okay? I know you like your therapist, but not everyone needs counseling."

Brett pursed his lips. It wasn't like him to be cruel, even inadvertently. Yet he had, to both Alyssa and Dane. In one day.

Fuck.

"Alright," Dane agreed, hesitantly.

"I just need to go," Brett mumbled, and he took off before Dane could say anything else.

———

BRETT OPENED THE door to his little apartment.

The building was in serious need of repair, his studio falling apart, but the owner and landlord apparently weren't concerned, never having done any kind of restoration.

The little room had been his life since his parents kicked him out the minute he graduated high school.

He hadn't bothered to move anywhere else. He didn't care he didn't have a bedroom; he didn't care rent was the cheapest in Tower City because a train that ran right outside his bedroom window blew its whistle faithfully every morning at four. He didn't care he ran out of hot water after a five-minute shower. Why should he? This place wasn't home. He felt about as comfortable here as he had when he lived with his parents.

He spread out on his futon, the thick cushion pushed into a flat pancake long ago, the bars of the frame digging into his shoulder blades.

God, he couldn't believe how he treated Alyssa.

Wearily, he threw an arm over his eyes. He didn't know what the hell his problem was when he was around her, even though she was prickly and had a bad attitude.

He blew out a breath.

Probably because of idiots like him.

Groaning, he pushed away from the futon to grab a beer from his little refrigerator, a small microwave sitting on top of it to save space. He leaned against the sink in his kitchenette and chugged half the bottle.

He didn't feel like eating but didn't have much in the way of food anyway. He stripped to his briefs, and settling on the futon again, pulled an old faded comforter over his body and flipped on the television.

His cell chimed with a text, and Brett opened the message from a woman he sometimes saw when he was in the mood for company, sex, or a decent meal. Deciding he didn't feel like any of those things, he ignored it and dozed in front of ESPN.

---

AFTER A SHITTY night's sleep, Brett showered and dressed in jeans and a white button-down shirt. They were clothes he usually didn't wear, and he was lucky they weren't wrinkled.

He left without making coffee, and his mind protested but he reassured himself he would grab a couple of cappuccinos on the way.

He stopped at a florist's shop just opening for the day and picked out a bouquet of, he didn't know what.

Afterward, he drove through the drive-through of a popular café and ordered two large coffees.

Driving carefully as to not spill the coffee or tip over the flowers that were sitting on the floor of the passenger-side seat, he made his way to Alyssa's apartment across town. It wasn't early, not in any true sense, but it felt early for him, and if Alyssa was a night owl, she may not be awake yet.

He would try anyway because he owed her an apology after the way he'd treated her, and it wasn't the way he wanted to ask for a favor. He wasn't sure why he was bothering now since asking her would produce a loud "fuck you," and he couldn't blame her one bit.

Outside her door, he tucked the vase into the crook of his elbow and held the coffees in their cardboard container. With his free hand, he knocked, and he shifted from foot to foot hoping she wasn't still sleeping.

The door swung open, and Brett stared. Alyssa's green eyes were on fire, her hair was mussed, and she looked as if she had just taken a tumble with some lucky man. He took an uncertain step back, thinking maybe she had.

"What the hell do you want?" Alyssa growled, tightening the sash of her terrycloth robe. "Can't you stay away from me? I really, really wish you would."

Brett thrust the flowers into her hands and stepped inside, ignoring her sputtering. "I brought coffee."

"That doesn't make up for it," she said, holding the clear vase away from her as if it were a bomb about to go off. "What the fuck are these?"

"I think they're flowers. At least, that's what they told me at the florist shop."

Brett tried for cool, for calm.

If he messed this up, he knew for goddamn certain he wouldn't get a third chance. No way in hell would Alyssa let him in again. He was surprised he'd gotten this far, and he could only credit his quickness and her befuddlement with the entire situation.

She followed him into her bright kitchen, comprised of white walls and hardwood floor like the rest of her loft, and he set down the cardboard container of coffees, carefully pulling them from the tight circles. "Here. Good morning."

Alyssa didn't turn when he offered her the to-go cup. She was staring at the flowers she placed on her kitchen counter in front of a silver and black toaster, her hands thrust into the deep pockets of her robe. "You need to go," she murmured.

"Hey. Here. Coffee. I need to talk to you about something."

When she turned, he was taken aback by the tears in her eyes.

"No. I don't want to talk to you. About anything. I'll

accept your flowers for hitting me with the door yesterday, but there's nothing we need to talk about. Please, just go."

Brett studied her face. Her brilliant green eyes were shadowed, her cheeks full and rounded, pink from sleep. Her mouth was pinched, her lips pressed into a thin line.

He waved the coffee cup in front of her and let out a silent sigh of relief when she finally accepted it and took a sip.

"What's this for?" she asked, narrowing her eyes at him.

Brett wandered into the living room and looked out her balcony doors at the Minnesota spring. There were still patches of snow on the ground, the grass a dingy brown.

The trees were budding with new leaves, and a brilliant blue was finally beginning to break up the grey winter sky.

He took a sip of his coffee. How could he ask her so it would make sense, so she wouldn't say no?

"I need a favor."

Barking out a laugh, Alyssa shook her head. "No. Whatever it is, no. There's nothing I can give you anyway, Brett. It's time for you to go. I have things I need to do."

Surprised, Brett almost dropped his coffee. He quickly righted the cup in his hand, but he stared at Alyssa, his mouth open.

She'd said his name. And it sounded so good coming out of her mouth.

"You don't know what the favor is yet."

"I don't care, and quite honestly, there is nothing you can give me in return to convince me to do it. Look," Alyssa continued gently, and Brett cringed. He wasn't going to talk her into it. "We don't get along. You can find someone else to do what you need done. Whatever it is."

Sensing this was his last chance, Brett blurted, "I want you to help me write a book."

"A BOOK?" ALYSSA glowered at him.

Was he out of his fucking mind?

"A book about what?" she asked confused, sinking into a chair at her table.

The sweet scent of the flowers drifted to her.

Alyssa had no idea what they were, some kind of white frothy things that looked expensive.

She tried not to look at them because when Brett thrust them into her hands they'd almost made her cry. No one had given her flowers before, not that she would ever tell Brett that.

"Running."

"You're crazy." Alyssa scoffed. "I write romances. *Romances*. You want to write a running romance?" She lifted her chin. "You were the one who told me I shouldn't be writing them anyway. 'Write what you know' is what you flung at me at Nikki's place. So, I don't know about romance, about falling in love, and I don't know about running. Ask somebody else."

Looking away, she tried not to cry. She knew about falling in love, the heartache. But unlike her characters, she had never gotten a happy ending. She was smart enough to know she never would.

"I was out of line," Brett said, perching on the arm of her stuffed grey sofa. "I tried to apologize."

"I didn't care about your apology then, and I don't care about it now."

She ran her fingers through her tangled hair. She'd had one of her nightmares last night and had woken tired and sick to her stomach. She felt gross, and she looked like shit compared to the crisp white dress shirt and soft faded blue jeans Brett wore.

"I want you to go. I don't want you here."

"Just listen for a second. It would be a manual, a running manual. From a beginner's perspective."

"And you want me to be the beginner?"

"Yeah." His voice was hopeful, eagerness shining in his eyes.

"I don't want to run. I don't want to write a book about running. That sounds like the most goddamn boringest thing to write about in the whole goddamn world."

She took a deep breath. Running. Fuck her. Oh, on second thought, no. She didn't want Brett to see her naked.

"Boringest? Is that a real word?"

"Artistic license," she said deflecting, waving her coffee cup.

Brett sat comfortably on the arm of her sofa like he belonged there. His blond hair glinted in the sun; his hazel eyes held a look that seemed almost . . . friendly?

He had balls, that's for sure.

She studied him as she sipped the cappuccino he'd given her.

Pairing his good looks with the crappy childhood Nikki told her about, well, it didn't take a genius to figure out he was a lady magnet.

Women loved fixer-uppers.

She wrote about men so broken she didn't think they would ever find love, and she was the one who created them.

Brett was hurt and damaged. She would screw herself spending time with him.

Not that she wanted to. She could spell prick as easily as anyone else.

"I don't think it would work," she said, trying to be as kind, but as firm, as possible.

She didn't want to work with him, even if she didn't have anything lined up right now. Her tour was done, her seminars completed. She was on her own for a few months, and it would be blissful.

It would be, dammit. She would make sure of it.

Brett sighed and ran his fingertip around the edge of the white plastic top on his disposable coffee cup. "All right," he finally said and stood.

Alyssa tried to ignore the hurt look in his eyes and failed miserably. "What do you want to write a book for, anyway?"

Rolling his shoulders in a stretch that he turned into a shrug, he gave her a wan smile. "I don't know. Boredom maybe. I'll, ah get out of here and leave you alone. I really am sorry."

"Yeah."

Alyssa followed him to the door, gripping the coffee cup.

She was glad he was leaving. She didn't want him to taint her living space any more than he already had. That she could picture him perched on the arm of her sofa was proof damage had already been done.

"I'll see you around," Brett said. "I guess with Nikki and Dane engaged we'll be seeing a lot of each other, parties and whatever the fuck. I really am glad they were able to work it out. Dane's a good guy."

After the door closed, Alyssa stood in the silence of her hallway and surprised herself by thinking, *You are too, Brett, you are too.*

"You're not considering it, are you?"

Squinting into the sunlight, Alyssa looked up at Nikki, thinking not for the first time how different they were and why they were friends.

Nikki Halstead was the quintessential blue-eyed blonde with legs that wouldn't quit.

Alyssa was the roly-poly dark-haired shorty.

They couldn't be any more opposite in appearance, yet they'd been friends since grade school. Their friendship had weathered many a storm. Nikki was her closest friend.

Alyssa took a deep breath of the crisp air. She liked spring. New beginnings and all that.

"No, not really. The thought of running, ick. You know I've never wanted to start. I don't know what would be more painful, running or writing about it. It sounds like it would be a few months of hell, no matter how much you tried to pretty it up."

Nikki laughed. "I know one thing for sure—you can only run if you want to. If you try to force yourself, you'll be miserable."

"What made you start running?" Alyssa asked curiously, tilting her head to catch her friend's eye.

"The solitude, maybe. The quiet. Time to think. The way I felt when I ran, how tired I was when I was done, but it's a good tired, you know? The sense of accomplishment when I could add distance bit by bit. And I like being outside."

"But you could have all that without running," Alyssa pointed out, trying to understand the appeal. "Another sport, maybe? You liked to swim, too."

"You're really considering this."

"No, I'm not. I just don't understand what you like

about it. You and Dane and Brett, you spend so much time . . ."

Bringing up Brett's name made her uncomfortable, and she looked away.

They were walking around a large pond, and ducks swam among the ice chunks that floated on the surface. The wind blew at her hair, the air warmer than it had been in some time, but it was still cold enough to make her shiver through her lilac puffer jacket.

Nikki nudged Alyssa's shoulder. "My running is your writing. The enjoyment, the sense of belonging. You get that with your writer friends, the conferences. I get that with my friends, the expos, Dane's store. We all want to belong, Lyss."

"Yeah."

"Is something wrong?"

Alyssa heard the concern in her friend's voice, but there wasn't anything she could tell Nikki about how she felt. There wasn't anything wrong. Things were the same as they always were.

Not right.

"No. You know I always get like this between projects. I want to take a break, yet I feel like shit when I'm not writing."

"You need a hobby. Or a man. Or both. Something to occupy your time."

"Well, it won't be running."

Alyssa was sure about that.

———

ALYSSA PUTTERED AROUND her office, straightening paper

clips, index cards, dusting her computer, and filing old notes.

She'd never felt so lost between projects before.

No deadline loomed; there were no writing seminars to plan.

Sure, she could write a book whenever she felt like it, hammer it out and turn it in, but threads of new plots slipped through her fingers, her mind unwilling to create new characters.

Today her thoughts were muzzy even with the brilliant spring sun illuminating dust motes drifting lazily through the air, and she felt lethargic even though she believed she had gotten a good night's rest.

She automatically reached for a chocolate bar to lift her mood, but pulled her hand away, biting her bottom lip. Yes, the chocolate would pick her up, but the sugar crash would drop her just as low.

The waistband of her jeans dug into her belly, the t-shirt she pulled on this morning strained over her breasts.

She needed to think about something other than food, and she woke up her desktop and typed in the address for the Tower City Marathon into her Google browser.

The website's colors were cheerful and bright, and pictures of happy people running previous races mugging for the camera flashed in a montage in the middle of the screen.

She wondered if Brett built the website himself, or if he hired a web designer. The site looked well put together and professional.

A menu along the top of the home page gave a visitor choices of event registration, expo information, frequently asked questions, contact us, or links to the marathon race sponsors.

After clicking on a link for the race's Facebook page, she looked through the photo album and stopped when she came upon a picture of Brett flanked by two tall brunettes. His arms were around their waists, and he was smiling, something she'd never seen him do. Medals hung from thick red ribbons which they wore proudly around their necks.

Changing her mind about the chocolate, she opened a king-sized Milky Way and reveled in the sweetness as the chocolate and caramel melted in her mouth.

She bet the two brunettes on either side of Brett didn't eat chocolate. They probably drank protein shakes and fancy water after yoga sessions.

After clicking out of the photo album, she scanned the posts. Now that the race was only a couple months away, people were tagging their friends reminding them to register, book hotel rooms, plan rides, and sign up for the after-race activities.

Scanning the event list for the weekend of the marathon, Alyssa couldn't help but be impressed. Brett did a lot of work. She'd heard Nikki talk about it often enough to know that the weekend of events took Brett all year to plan. Then it went around and around again.

Alyssa clicked the back button to the marathon page and clicked on the volunteer link. Pages of volunteer opportunities leaped out at her, everything from manning a water station along a race route to handing out medals to kids at the youth run. She smiled at that. It would be fun to hand out finisher medals to children proudly crossing the finish line.

Her smile faded. Running was not for her. She'd never been interested. It was Nikki's thing, and it had served her well—she'd met her future husband thanks to a hobby she enjoyed.

She took another bite of her candy bar and flattened the gooey bite between her tongue and the roof of her mouth as she considered Brett's motives.

He wanted to write a runner's manual, and he wanted to train her and write about it. She didn't understand why because she knew the marathon took all his time. Even with Dane's help, Nikki said Brett hardly had time to himself.

Maybe she kicked him out too quickly yesterday.

No.

She couldn't forget what a jerk he was. He wasn't nice; he'd only been pretending because he wanted to use her, her writing skills, her connections.

He probably assumed she could help him find a publisher, but he could write the book on his own and shop it around. If it was well-written and contained helpful information, he could easily find a buyer. Putting on a marathon of this size was an achievement, and that gave him credibility in the industry.

He may not act like it, but Brett Sommers was a minor celebrity in town. The city council loved him, the mayor kowtowed to him because of the tourist dollars he brought into Tower City every spring, and local businesses scrambled to sponsor the race for advertisement opportunities.

Alyssa forced herself to open a new Word document and begin a few lines of a new book she'd been loosely plotting. Guiltily, thinking about protein shakes and fancy water, she finished off her candy bar in a sugary mouthful.

---

MARATHON HEADQUARTERS WAS a madhouse.

The shipment of shirts for the half marathon race hadn't come in when they were supposed to. Race t-shirts were part of the swag bag runners received when picking up their bibs at the race expo. Each race was represented with its own t-shirt and decorated with a unique race decal.

Brett was getting nervous, and when the line disconnected, he slammed down the phone. Half an hour on hold with the shirt vendor had yielded zero results.

"I need Nikki to call these people. She has more patience than you and me put together, and I need those shirts."

Brett dry washed his face in frustration. That's what he deserved for trying to save a couple bucks by going with a new vendor.

"She's at the store," Dane said, talking on a phone of his own at a desk near Brett's.

From this side of the conversation, Brett gathered the water vendor was giving Dane a difficult time as well.

The Tower City Marathon gave away thousands of bottles of water. After running a race, the participants drank two, three, even four. The bottles were inexpensive; they were giving Dane the run around on a delivery date.

The variety of protein bars that would be handed out at the end of the races were the only things going his way. The pallets were already sitting downstairs in storage.

The next task on Brett's list was contacting the local grocery store and checking on his order of bananas. He felt like he made the same phone calls over and over again confirming things, but he couldn't leave anything to chance.

Later, he would go by an outdoor athletics store and pick up coupons that would be stuffed into the swag bags.

The race was two months off, but everything Brett could accomplish before then was one less headache the month of the race.

"She can spend the day here tomorrow, right?" Brett asked.

He needed all the help he could get. He was beginning to feel a little desperate, and he felt like shit asking for help as he was the only one earning a wage putting the race together.

"She'll be here," Dane said, still on hold. "She has her own phone calls to make for the women's race—Hey . . ."

Brett turned away when Dane resumed his conversation.

He pressed the heels of his hands over his eyes. Year after year it was the same thing: shirts, water, bars, website issues.

It would never get easier.

Black dots obscured his vision, and he blinked to clear them.

People milled about, some on cell phones completing tasks they were assigned or volunteered to do, or they were laughing, joking, hanging around buzzing from the energy.

Runners were a cheerful bunch, and they stuck together. They were loyal, and if Brett needed something done, in five seconds he would have ten people lined up to do it for him. That didn't feed his ego or give him a sense of entitlement—it made him humble.

He wasn't the only one who wanted Tower City to have the best marathon in the country.

A short woman with black hair walked down the hallway, but a group of runners talking about a race in a nearby city blocked his view. She may be the reporter who was scheduled to interview him for the Tower City Journal.

When the group moved away, discussing where to order lunch, Brett saw it was Alyssa walking toward him.

Dane grunted in surprise, but he was still on the phone and couldn't say hello.

He should have stood, should have greeted her, but he was too stunned to do anything but stare as she approached.

She moved uncomfortably around the runners wearing their sleek gear, and he knew what she was thinking. Slim runners, their health sparkling in their eyes, in their laughter, contrasted with her pallor, her exhaustion, her size.

He could only gape at her as she planted herself in front of his chair, her ill-fitting clothes stretched to their limits, her hair a wild mess. A huge black bag hung from her shoulder; her car keys dangled from her hand.

She growled in the back of her throat, sounding like some pissed off little cat, spitting her fury.

He suppressed a laugh knowing she could inflict the same amount of harm as Nikki's kitten: none.

Her eyes snapped at him, the color rising in her cheeks.

All the laughter he was trying to contain died when she opened her mouth.

"I'll do it."

# CHAPTER TWO

You're not the boss of me—Alyssa

Stop whining—Brett

---

A LYSSA REGRETTED THE words as soon as she spoke. That Brett sat gaping at her, his mouth hanging open like a guppy, didn't make her feel any better.

She pushed her purse strap farther up her shoulder, her skin prickling with embarrassment as his eyes focused on her in disbelief, and she shifted her weight from foot to foot wanting to bolt.

She was about to turn on her heel and leave when Brett finally croaked, "What?"

Glaring, she fisted her keys in her hand. "Forget it."

She turned away. This was a stupid idea, and she should have never come.

"No, wait." Brett stood and grasped her shoulder.

She spun around preparing to let him have it for

touching her, for making fun of her, until she saw the hope in his eyes.

It took the edge off her rage, but she still felt like a stupid fool.

People were staring at them and whispering to each other behind their hands.

Alyssa knew what they saw when they looked at her.

"Really? You'll really do it?"

Her attention jerked back to Brett's face, and she sighed. Because she didn't trust her voice, she nodded.

A huge grin spread across his face, and he squeezed her shoulder.

In her discomfort, she'd forgotten his hand was still resting along the curve of her neck and she pulled away, unaccustomed to a man touching her.

"Why?" Brett asked, letting his hand fall to his side.

She cringed under his gaze, but she owed him the truth. If they were going to do this, work together, run together, they needed to start off on the right footing, so to speak, and she would need to start with honesty. "I don't know for sure. I need a change, I need something different . . ."

She faded, not sure where to go from there. She *was* looking for a change, but she wasn't sure this was the kind of change she should be looking for.

Brett nodded, and then he gestured around the office space. "Has Nikki told you anything about the race?"

She shook her head. Nikki had spoken some about the marathon and the events surrounding it, but Nikki avoided too many details simply because she knew that Alyssa didn't care.

"We have hundreds of volunteers," Brett said, launching into a speech that sounded like something he'd repeated many times before. "And we need them. Marathon weekend starts Thursday morning when the expo opens. We need volunteers to not only put the expo together but to work it as well. It's held in the Tower City Community Center."

The Center was the main venue for any large event Tower City hosted.

Singers held their concerts there, truck pulls, roller derby, Disney on Ice, anything and everything was held at the Center. The fact that the Center was the expo's venue wasn't a surprise, and it told her how large it had grown since the first year Brett had put it together.

He tugged on her hand and led her away from the crowded room.

Dane's eyes bore into her back, and she wondered how long it would take him to call Nikki and tell her that she was there.

She pulled her sweaty hand out of Brett's grasp, but he didn't say anything.

The office was warm, and she hadn't taken off the jacket she'd worn to ward off the early spring chill. Perspiration trickled down her sides. As Brett led her down a quiet hallway, she took one last look over her shoulder.

People were standing around, talking on their phones. Two women were seated on a beat-up love seat comparing their toes, for what reason Alyssa had no idea.

A group of women stood off in the corner drinking coffee and laughing. She saw why Nikki would enjoy coming here, laughing with friends, being involved. It was that type of place, and Nikki was that type of person. Her friend probably knew everyone here.

The camaraderie made Alyssa uncomfortable. People wanting to talk to her, in general, made her want to hide. She was a writer, a loner. She didn't want to be there, and when the laughter died behind them she blew out a breath in relief.

"These are some smaller offices that came with the rental space," Brett said, jerking a thumb at an opened office door. "I'll use one if I have to make an important call, but otherwise I'm out in the main area."

Alyssa shot him a look of surprise, and she was chastised when his cheerful expression turned stony.

"What? You think I'm not a team player? That I'm some asshole bossing people around? Look, it *does* take a lot of people to put on this goddamn thing. The expo runs Thursday all day, and after the expo closes for the day, we have the youth run. Over five hundred kids ran last year. *Five hundred* squealing kids."

Alyssa let a small smile slide across her lips when he shuddered.

"The expo runs all day Friday too, and during that time we hold a speaker series. These speakers are set up sometimes years in advance. Elite runners can be booked solid because of other speaking engagements and races they've committed to, not to mention their training schedules.

"Friday night is the 5k fun run/walk and that starts at seven o'clock. Then Saturday morning bright and early the full marathon starts at seven-thirty, the half at eight, and the 10k at eight-thirty. We need volunteers every step of the way. Jesus Christ, I need volunteers to keep track of the volunteers. This race is getting insane."

She nodded, understanding a little bit of what he was saying only because she'd skimmed the website earlier in the day.

Volunteers to herd volunteers. She could believe that.

"What's Dane helping with?"

She stuck her head into a couple of the smaller offices.

One had been converted into something of a break room, and a coffeemaker sat on an empty counter near a sink, a family-sized canister of Folgers pushed against the wall.

Mismatched mugs, some decorated with the Tower City Marathon logo, littered the counter, and two lined with old coffee rings sat in the sink, waiting to be washed.

He waited until she finished looking around to answer.

"He's on the phone with the water distributor. Sometimes there're glitches, and it takes a hell of a lot of patience to clear things up. I need Nikki to call my shirt supplier. The shirts for the half marathon haven't come in yet, and I'm pissed. I can't deal with stuff like that without wanting to yell at somebody."

"And here I thought that was a natural state for you," Alyssa said, rolling her eyes.

"It is." Brett crossed the hallway to an old service elevator and jabbed the button with his thumb. "We have storage down here," he said as the doors slid open.

"I don't need to see it," she said, refusing to step into the dim box.

"If you're going to be writing about this you might as well see the whole thing." Brett stepped into the elevator and held the doors, waiting for her to join him.

Alyssa balked. The elevator looked old, and its intestines creaked.

"I've ridden in this thing a million times."

"Fine."

Brett took his hand away from the entrance, and the doors closed with a soft squeal.

"That makes me feel totally safe."

She pressed herself against the wall farthest from Brett and clutched her purse straps.

Her discomfort wasn't caused by the elevator, or the way it swayed as it lowered them down.

No, it was from being in such close proximity to Brett.

She didn't like being around men. It was simple cause and effect. She allowed herself to be around a man, maybe even let herself get close to him, she got hurt.

"It always does that," he said, defending the elevator, scowling at her.

"I thought we were writing a manual anyway? Why do I need to know about the marathon?" Alyssa tried to focus on the book.

Not how it felt to be in the little cube with Brett. Hmm, how did it feel? Like she'd just run a million miles and was having a heart attack.

"Eventually they'll go hand in hand. I haven't met a runner who didn't race. We all get addicted to the swag."

"Swag?" Alyssa rolled the word around in her mouth like a bite of a vegetable she didn't want to swallow.

"The medal, the shirts, pencils, pens, pedometers, anything that's handed out at the expo. There are booths from the hospital, chiropractor offices, health food stores, Dane's store, reps from other races. Companies selling running gear set up booths, too. We get it all, and runners collect what the vendors hand out. Can never have enough fucking energy chews," Brett muttered as the elevator landed with a loud thud.

"If you don't like doing this, then why do you?"

She followed him as he stepped into a dark space that smelled musty and dirty.

Without warning, Brett stopped and Alyssa plowed into his back. "Sorry," he said, his voice unnaturally loud in the quiet.

The elevator doors closed, shutting out the light.

Standing in the dark, the only sound Alyssa heard was her own breathing.

"No problem," she whispered, easing away from him.

She couldn't see where she was going, and she put her foot down gingerly, not wanting to bump into anything else.

"It's not that I don't like it. It's just that I don't like it."

His chuckle made Alyssa's hair stand on end. As his low raspy laugh faded, wisps floated through the dark making her shiver.

"What?" She had forgotten the question.

"Why I do this." Brett flipped a light switch and with a low buzzing, fluorescent bulbs blinked on.

Yeah, this was good light. The gross kind in fitting rooms that made her appear sallow. Not her best look, though, nothing was anymore.

She flinched when he flicked a glance at her out of the corner of his eye.

"It's like any job. Good points, not so good points. There are worse things I could be doing, and not much better. The pay is shit, but honestly, I can't say there's anything else I would rather be doing."

Pallets of cardboard boxes took up a lot of space. The room stank, the lights flickering in their fixtures. The brick walls were painted beige, and the industrial carpet covering the floor matched the dull color.

*This* is what he wanted to show her?

"The delivery door is over there," Brett said, pointing across the room to where the floor slanted, and a roll-up door, similar to that of a residential garage, was closed tightly, not even thin fingers of light shining through. "We'll store the water down here, too, when Dane can finally get that figured out."

Warily, Alyssa watched as Brett took a pocket knife out

of his warmup pants and stepped to a pallet stacked high with brown cardboard boxes. He cut through the plastic and opened the top box.

"Here, what do you think?" Brett handed her a bar wrapped in brown paper, a picture of a man climbing a mountain drawn on the front.

It wasn't going to taste like her Milky Way, she knew that for sure, and Alyssa cautiously took a bite.

She let the piece of protein bar sit in her mouth, but she desperately wanted to spit it out. "Why does it taste like tree bark?" she asked after forcing herself to swallow.

"It's good for you. And if you really want to do this with me, running is only part of it. You have to eat, and eat well. Garbage in, garbage out. You can't run on chocolate and soda pop. It won't work.

"Look, Alyssa, it's really great you want to do this, but, if you don't do it right, you'll want to bail before you start. I don't want that to happen. It *can't* happen. I'm invested in this book, and I want you to be, too."

Brett leaned against the pallet, his legs crossed at the ankles. He looked like a model for the protein bar company. Alyssa remembered the girls flanking him in the photo on the marathon's Facebook page.

"Yeah," she whispered, the bar clutched in her hand. Tears pricked her eyes, and she looked away, mortified.

"Hey, what's this?"

The concern in his voice made the dam crack, and before she could stop herself, she stepped into Brett's arms and cried into his Tower City Marathon shirt.

---

BRETT WAS USED to tall women.

Women who could look him in the face, without heels. The top of Alyssa's head didn't even reach his shoulder, and he was brought back to his university days when he held Marta . . . No, he didn't want to think about her.

That he'd been able to keep in touch with her was enough for him, and regret seared his heart at the thought of her.

Dane and Nikki met up with her at the running retreat they'd attended last year, and Dane wisely had not spoken of her—not to tell him how good she looked, not to tell him how happy she was without him, not to tell him if she still missed him after all these years.

It wouldn't have made a damn bit of difference. What was done was done, and there was no going back.

Not even if he wanted to.

Not that he did.

That part of his life was over. Now, holding Alyssa the way he would have held Marta made his stomach lurch and a cold sweat bead over his skin.

He didn't know why Alyssa was crying. He didn't know a lot of things about her and didn't want to. He wanted her to run and help him write his goddamn book. That's it.

He didn't want her problems, didn't want her baggage. He had enough of his own, and he was tired of carrying it.

He couldn't handle anymore.

"Hey," he snapped, nudging her shoulder.

When she pulled away, he ran a hand over his t-shirt, and his palm came away wet.

Alyssa, her face pink from sobbing, stepped back.

"S-sorry."

Her voice, husky with tears, made his cock stiffen.

He hoped like hell his baggy warm-up pants hid his boner. If Alyssa saw that, he'd never convince her to help him. They didn't have to get along, but they had to be able to at least tolerate each other. She wouldn't let him near her with a ten-foot pole if he even so much as hinted sexual attraction.

"What the fuck was that?" Immediately, he regretted the way he spoke to her.

She shut down, a hard, blank look taking over her face, and that made him feel like shit. When the hell had he turned into such an asshole? Oh, that's right. He'd always been one. "Don't do that."

Alyssa jammed the protein bar into her jacket pocket and wiped the tears from her cheeks. "I better go."

"Wait."

She turned around, the flat look in her eyes, tears shining in the piss-poor lighting.

He owed her something, for being here, for facing him after the things he'd said to her. He was a prick, and she knew it, but she still came, told him she would work with him. But what in the fuck could he give her in exchange?

He'd never felt like he owed anybody anything. He didn't give a shit about anyone because no one had ever given a shit about him, except Marta, and look how that turned out.

"You need running clothes if you're going to do this. Decent shoes. Nikki's at the store now. Go buy gear."

"If?" Alyssa pounced on the word. "You're giving me an out? After I told you I'd do it?"

Brett nodded. That's exactly what he was doing. Giving her an out. Because he wasn't sure if this was such a good idea anymore.

With the straps of her purse gripped in her fist, Alyssa took a deep breath in and let it out as she stared at the delivery door across the room.

Brett dreaded her answer. He dreaded she would say yes. He could still feel the warmth of her back beneath his palm, her long, tangled mess of hair brushing his arm.

He dreaded she would say no. Somehow this book had turned into something important to him, and even if he found someone else to help him, it wouldn't be the same book.

He needed her.

"I'm not a quitter."

Brett sagged in relief.

"Fine. Go get some gear. Nikki will help you find shoes and clothes. I'll bum your number off Dane, and I'll text you about our first session. I need to get back upstairs. I'll talk to you later."

Instead of waiting to go up with her in the elevator, he flicked off the lights, and in the dark, turned around a corner. After he heard the ding of the elevator and the doors squeal open, he sank against the wall and slid to the heels of his shoes wondering what in the hell he'd just done.

---

"I LOOK STUPID." Her reflection met Nikki's in the fitting room mirror, and her best friend wrinkled her nose.

"You do not. Everyone starts somewhere or they wouldn't make running clothes in your size. I still don't understand what you're doing, explain this to me again. Here, it's chilly outside, you'll need a running jacket, too."

Alyssa took the black running jacket and slid it over the running t-shirt she was trying on.

Nikki called it some kind of wicking material. Whatever the hell that meant.

She rather liked the jacket though, slipping her thumbs

through the holes in the sleeves. Pockets were everywhere, and the material was stretchy and comfortable.

The running capris felt good too, but they made her thighs looked like sausages, and even in black, her butt looked huge.

*Dumb ass. Because it is.*

She bounced on her toes in the new running shoes and stopped, dismayed when her breasts jiggled in the mirror.

That was not a sight she wanted Brett to see.

"I don't know what I'm doing, either. I'm tired of being alone, I'm tired of being made fun of. I'm tired of men treating me like shit. And for some stupid reason, I want to help Brett. The writer in me knows this book is a good idea. It could turn into something big."

She sat on the bench that took up one wall of the small fitting room.

She didn't understand why Brett had left her there alone in the dark, or where he'd disappeared to.

The building was unfamiliar to her, and she only knew how to get out the way she came in.

She'd made her way back upstairs, down the hallway, past the empty offices, and into the large room where she'd met Brett in the first place.

Dane had still been on the phone, and she'd been able to avoid speaking with him. Relieved she didn't have to answer questions or make small talk, she'd scurried through the group of loitering runners and out into the parking lot.

Nikki knelt in front of her. "Those are good reasons, but they're not enough. You have to want it for you."

"Pffft. It's enough for me."

Nikki shook her head in frustration.

"You think I'm kidding, or telling you some self-discovery, hippie-chick shit, but this is real. Running, just starting out, is *hard*. If you don't have the motivation inside yourself, you're going to quit."

"Brett won't let me quit."

"He can't make you run," Nikki disagreed. "You get out there on our path, he can't make you run."

Alyssa lifted her chin. "I won't quit."

Nikki sighed. "Okay. Don't say I didn't warn you. You can have a million reasons, but if any of those reasons aren't for you, then it won't matter how many you have."

Afraid Nikki was right, Alyssa waved off her friend's concern. "That's going in the book."

Nikki frowned. "Are you all set then? You got enough stuff?"

"I think so. This is going to cost a small fortune. A third world country could eat for a year on what I'm spending."

Opening the stall door, Nikki laughed. "Actually, Dane told me to comp it all—business expense," she said over Alyssa's protests.

"I can't accept that."

"I don't think you have a choice," Nikki said, leading her to the cash register. "Are you wearing all that home?"

Alyssa looked down at her new running shoes. She'd forgotten to wedge her ass back into her jeans, the running material feeling more comfortable than her regular clothes. "Yeah, I guess so. They aren't so bad."

"They're tough to get off in a hurry if you know what I mean." Nikki giggled and winked.

"I'm not going to need to know that."

"You're right, you're not. Stay away from him." Nikki scanned a tag of a running shirt and shoved it into a white bag decorated with the store's logo.

The severity in Nikki's voice caught Alyssa off guard, and a blush crept over her face.

"Alyssa!" Nikki hissed. "Stay away from him. He'll chew you up and spit you out. Don't fall for him."

"I'm not! I mean, sometimes he looks . . ."

She didn't know how he looked. She pictured him perched on the arm of her sofa, holding his disposable cappuccino cup, asking for her help.

His defeat when she said no.

The hope when she'd changed her mind and said yes.

She couldn't explain how all those emotions filtered through his hazel eyes made her feel, how those warm, fuzzy confusing feelings fought with the truth.

He thought she was fat, a loser who couldn't keep a man.

To him, she was only a woman who wrote books about a topic she knew nothing about.

The memory of him shoving her aside, his flinty expression as he rubbed her tears off his shirt, made her grimace.

No, Nikki didn't have to worry.

Brett would never touch her. He was using her, and she could never, ever forget that.

Nikki finished bagging her running gear and carried the bag around the counter. "I don't know what his story is. Even Dane doesn't know. He thinks it has something to do with Marta, a woman they went to college with, but Brett never said anything to anybody, and neither did she."

Alyssa took the bulging bag from Nikki. Running bras, pants, capris, shirts, headbands, and the box that contained her old shoes stretched the white plastic. The handles dug into her skin. "I can take care of myself. I'm tired of being hurt."

Nodding, Nikki agreed. "And that's what he would do, I know it."

Walking to her car, Alyssa sighed, because she knew it, too.

———

Alyssa set aside a novel from a new author she'd been trying to read and wandered restlessly around her apartment.

If she'd been in any other circumstance, she would've been elbow deep in a bag of chips, but Brett's "garbage in, garbage out," comment stuck, and it annoyed the hell out of her.

Hungry, pissed, and maybe even a little bored, she rifled through her kitchen looking for something to acceptable to eat.

She didn't find anything.

He hadn't told her when he wanted to run, and she didn't know when he was going to want to start the actual writing process. He may not be able to start the book for months if he was swamped with marathon duties.

Something he could have told her.

Just as she was about to succumb to the huge bag of Cool Ranch Doritos she kept in her cabinet, someone pounded on her door.

She didn't want to quit or sabotage herself before she even began. If she was going to be in it, she was going to be in it all the way.

"I'm coming," she yelled when more pounding threatened to bust down her door. "Hold on!"

She yanked it open and was surprised to see Brett on the other side holding bags of . . . food?

He hadn't been beating on the door; he'd been kicking it with his foot.

"Are you going to let me in, or what?"

"What are you doing here?" she asked, stepping aside.

"I'm here to clean out your kitchen. I don't trust you."

Alyssa would have been offended if he hadn't been so close to the truth.

She scuffed her toe along the hardwood flooring.

"Ah-huh," Brett said, letting himself into her kitchen as if he belonged there. "I know a guilty look when I see one. I probably shouldn't have left you alone this long. What's the damage today?"

"Nothing!" Alyssa defended herself. He didn't have to know she'd been about to drown herself in chips.

Brett set the bags down on the floor near her small rectangular kitchen table.

"I'm getting rid of anything you shouldn't be eating."

He hung his jacket on the back of a chair and started randomly opening cabinet doors. Hitting pay dirt, he growled.

"Really?"

He held out the family-sized bag of Doritos that had been in her sights.

Shaking his head, he set the bag aside and kept digging. More chips, cookies, her emergency stash of chocolate truffles.

The pile grew, and Brett made himself comfortable on his knees as he reached into deep storage spaces.

"How long have these been back there?" Brett asked in disgust, holding out a half-finished bag of Cheetos.

"I thought I finished those."

"And you wonder why you look the way you do."

"I've never wondered," Alyssa said bitterly, too hurt by the pile of junk food on the floor to take his comment personally. "I've just never done anything about it."

"That ends tonight."

"Is there going to be a food plan in the book then?"

Alyssa hadn't considered having to cook as part of this arrangement. She didn't cook. She snacked. All day. And Brett was about to take her main food supply away.

"No. I'm not a chef. But I can at least help you. This stuff is disgusting." Brett stood and began opening and closing cabinet doors at eye level. "Don't you eat real food?"

"That *is* food."

"Campbell's Chicken Gumbo Soup is not food. It's a disgusting mess of MSG."

"It's good."

Brett pulled cans from the shelf and set them on the counter. "It's toxic. We'll donate what we can to the food shelf, and anything open is going into the trash."

Alyssa scowled as he cleaned out her kitchen. He saved the fridge for last, and she blew out a relieved sigh when he left her cheese alone.

"You don't drink soda?" Brett asked, surprised.

Alyssa shook her head. "Mostly I drink coffee."

"You need to start drinking water. Your muscles and organs depend on it. Your skin will perk up, your eyes will brighten." He tugged on a lock of her hair. "Your hair will look better. Your body needs water."

He pulled out a large yellow container of chocolate chip cookie coffee creamer. "Stop this. It's full of sugar. Use half and half or pay for whole cream. It's expensive but worth it. Zero carbs."

"You're throwing away my whole kitchen."

"You can't run on this shit, Alyssa."

Alyssa groaned. She knew she couldn't.

After throwing away most of her junk food and pushing the rest aside, Brett dug into the bags he brought.

"This is real food. You'll need to go to the grocery store every couple days. Bananas, apples. Lettuce, tomatoes, cucumbers. Make a salad for God's sake. Fish. Chicken. Eat lean."

He pulled out bags of frozen vegetables.

"Broccoli, cauliflower. Stop eating sugar. No pasta. Stop eating potatoes. Scramble eggs. Oatmeal." Brett showed her a package of low-carb tortilla wraps. "Use these for sandwiches instead of bread. Fat is your friend. Stay away from sugar."

Alyssa started putting the groceries away, but she stopped short as Brett pulled a skillet from her pots and pans. "What are you doing?"

"I'm making us dinner."

"You know how to cook?" she asked, her eyebrows raised.

"Nothing fancy, but I run marathons. I need to be able to feed myself or I could never finish twenty-six feet much less twenty-six miles. The training alone is a tremendous strain on your body."

"I'm not running a marathon." She would never attempt twenty-six miles.

"Not a full," Brett agreed, adding a pad of butter to the skillet.

Alyssa's mouth dropped open. "I'm sorry?"

"There's more than enough time to get you into shape to run the half at Nikki's women's run in October. There isn't enough time to train you for the half in June, but by October you should be able to run a three-hour half marathon, no sweat."

"You think I'm going to run non-stop for three hours? You're out of your mind."

Brett laid two pink salmon filets into the melted butter

then added water to a pot. "You've got over half a year to prepare. Running thirteen miles will be nothing to you by then."

"You're going to stick with me for seven months?" Alyssa asked skeptically.

Seven months of Brett incessantly harassing her about her running schedule, overseeing her diet. That could have been a dream come true . . . or hell on earth.

Brett opened his mouth, then shut it, then opened it again. "Well," he said, turning on the burner under the water, "I hope it doesn't take that long to write the book. When we're finished, Nikki can run with you."

"I guess so," she muttered.

She shouldn't have been surprised. She knew all along Brett would drop her once the book was done, but it still hurt.

Throwing a steamable bag of broccoli into her microwave, Brett frowned. "What? You don't want me dogging you all the time, and anyway, I can't. You're going to have to run by yourself sometimes until this marathon is over. I'm not going to be able to spare time for you every day." He flipped the salmon filets over, then sprinkled salt on them. "You'll have a lot more fun running and gossiping with Nikki, and if you really take to it, you'll enjoy running alone. It's what most runners appreciate anyway—time to themselves."

Alyssa conceded that was probably true. Writing was a solitary activity; she was used to being alone. To be contrary she said, "I doubt I'll keep running after the book is done."

"Suit yourself," Brett said, shrugging. "Grab me a couple plates, will you?"

Brett plated salmon, rice, and broccoli. She eyed the

meal with suspicion, and she heaved a sigh when he placed a glass of water before her on the table.

"This is what you eat." Brett pointed at her salmon with his fork. "Protein." He moved his fork to her pile of brown rice. "Good carbs." He jabbed at the broccoli. "Vegetable. The greener the better. Spinach. Kale. When it gets warmer, the Tower City farmer's market sells great produce, and it's cheap."

She frowned and forked a small bite of salmon into her mouth.

Brett had browned it perfectly, and the butter and salt enhanced the flavor. "I'm still not clear what I'm getting out of this."

"You know, or you wouldn't have decided to do it. You should get your numbers done. They would be an interesting addition to the book." Brett took a gulp of water.

"My numbers? You mean you want me to go to a numerologist or a psychic?"

"No." Brett laughed. "Your numbers, like your cholesterol, your blood pressure. When was the last time you had a check-up at the doctor?"

Alyssa crossed her arms.

Unaffected, Brett ate the meal he'd prepared.

He was always calling her fat, unattractive, and unhealthy, yet, unbelievably, she was almost . . . content to sit here with him.

His eyes were twinkling, and he exuded the health that came with being fit. The health displayed by the other runner volunteers at marathon headquarters that Alyssa had envied.

"I can't remember. Probably not since I was a kid."

Brett dropped his fork, and it clattered onto his plate. "You haven't had a check-up for twenty years? You need a physical. I want to see your numbers. We can track them and show our readers through concrete proof that exercise, running, in this case, is good for you. Eat your food. Your body is probably going into shock because there's no Red Dye Number Seven."

Alyssa finished her meal while Brett cleaned up. "I can do that. Just leave it in the sink," she said as he washed the skillet by hand.

"I've got it." He rinsed it and set it into the white strainer to dry. "I'll see you in the morning."

Dinner hadn't been that bad, and she was almost disappointed he was leaving so soon.

*Well, what did she expect, he would hang out all night?*

His words sank in.

"In the morning?" she asked, alarmed, following Brett to the door.

"Yes. Tomorrow. Our first run. I don't know how you want to go about this. If you want to write your impressions on your own, or if you want to wait and write together?"

Brett looked uncomfortable, and she liked him looking off-kilter. Like she'd felt from the moment she'd told him she would participate in this crazy scheme.

"I'll write a little bit, but I think it's best we write together. It will save us time later if we have areas where we don't agree."

Brett flashed her a grin, and her stomach churned.

She blamed the fish.

"Sounds good to me, though between running with you and the marathon, we may be emailing back and forth for a while, until I can get a little bit of my free time back."

That suited her; she didn't want him in her loft.

When the time came for them to sit down regularly at a computer, they could do it in his office. She didn't mind writing through email. She once collaborated with two other writers on a romantic anthology, and it had gone well.

"Anyway," he said, cracking the door open, "I'll be here at six. We can run out back. The paths are nice. I've been on them with Dane quite a few times."

"*Six?*"

Alyssa tried to wrap her mind around the early time and failed. She was a night owl; often she stayed up all night writing. There was nothing like the desolation, the loneliness, at two in the morning to help her set a dull and dreary scene full of heartbreak.

"That doesn't work for you?"

"No!" If Brett was willing to change the time she wouldn't waste her chance. "I do my best writing in the middle of the night. Getting up and out by six would be impossible."

"In the evening then," Brett said easily. "I'll be by tomorrow night at seven."

Grateful he acquiesced so quickly, she smiled. "Thank you."

"Alyssa—"

She met his eyes. "Yeah?"

"I don't want to make this hard for you. I get that you're doing me a favor, and I'd be stuck if you changed your mind. So . . . thank you. If running in the evenings is what you want, I'm happy to do it."

Alyssa blinked. "Oh. Um. Okay. Goodnight, Brett."

"Goodnight, Alyssa. Keep your hand out of the cookie jar."

Alyssa sighed as the door closed behind him.

There was no chance of her sneaking a cookie.

Brett had thrown them all away.

ON THE DRIVE to her apartment from headquarters, Brett wondered if Alyssa would show.

She hadn't shared why she changed her mind about helping him, and he probably didn't want to know.

People ran for a lot of different reasons. Maybe she was tired of being overweight. Maybe she was bored. It was none of his business; he just thanked his lucky stars he convinced her.

As he pulled into a guest parking space at Alyssa's building, the tension that had built during his hectic day eased.

Brett climbed out of his crappy car.

Almost everything he owned was from high school. His studio apartment, his car. Even some of his clothes he'd worn his senior year, back when he was a scrawny kid at seventeen.

He was surprised to find Alyssa pacing the sidewalk in front of her building's front door.

She either didn't want him to come up, or she was being courteous. It didn't matter. He wasn't in this for the friendship. He wanted to write a book. Branch out career-wise. That was it.

Brett studied her as he approached her pacing form. Alyssa's dark hair was pulled into a messy pony tail, and she was wearing too many clothes.

Even at the run/walk pace he'd planned for them this evening, she would be sweating like a pig in no time.

Strain shadowed her face. Her eyebrows were gathered into a frown, and from the hard set of her jaw, Brett guessed she was gnashing her teeth.

"You're overdressed."

"What?" She balled her hands into fists and widened her stance.

"You're going to be too hot," he said, tugging on her purple puffer jacket.

"It's cold out here."

"No, it's not. Bring your jacket back upstairs. If you wear it, you'll want to take it off half way through our run, and you'll have nowhere to put it. The sleeves are too thick for you to tie around your waist, and you won't want to leave it behind. Put on something lighter if you have to, but don't wear this. I'll meet you on the trail."

Brett walked around the corner of her building to the cement paths behind her apartment complex.

It wouldn't be a bad area to live in if he cared to change his living situation, but he didn't. He didn't care about much of anything in his life right now except the race and the book.

He wished he were more like Dane who, amidst an imminent divorce and his parents' emotional abandonment, still went ahead with his dream of opening his own store.

Hell, he wished he *had* a dream. Any dream. The book was a good start. It was just too bad the project was so damn dependent on the woman stomping over the grass toward him.

"You look better."

"I'm cold."

Brett huffed in amusement. "You are so goddamned contrary."

Alyssa stuck out her tongue.

"Knock it off. We'll warm up a bit. Remember how you're feeling, what you're thinking. These first few experiences will help first-time runners who might be apprehensive about starting a running routine."

Alyssa remained quiet, and Brett tried not to think anything of it.

She was moody, hot-headed, and bitter.

Normally, she was the type of person he would stay away from. She was too much like himself, and he didn't need the stress and worry of being around someone like that.

Marta had always been happy and cheerful until—

That didn't matter anymore. The past was the past. That Marta still touched base with him shocked the hell out of him, but in a way, it was comforting, too.

"Let's run for a bit. Slowly. Don't burn out. Try to keep it fun." Brett started running lightly, more of a hopping on his toes, and Alyssa kept pace beside him not saying a word. He looked at his watch as they ran, deciding to run a minute and walk five.

He'd looked up some online training schedules for beginners and tweaked them with Alyssa in mind. He would have to tell her, and they could include plans in the book as an additional resource.

He liked to run in the quiet as much as any runner, but after awhile Alyssa's silence began to bother him.

"Something going on with you?" he finally asked, slowing them down to a walk, noting the time. He had a GPS watch somewhere. It was equipped with a run/walk feature that would be useful for these first few runs.

"Nope," she said, staring at her toes.

She didn't look half bad in her running gear. Because she had bought it all at Dane's store, everything was stamped with the Tower City Running Company logo.

Black capris were printed with hot pink letters down her leg, and a matching hot pink t-shirt peeked from her black running jacket.

She looked like a runner.

Plus fifty pounds.

The new diet and exercise regimen would take care of those. Quickly, too, if she kept up the exercise on her own like she promised.

Thinking about her diet suddenly made her bad mood make sense.

"You're going through sugar withdrawal," he said, pleased he figured it out. "Sugar is addictive. When you stop eating it your body craves it. It's a drug. Like caffeine."

He paused.

"What have you eaten today?" His eyes widened when she started sniffling. "What is it?"

"I haven't eaten anything!" she wailed. "I don't know what to eat. I can't cook."

"Fuck. Alyssa, it's seven o'clock. You haven't eat anything all day? You're starving yourself. Come on."

Grumbling under his breath, he led her back to her apartment.

---

"So HE MADE me a turkey and bacon wrap with tomatoes and lettuce on lavash bread. Nothing ever tasted so good in my life."

The next evening, Alyssa ran/walked with Nikki, after Nikki finished her shift at the store.

She'd barely seen her friend since Nikki had gotten engaged to Dane, and run/walking now would have two purposes: catching up and getting in her work out.

The night before, Brett had abandoned their first run and walked her back to the loft where he'd proceeded to fix her dinner.

He wrote out a meal list for her to consult when she was hungry and had no clue what to eat.

Items she thought she'd never be allowed to eat topped the list, and she had eaten well all day.

But Brett hadn't lied—there wasn't a grain of sugar anywhere near her meal plan.

"You feel okay today?" Nikki asked, leading them into a jog.

Alyssa huffed as she forced her legs to move. Training with Nikki would be just as bad, or even worse, as training with Brett. She could sweet talk him into giving in sometimes. With Nikki, there was no chance in hell.

When she lagged behind, Nikki shouted, "Come on, don't wuss out on me."

Alyssa increased her effort and managed to keep up until Nikki slowed them down to a walk again.

"Is this how you started?" she gasped, her legs burning.

"It's how we all start out, unless you run as a kid, high school track like Dane and Brett, and you have that natural energy at your back that you bring with you. I didn't, and this is exactly what I had to do."

Evening was Alyssa's favorite time of day. The sun had just gone down—the rays still lingering in the sky making purple and pink glowing streaks. A few early stars twinkled. The half-moon glittered white and bright.

A contentment she hadn't felt in quite a while enveloped her.

She was trying to take control of her weight, she was spending time with her friend, and her professional life was on track.

The only thing she lacked was a man, but no matter how good things went, she knew a relationship wasn't in her future.

She wanted to ask Nikki how her wedding plans were going, but the fact was, she didn't feel like knowing. There was a bitterness, a jealousy, of Nikki that Alyssa didn't want to admit to feeling because Nikki had what Alyssa so desperately wanted.

She wasn't getting any younger, and to find a man, a man worth loving, a man worth keeping, would take time.

She wanted children, but she would never have them.

Maybe she would adopt a cat the way Nikki had. A kitten that would wrap her body around her computer monitor the way so many of her writer friends' pets did.

"Want to come up?" Alyssa asked as they approached her building. She was glad Brett forced her to leave her puffer jacket behind yesterday. It taught her how to dress, and she gave him the credit he deserved. A fine sheen of sweat coated her body, the evening breeze cooling her. She would have boiled wearing her jacket.

"No, thanks. I need to head home. Dane's lease is finally coming up for renewal, and we're both downsizing. Brett, I think, is going to luck out into some furniture whether he wants it or not. He's been sleeping on an old ratty futon for over ten years."

"It will help not having to pay two rents," Alyssa said.

"Dane wants us to pay for most of the wedding ourselves, but I talked him into letting our parents help, at least a little bit. I'm meeting with Peg and my mom later this week to look at a few places for a reception. I liked where Kayla had hers, but I need to ask her how much she spent. We have to book the venue pretty soon, even if we're not getting married until next spring."

Nikki absently twisted her engagement ring as she explained her wedding plans, and Alyssa watched with envy.

"Hey, Lyss?" Nikki asked hesitantly.

"Yeah?"

"Will you, you know, be my maid of honor?"

Alyssa thought of all she would be required to do in the role: lunches, teas, the bachelorette party, the bridal shower. All the wedding dress fittings she would be asked to attend, the bridesmaid dress she would be forced to wear.

There was nothing she wanted to do less.

"I would love to."

## CHAPTER THREE

It will get worse before it gets better—Brett

Fuck off—Alyssa

---

A LYSSA APPROACHED THE gym with trepidation.
Brett told her to do some kind of cross-training, but she'd had no idea what she could do.

When she asked Nikki, Nikki suggested joining a gym and taking classes. Step aerobics, Pilates, or yoga would all qualify as cross-training.

Also, Nikki pointed out, if it was raining or in the wintertime when temperatures grew too cold to run outside, she would already be familiar with a gym, and she could use a treadmill so she wouldn't miss her runs.

Alyssa doubted she would still be running in the winter, and she *really* doubted she would run the half marathon in the fall, even if she signed up and paid the registration fee.

It didn't sound as if Brett intended to stick with her that long, and she couldn't do it on her own.

But for now, she was in it, she would follow Nikki's advice, and she found herself at the biggest gym in Tower City.

Boasting a juice and smoothie bar, his and hers steam rooms, and a million treadmills and exercise classes, it seemed the most practical choice. The gym was also open twenty-four-hours a day, three-hundred and sixty five days a year, and there would be no excuse for her to skip workouts.

She opened the gym's heavy glass door and stepped to the guest services counter.

"Can I help you?" asked a perky blonde who sat behind a computer wearing a headset with a microphone positioned in front of her mouth.

"I need to sign up."

The blonde shoved a clipboard with a thick stack of papers and a pen at her, and she filled out paperwork, for what seemed like hours.

When she was finally finished, she was hungry, had to go to the bathroom, and wanted to go home.

She stood self-consciously, watching people drift in and out of the gym. Everyone looked so fit and healthy.

When the blonde returned her credit card, Alyssa slipped it back into her wallet.

"Thank you," she muttered.

She hadn't brought her clothes or running shoes.

Her intention had been to sign up and run, literally, out the door.

"Wait! I'll have Tom give you a tour. He's a personal trainer. If you're interested in some sessions, let him know." The woman lifted her eyebrows in question.

"I'll think about . . . it . . ." Alyssa faded as the most gorgeous man she'd ever seen came her way.

"I'm Tom," he said, holding out his hand to take hers. "Just getting signed up? Welcome to the club. This is a great place to work out."

Alyssa stared into his friendly bright blue eyes, framed in the corners by little wrinkles that squished together when he smiled at her.

Drawn into his welcoming gaze, she involuntarily smiled back.

She followed him through the gym, watching as he demonstrated the workout equipment, showed her where the women's locker rooms were located, and where the fitness classes were held.

Tom handed her a sheet that listed all the exercise classes and their times. "What do you think you would be interested in?"

Squinting into his face, she tried to find signs he was making fun of her, or mocking her, but there was nothing but genuine kindness and interest.

"I'm not sure," she admitted, fingering the paper that contained a grid of colored squares, descriptions, dates and times of classes.

"Would you want to maybe, ah, grab a smoothie and chat for a minute? I have fifteen of them before my next appointment shows." He ran his fingers through his short-cropped chestnut brown hair and smiled at her, a deep dimple in his cheek flicking flirtatiously.

Taken aback by what seemed to be sincere friendliness she blurted, "Sure," but she regretted it before the word had finished coming from her mouth.

"Great!"

She followed him to the juice and smoothie bar and sat

awkwardly on a high-backed stool. She hung her purse on the backrest and perched her feet on the highest chair rung. She was short, but the extra weight she carried canceled out the cute petiteness her height could have given her.

"Pick your poison," Tom teased, leaning toward her, resting his arm on the back of her stool.

A menu written in bright pink chalk on a blackboard leaned against the wall behind a line of blenders.

She scanned it, searching for something palatable.

"Ummm."

Tom laughed and casually tugged the ends of her hair.

Alyssa inwardly flinched but was proud of herself for not pulling away. She was so skittish around men, one couldn't casually touch her.

Brett was always brushing against her in some way.

Between Brett and Tom, she'd been touched by a man more in the past few weeks than she had in years, and the idea made her uncomfortable.

She didn't want a man paying attention to her. When they did, when they bothered, in the end they always pushed her away, and never had she walked away unscathed.

Tom pulled her from her thoughts. "What's your favorite fruit?"

"What's fruit?" she asked wryly.

Tom laughed.

After they ordered their drinks, a watermelon concoction for her, which tasted like a virgin margarita, and some goopy green sludge for him, they talked about why she was joining the gym, what she wanted out of her membership, and if she was interested in training sessions, particularly with him.

"I'm umm, helping Brett Sommers write a running

manual," she said, grazing the tip of her finger along the ridges of her clear plastic smoothie cup. Voicing out loud to a stranger what she was doing with Brett made it sound silly.

Tom grinned. "Hey, I know Brett. The marathon director. He's pretty cool. I run the 10k most years, and the gym sets up a booth at the expo to sign up new members. I work that, handing out information about the gym, training sessions, the classes, all that stuff. That's awesome, Alyssa."

"Yeah. He wanted to write a manual for beginners, and I'm his guinea pig."

"And the gym? Where does this place fit in?" Tom asked.

"Cross-training. Obviously, something I know nothing about." She wanted to set the elephant free.

Tom laughed again and tugged the ends of her hair.

Alyssa kind of wished he would stop doing it, but at the same time, if he did, she'd be disappointed.

"So, you write?"

Alyssa's mouth dropped open, shocked he wasn't going to mention her weight.

Well, he saw fat people every day; what she looked like was probably old news to him.

"I'm a romance writer," she said, taking another draw of her smoothie.

"That sounds fun," Tom said, then finished his drink, tipping his head back so the last of the sludge could slide to the edge of the cup. "My time is almost up, but hey," he fished into the pocket of his workout pants, "here's my card. Call me if you want to sign up for some personal training sessions. I make my own schedule, and I'll fit you in ASAP. I can help you run faster, better. Or, call me, just to call me."

Alyssa blinked.

He was flirting with her.

"I will." She took the card from him and folded her fingers around the sharp corners of the coated paper rectangle.

"I'll look forward to it. Welcome to the gym, Alyssa. See you later."

She watched him walk away, the black gym t-shirt stretched tightly across his shoulders, until he slipped through a door marked PRIVATE.

The girl behind the counter cleared her smoothie cup, and Alyssa slid the class schedule off the countertop.

Maybe it wouldn't be so bad after all.

---

BRETT SLAMMED HIS forehead against the desk, and Dane jerked in surprise, spilling hot coffee over the rim of his Tower City Marathon coffee cup.

"What the fuck?" Dane asked irritated, flicking his fingers to rid them of the scalding liquid.

"The photography company just pulled out of our race. They went bankrupt."

Sick dread filled his stomach as the meaning of the words took hold. He wanted to throw up, and he swallowed against the bile rising in his throat.

Photos were taken along the courses and videos were filmed at the finish lines so each runner could search their bib numbers to look at, and purchase, pictures and short clips of themselves running their chosen race. The company also took candids at the expo, the speaker series, and the finish line party.

The date had been booked since last year.

He was really and truly fucked.

Brett raised his head but saw nothing except red rage.

"Holy shit," Dane said, leaning against Brett's desk. "What are we going to do?"

"What do you mean, what are *we* going to do?" Brett asked. This was no one's problem but his.

"We're in this together. Whatever you need, I'll do it. What should we do first?"

Brett rubbed his eyes in defeat. "Nothing we can do. That company serviced more races than just us. We're all screwed. No use scrambling for another company. No one could do it at such a late notice, and with the other races in need, I'm not getting into a bidding war for our date, even on the off-chance there was someone who could do it."

The two men sat in silence, the bustle of the main room drifting in from down the hallway.

Brett had used the small office to make phone calls, not feeling up to visiting with anyone, just wanting to get his shit done and go home, and he was relieved he had.

That hadn't been a call he needed to take with people watching him. His volunteers would know right away something was wrong.

Dane snapped his fingers. "What about Marta? Do you think she could pull some strings?"

Brett sighed. He didn't know which was worse, dealing with the fallout that would happen when he announced there would be no photographs of the race this year, or calling his old college flame.

He shook his head against Dane's idea. "There's nothing Marta can do. I'll put off making the announcement, though once someone finds out, the news will probably spread like wildfire through social media. Fuck. I guess what you can do is start making some calls and see what you can do about lining up a new company for next year. Other races will be clambering too, so it wouldn't hurt to be first. Thank God we already have the date ironed out."

"I'm on it." Dane saluted Brett and left him alone, and Brett slumped behind the huge metal desk he'd swiped from a closing elementary school.

His head throbbed.

The last thing he wanted to do was run with Alyssa tonight, but he still didn't trust her to do what he wanted without dogging her heels every step of the way.

He hadn't spoken with her in a couple days. That worried him, but there wasn't much he could do about it.

With the race five weeks away, phone calls, errands, and interviews pulled him in a hundred different directions. He had to look on the bright side—if Alyssa fell back into old habits, failure and repercussions of slipping off track could be a good chapter to include.

Brett fielded some calls, chatted with a few volunteers, updated the Facebook page, and checked the new number of race registrations. The numbers were growing before the final fee increase that was set to happen in at the beginning of May before the race.

"Heading out?" Dane asked as Brett stepped into the large hub where he and other volunteers were still hanging around, killing time or finishing up little projects before leaving for the day.

The Minnesota spring was taking its sweet time warming up this year, and Brett slid on a running jacket over his t-shirt.

"Yeah. Running with Alyssa later, and I've been teaching her how to cook a little."

"Nikki told me she joined the Tower City Fitness

Center," Dane said, tapping a pencil on the desk where he'd been making phone calls.

"That's good." Brett paid for a membership there, and he knew Nikki and Dane did too.

"She seems to be going all out. Have you two written anything yet?"

"Nope. I need to talk to her about it tonight. She's been running, so we should be able to pound out a chapter soon." Brett ran a hand through his hair. "Fuck. What I really just want to do is go home, plow through a bag of chips, and drink a six pack. Fucking marathon."

The comment earned him looks from the other runners, some giving him sympathetic smiles.

Dane laughed. "What kind of coach are you? Is that advice going in the book? 'If you get pissed, drink beer, gorge on chips, and blow off a run? There's always tomorrow.'"

"We've all done it. Christ. This marathon has been hellish this year."

"Cancel on Alyssa, go home, and get some sleep. Are you in shape enough to run it?" Dane asked.

Brett snorted. "I couldn't even fuckin' run the half now, no matter how hard I tried. Last long run I had was with you around Christmas."

He didn't need Dane's smirk for the irony of it to hit home, and just to get the last word in before he left, he gave Dane the finger on his way out the door, much to the amusement of the other volunteers.

———

BRETT WAS TEMPTED to skip Alyssa's, but he found himself parked in her lot before he could change his mind.

He made his way up the stairs of the apartment building, and the fragrant aroma of pot roast met his nose. He wasn't in the mood to teach Alyssa how to cook anything tonight, so he hoped she wasn't hungry, waiting for a lesson.

Pain hammered through his skull, and for the first time in a long time, he wished he were on his way home to a woman who had dinner waiting for him. Roast beef, potatoes, carrots and dinner rolls. Gravy. He didn't care about the starch. Not tonight.

The smell strengthened as he walked down the carpeted hallway to Alyssa's loft. For one unbelievable moment, he thought it was Alyssa who was making dinner, but he brushed the ludicrous idea aside.

He knocked, his stomach growling, mental fatigue almost knocking him off his feet.

The door swung open, and Alyssa shot him a look of distaste. "You look like shit."

Her criticism didn't do much for his mood, and he scowled. "I've had a piss-poor day, thank you very much. Are you going to let me in or what? And what the hell? Are you cooking?"

"Yeah. I've had a roast in the slow cooker all day. Just some broth in it. I made cauliflower with cheese sauce, and there's cottage cheese. Wild rice. Not too bad, huh?"

She sounded damn proud of herself. Her face was slimming down, her hair gleamed. Her running t-shirt didn't look as tight, though he couldn't be sure, he backpedaled, because he didn't spend time looking at her breasts—much. He felt a twinge, of, he couldn't put a name to it. Her slimmer face was almost . . . disappointing.

And since when had he liked chubby women? Since never, that's when.

He forced himself to think of the leggy women runners

he'd dated, the feel of their long, slim legs wrapped around his waist during mind-numbing, or mind-blowing sex, whichever he needed at the time.

"No, not bad," he said, pushing past her and flopping onto her couch.

Ignoring her disgruntled look, he shifted to make himself more comfortable. He kicked off his shoes, and unbelievably, his tension drained away.

As if by magic, a bottle of beer appeared near his elbow on the coffee table, and he looked up to find Alyssa scowling at him. "We can eat whenever."

Brett brightened. "You're going to feed me?"

"That was my idiotic plan," she mumbled.

Closing his eyes, he listened to the calming sounds of her shuffling things around and plates being set on the table. He roused himself and sat up so he wouldn't fall asleep.

Alyssa apparently appreciated comfort, and the couch was pleasantly padded and long enough his feet didn't touch the armrest.

She placed the platter of pot roast in the center of her little table. "Dish up," she said, taking a seat. She lifted a glass of sparkling water to her mouth.

"Good?" Brett asked, filling his plate.

"If I imagine hard enough, the orange flavor tastes like the orange pop I used to drink as a kid."

They ate in companionable silence, Brett filling his plate two more times.

Besides eating at Nikki's, he rarely ate a home-cooked meal. Sometimes when he had a girlfriend, she would cook for him, until the domestic claustrophobia took hold and he booted her ass to the curb.

No chance of that with Alyssa. He leaned back in his

chair and took a pull from his beer. No way would he ever tangle with this little minx.

"I was thinking instead of running we could write for a while, get that going," Brett said before Alyssa began clearing the table.

"That sounds okay. I went to the gym this morning anyway. I'm a little sore from a step aerobics class."

"Don't overdo it. You don't want to burn out."

"I know. It was just to try it out; I've never gone to one before. Then I had a wheatgrass shot with Tom at the juice bar. God, that was gross."

Brett frowned and wasn't happy with the prickle of apprehension that trailed over his skin. "Who's Tom?"

"Oh, the trainer I've started seeing. We met up to go over some sessions, make a plan. He knows I'm running with you, and that I'm helping you write a book. He thinks it's pretty cool. His words, not mine."

"Oh," Brett murmured, not able to pinpoint why that made him relieved. "That's not bad. Just don't wear yourself out. Running and the book should be your first priority."

"I know," Alyssa said, rolling her eyes.

After the leftovers were put away, Brett followed Alyssa up the wooden stairs to her loft, and he looked around with interest.

A massive desk sat in a corner, but instead of it butting up against the wall, it was turned, affording her a view of the stairs.

"Paranoid?" he asked, amused.

"Sometimes I write romantic thrillers. About the time I wrote a creepy one, I went through a crappy breakup. It made me a little nervous to be up here alone, but I never bothered to move the desk back. It's heavy, and with all the computer wires, it takes me all day."

Brett bristled at the thought of someone hurting her, then remembered he had, the very first time he met her.

As she took a seat behind her desk and logged into her computer, he walked around the loft, taking in the sloped ceiling and the pictures hanging on the walls. "You're pretty famous, huh?" he asked, realizing the posters were the covers of her books.

"Not really. Not Nicholas Sparks famous, or Nora Roberts famous. None of my books have been turned into movies. Not even a special series on the Hallmark Channel. But that's okay. My books sell all right. My publisher is happy, and I'm sitting in the middle of a pretty good contract."

Brett appreciated her honesty and her modesty, but from what Dane told him, Alyssa frequently attended writing retreats to teach and went on book tours where she was mobbed every time.

He fell into a huge adult-sized bright pink bean bag chair. The foam inside conformed to his body, cradling him. "Nice."

"I read there a lot."

They worked on the book, Brett saying ideas out loud as he thought of them, Alyssa turning his thoughts into sentences and paragraphs, and eventually, the introduction and the first draft of the first chapter were complete.

Brett was fighting off sleep when Alyssa lifted her arms above her head to stretch.

"So, what got you all pissy today?"

He groaned and buried his head into the soft fuzzy material of the bean bag chair. "Don't remind me."

If he could have hidden there forever, he would have.

When Alyssa didn't comment, he said, "The photography company went bankrupt so there won't be any photos of the races and runners this year."

"Is that a big deal?"

Brett laughed without humor. "Fuck, yeah, it's a big deal." He went on to explain how runners loved to buy their pictures and watch themselves run, or some cases, limp, across the finish line. "You've seen our Facebook page? The website?"

Alyssa nodded.

"Who the hell took all those pictures?" Brett sighed. "Sorry."

"I didn't realize."

"Not many people do. Look, I should go. We made decent progress today, huh?"

"Not bad. But it's getting dark. You should just take a catnap or something. I don't want you to fall asleep while you're driving home."

Alyssa's suggestion sounded like heaven, and before he knew it, he was out cold.

---

ALYSSA LET BRETT sleep in her apartment overnight.

She didn't like the thought of him being in her loft, sleeping there, and she wasn't about to tell him he was the only man who ever had. She didn't want him to get any ideas that she liked him or something.

Last night, he'd seemed . . . she didn't know. Lost, maybe.

Alyssa made coffee and decided to make omelets when Brett woke up. She'd practiced the other day, watching a YouTube video.

Her first attempt had been okay, and then she'd tried

again because she'd still been hungry. It had worked rather well, and she was confident she could make Brett something presentable, and bonus, edible.

While she leaned against the counter sipping her coffee, she thought about what Brett told her about the photographers.

She *hadn't* thought about who had taken the pictures she looked at online, and the runners probably didn't either. They only wanted to go on the website and look at them with their friends.

Alyssa couldn't guess how many photographers it would take to put a project like that together. She'd never run a race, and she didn't know how many photographers were stationed along the route.

The stairs creaked, and she reached for the sash of her robe to make sure it was still tied. She wore a modest pajama set under the robe, but she was unaccustomed to having a man around, and the tank top of her pajama set made her feel exposed.

"Why didn't you kick my ass out?" Brett growled sleepily, rubbing his face.

"That would have been rude. Besides, you were dead to the world. When was the last time you had a decent night's sleep?"

Brett opened his mouth, but Alyssa cut him off. "I don't want to hear about your sexcapades."

He barked out a laugh. "Sexcapades?"

It sounded silly, and Alyssa laughed too, while she filled a mug with coffee. Catching his eye when she turned to hand him the mug, she drew in her breath.

His hair was mussed, his eyelids were still droopy with sleep, his jaw shadowed with whiskers. His clothes were rumpled.

It was all she could do not to lick her lips.

He looked like every male fantasy she'd ever had. All her dream men and all her books' heroes wrapped up into one living, breathing man who just happened to be standing in her kitchen.

Heat pooled in her belly, and she thought maybe he felt it too, the way he stared at her and ignored the mug in her outstretched hand.

Then he grinned, and the delicate moment was broken.

As he took the cup from her, she fought off disappointment. She didn't want a relationship with him, even though the memories of the way he'd treated her were growing fainter with every passing day.

"Do you want breakfast? I've been practicing omelets," she asked, forcing cheer into her voice to smooth over the awkward silence.

"Sure. You've gotten into this cooking thing."

"Kind of." It was either that or starve.

While she assembled the ingredients, he sat at her little table sipping his coffee.

Alyssa felt him watching her, and she wished she could capture his attention like the glamazon runners who hung around marathon headquarters.

On the other hand, if she ever did grab his attention, she didn't know what in the hell she would do with it.

"Tell me about this photography nightmare you have going on," she asked, cracking eggs against the rim of a clear bowl.

As she listened to him fill her in, her mind began to churn with possibilities, and, perhaps, a solution. "How many photographers are we talking about?"

Brett shrugged. "I'm never sure. Twenty? Thirty? Forty? We have them along the routes. We have to keep in mind they need breaks, maybe they have to piss, whatever. Then all the shit before and after the races. All I know is with that company going out of business, they fucked me over. There'll be hell to pay, and I'll be the one paying it. Can't keep everyone happy."

Alyssa concentrated on folding the omelet over and was proud of herself for not breaking the eggs.

The omelet was perfect.

So was her plan, if she could make it work.

After breakfast, she told Brett goodbye and made a call that would put the steps in motion.

## CHAPTER FOUR

Working out can be fun—Brett

Make someone suffer with you—Alyssa

———

W HEN ALYSSA WENT to the gym for a workout
session with Tom, she found him already in the
lobby waiting for her, a twinkle in his eye and a gleaming
smile on his face.

"Hey," he said, holding the door open.

"Hi," she said warily as he took her gym bag.
"What's up?"

There was something different about the way he looked
at her, and he bounced on his toes, excitement radiating
off him.

"How much time do you have today?" he asked, leading
her to the women's locker room.

"Why?"

She'd been prepared to do their usual work out—some floor work, maybe time on an elliptical machine.

Alyssa liked the floor workouts best: obstacle courses, an exercise that reminded her of hopscotch, throwing balls that weighed a ton.

After floor workout days she could never move, but she preferred them over using only the treadmill or the bike, feeling like she was working out her whole body and not just her legs.

Tom laughed. "Are you always so suspicious?"

"I prefer to call it curiosity," she said, stopping near the locker room door and holding out her hand for her bag.

"I was thinking of doing something else today."

"Oh."

She didn't like the sound of that, but in the weeks she'd been working out with Tom, he'd always been a polite and professional gentleman.

"I have all day," she said, deciding to trust him. "What did you have in mind?"

"A run through the park?" he asked.

That wasn't what she'd expected at all, and she felt it fair that she warn him. "That sounds fine, but I'm not very fast yet. I still do the run/walk thing. Is that okay?"

"Yeah, of course. I'm rusty myself," he said, finally giving her the pink duffel bag. "Change your shoes, and meet me in the lobby, okay?"

"Yeah. I'll be out in a second." After Alyssa stowed her purse and her bag, changed her shoes, and went to the bathroom, she found Tom chatting with the guest services girl.

"Ready?" he asked, pulling his keys out of the pocket of his running shorts.

"Have fun you two," the girl said, winking before turning away to answer a call.

He drove them across town, and Alyssa hummed along with the radio. "What made you decide to do this?"

"It's nice to get out of the gym sometimes," he said, parking his car near an evergreen tree in a park along the outskirts of the city. "I get tired of listening to the loud music and treadmills going all the time. Every once in a while I like to go outside."

She'd never been to before this park before. Trees and distance muffled the city traffic, and she was slowly beginning to understand why Nikki spent so much time with Dane at the state park.

It made her feel special he'd asked her to meet outside the fitness center, but he probably brought a lot of his clients out there to try something new. She shouldn't feel special. It wasn't as if this were a date.

Tom led her through a variety of stretches to wake up their muscles. "I need to start running outside more. I signed up for the 10k, and I need to get used to being on a trail again. Running outside is more difficult than running on a treadmill. Have you noticed that?"

He stood and held out his hand to pull her off the grass.

She didn't want his help, but she didn't want to be rude, either and there was no polite way to heft herself from the ground. He took her hand, his callouses rubbing against her skin. As soon as she was steady on her feet, she tugged her fingers out of his grasp.

"No, not really," she said. She didn't compare running inside to running outside. Both were torture to her. "I'll have to ask Brett about that. It might be worth putting in the book."

"That's a good idea. Especially if your readers will want to race. It's always smart to run outside and get used to it, even run the race route if you know it." He paused. "Are you running in a race?" Tom asked as he started an easy jog down the paved path that ran along the river.

The lazily-moving water and the sun warming her skin made her relax.

Brett had beat not overdressing into her so hard that sometimes she underdressed instead.

Spring was always an iffy time of year in Minnesota, and more than once she'd been cooler than she liked to be on a run. Today could have been one of those days if the sun hadn't been shining. "I doubt it. Probably not."

"You could run the fun run 5k the night before the other races."

"Maybe."

She thought if she'd there she'd be volunteering, not running a race—Brett always needed another pair of hands. And he had the photography issues she was still working on. That might take up some of her time that day, too. If her idea panned out.

"I'll have to check with Brett. He might need help."

"Well, if he doesn't need you, you should think about it. It's only three miles."

Heart pounding, Alyssa stopped to walk. "Are you working for Brett now? Public relations?"

Tom laughed. "Maybe. It's a fun weekend, and aren't you going to put the marathon in the book?"

"No. At first he wanted to write about the history of the marathon since he's been in on it from the beginning, but he wanted to do the manual first. He'll probably turn that into a different book with someone else's help."

Tom cleared his throat. "I have an idea. How about you and I walk it and then maybe grab drinks afterward?"

"What?" she asked, her eyes meeting his. "I'm not sure."

Her skin prickled. She looked away and started jogging. "That's a long way off."

"Good point. How about I try to convince you over dinner tonight?"

Alyssa couldn't believe this.

She tried to remember her last date and failed; it had been that long ago. Now Brett was at her place all the time and this thing with Tom.

She couldn't pretend she hadn't felt something when they first met, but she ignored it, thinking that was how all his female clients reacted to him.

He was smart and funny, and kind. Not to mention hot.

A girl would have to be blind not to be into him—but feelings like that weren't real.

"I can't. I'm working with Brett tonight."

"Tomorrow?"

Slowing to a walk, she asked, "Will you give up if I say no?"

"Yeah." Playfully, he yanked on her ponytail. "I like working with you and don't want to creep you out."

It was already too late for that, but it wasn't his fault she spooked too easily around men.

He hadn't done anything wrong. In fact, he'd done anything but. Not finding any reason to decline besides her own apprehension, Alyssa said, "Okay, then."

"Is that a yes?" Tom grinned.

"Yeah, but it has to be healthy, or Brett will kick my ass."

"I can do that. I suppose I better turn this into a real workout or Brett will kick *my* ass."

Alyssa trotted ahead, laughing. "Come on, hotshot, show me what you got."

Tom treated her to a dazzling grin and said, "More than you can handle."

They turned the run into a game of tag, and before they knew it, they'd gone five miles. Hot and sweaty, she gasped, leaning against his car in relief. Her hair was falling out of her elastic, and her tank top clung to her skin. "I'm never going to be able to walk again. But that was a lot of fun."

Too close, Tom rested against his car, but she was too tired and sore to muster the energy to move out of the way. He was invading her personal space, but there was no reason to mind. He'd back off if she told him to.

He tucked a piece of hair behind her ear. "I'm glad. I want you to like hanging out with me. Would you mind if I . . ." he whispered.

Holy shit! He wanted to kiss her.

"Don't be scared of me, Alyssa."

"Tom—"

"I'd never hurt you." His murmur was almost lost over the wind blowing through the tree branches that hadn't yet started to grow new leaves. Cupping her cheek with his hand, he lowered his head.

She wanted to cringe away, but she made herself stay in place.

He brushed her lips with his, and she trembled.

It'd been so long since she'd been kissed, and with such . . . She couldn't pinpoint exactly what was in the kiss, but it wasn't desire or passion, or if he felt that way about her, he kept those feelings out of it.

Maybe he knew her better than she thought he did. Or maybe she wasn't doing a very good job hiding her skittishness around him.

He broke the kiss but didn't pull his hand away from her face. "I would never hurt you. Come on, I'll take you back to the gym."

With her hands twisted in her lap, she sat in the passenger seat, sweat drying into a salty paste on her skin.

After he parked in the employee parking, he sat for a moment staring out the windshield at the grey-bricked building. "I like you, Alyssa. I hope you like me, too."

She didn't know what to say, and scared things were going too fast in a direction she didn't want to go, she fled.

---

SHE ITCHED TO talk to Nikki about Tom, but Nikki was working at the running store and with the race only weeks away, they were busier than ever. Nikki wouldn't have time to talk to her, and Alyssa sat on her news for the rest of the day.

By the time she made it to marathon headquarters that evening to write with Brett, she was bursting at the seams with the need to tell someone, *anyone*, that Tom had asked her out. And for God sakes, tell her what she should do. While she was excited about it, Tom's invitation had scared her shitless, too.

Brett was on the phone when she let herself in. Everyone was long gone for the day, and it was just the two of them. This was the time she liked best. Not being alone with Brett, of course, but the empty office space. No one gawking at her, no leggy runners eyeing her while trying to look like they weren't.

By now everyone knew she was helping Brett write a book. Everyone knew she was running and they would weigh her, guessing how many pounds she'd lost since starting this whole thing.

She liked being at headquarters after business hours.

She could feel a part of it without the judgment of the runners and volunteers who belonged there.

Quietly, Alyssa unpacked the carryout containers of salad and packets of dressing she'd brought for a late dinner.

He raised his eyebrows, and she shrugged. She'd been hungry all day, thanks to Tom and the run. Her cheeks heated at the thought of Tom's kiss.

Brett frowned at her.

Feeling guilty thinking about another man while Brett was only a foot away from her, she broke their gaze and stared at the top of his cluttered desk.

She didn't owe Brett anything but her time. She shouldn't feel guilty about spending time with another man, especially since he was her trainer and helping, in his own way, with the book.

Brett wouldn't care as long as spending time with Tom didn't interfere with the time she promised him to write. She shouldn't care, then, either.

"Okay, thanks, bye." Brett hung up the old-fashioned rotary phone. "I've been confirming expo booths all day," he said, stretching his arms above his head.

"Is there still a lot to do?" Alyssa asked, pulling the tops off the salad containers.

"Nothing new, just calling to confirm things. I don't need any more surprises."

Poking at her salad with a white plastic fork, she said, "That reminds me—"

"I saw your numbers. What a disaster. I'm glad we decided to put them in the book."

Wincing, Alyssa popped a cherry tomato into her mouth.

She'd been appalled when her numbers came back from her general practitioner.

Her blood pressure was out of this world, her bad cholesterol through the roof, her BMI off the charts.

Her doctor almost fainted when he read her the results and had been relieved to hear she'd started an exercise plan.

He'd offered her a referral to a dietician, but she turned it down thinking Brett's menu to be an improvement over everything she'd been eating before she started running.

"Did you run today? I won't feel like it after this. I've had a long day, and I want to go home."

"Yeah, this morning, with Tom. He took me to a park along the river. It was nice; I've never been there before."

Brett narrowed his eyes, and Alyssa's bite of salad turned to dust in her mouth.

"Do you see him a lot?"

Alyssa didn't want to admit she saw Tom close to five times a week.

It seemed wrong, somehow, she was spending time with another man even though Brett had been the one to make her start cross-training in the first place.

Even if she wasn't scheduled to do some kind of workout, Tom always managed to find her to walk with her on a treadmill, or meet at the juice bar for a smoothie before she left for the day.

She liked hanging out with him, but as Brett stared at her, her face heated with embarrassment.

"A few times a week. With the race coming up, you and Nikki are busy all the time."

"You're buying company? Most people aren't going to be able to do that. We have to be honest. How are we going to include you paying for a training buddy when a lot of our readers are going to have to do this on their own? Did you think about that?"

Alyssa swallowed past a lump in her throat.

She and Tom didn't always workout, but Brett wouldn't care.

In fact, telling Brett might make it worse.

"You're the one who told me to join a gym, and I did. Why did you tell me to cross-train there? You didn't tell me this was a poor-man's manual. If money was an issue, you could have told me to buy some workout DVDs from the five-dollar bin at Walmart. And I'm not buying company," Alyssa said, near tears.

She dug around the bottom of her purse for the memory stick they used to save their book. "For your information, Tom likes spending time with me."

She closed her mouth, hating how that sounded. She wasn't anything to Brett, and who she dated or didn't date, wasn't any of his business. She never asked him who he spent time with when they weren't writing, and she had no plans to start. All those volunteers hanging around, they did more than make phone calls for him, she was sure of that.

She slapped the memory stick into his palm.

"Fine. We'll make a note to add a section of different cross-training choices and their prices. You should learn to work out alone. If you get used to company when you run, you won't go when you don't have anyone to run with you."

"I guess we'll have to put that in there, too," Alyssa mumbled, her appetite gone.

They worked on the book, stopping around ten.

Alyssa realized they could only write as quickly as her progress.

Brett warned her it would be slow, so a lot of the book was her impressions, her feelings as she ran.

It was mortifying to write those sections in front of Brett. The struggle to keep going when a stitch in her side threatened to rip her apart. When her muscles ached so badly she felt like she'd been hit by a truck. When the only thing that made her move her ass was the threat of failure and the humiliating "I told you so" look in his eyes if he found out she was a quitter.

When she was so tired of being overweight but she knew running and eating right were the only things that would help.

"That's good stuff," Brett said, saving and closing the document. "It's from the heart, and first-timers will connect with you. Those are passages people could go back to, over and over again, so they know they aren't they only ones experiencing things like that."

"Yeah, I guess," Alyssa said, raw from exposing her feelings. What she'd written tonight was all the more truthful because she was still sore from her morning run with Tom.

She groaned as she stood, her thighs trembling with the effort. She'd had so much fun chasing Tom, and being chased, it hadn't seemed like working out at the time. It felt like it now, though, and all she could think about was a hot bath.

"You and Tom get a little hot and heavy?" Smirking, Brett pushed way from the desk.

"At least he makes it fun," she snapped, her patience gone. She'd spilled her soul tonight on those pages, and Brett couldn't even be nice to her.

"I make it fun," he muttered.

"About as fun as a root canal. I'm going home."

"Wait, come here."

"What?" she asked warily. After his attitude tonight, she didn't trust him.

"Come this way."

Alyssa followed him down the back hallway. It was

unnerving being alone with him, and she thought of Tom's lips on hers.

How would Brett kiss? He was too crabby most of the time to be gentle. He'd be impatient, rough. He'd manhandle her, and she swallowed at the thought, heat making her skin slick with a fine sheet of perspiration.

He opened the door to a small room with a massage bed placed in the center. "I'll rub you down."

Alyssa whipped around.

---

"What? That's another thing we offer after the races—massages. Twenty dollars per fifteen minutes. The money goes toward charity, and the therapists who volunteer their time get paid with mall gift cards the mall donates. It's win-win. Everyone pats each other on the back around here. Hop on. I told you not to overdo it."

"That's really sweet," Alyssa said, tentatively stepping into the small room.

"It's how it works," Brett said, pushing her closer to the massage table. "Most of the time I feel like a beggar, but it's for the good of the marathon. Now lie down. Where are you sore the most?"

"You don't have to do this. I can go home and take a bath."

"I know what I'm doing. I've done it before." Brett took a deep breath to calm down, but he'd been in a shitty-ass mood all evening and Alyssa bringing up Tom made it worse. He should let her go, and he should go for a run to let off some steam.

But he didn't do either of those things.

"I bet you have," Alyssa muttered, but she hoisted herself onto the table.

"Oh, please. I can't pretend I'm a monk. Where do you hurt?"

"My legs, mostly. I think I went farther than I ever had. We lost track of time."

Brett gritted his teeth, pulling off her running shoes and peeling the damp socks off her feet. Her toenails were painted pink, and the skin of her arch was soft under his thumbs.

"Are you going to put your running history in the book?" Alyssa asked.

"Nah. I can do an 'about the author' page in the back, or maybe I'll write a short intro for the beginning. I don't need to be a part of it."

"How long have you been running?"

Brett started on her other foot. "Since I was a kid."

"There isn't track in elementary school."

"Not in school."

God, he didn't want to get into this now, but the quiet room, her warm skin under his hands, her soft voice slithering down his spine. It made him feel like he could tell her anything.

He moved to her calves and rubbed at the knots he found in her muscles. "My parents didn't want me. I'm sure you've heard this from Dane and Nikki by now. I knew they didn't want me, and I kept trying to run away. One night I managed to stay out all night."

"Didn't your parents look for you?"

"No."

Alyssa pulled her leg from his grasp and sat up.

He let her, lost in that night, the little boy he'd been. He leaned a hip against the table.

"What happened?" she asked.

He took her hand, started to rub at her knuckles the way he'd been kneading the knots in her legs. "The cops found me. Bought me a hot chocolate and a donut and brought me home, I don't remember now. Four in the morning? My parents didn't care I was gone."

"How old were you?"

"Five or so. It's pretty cool to ride in a cop car when you're five."

He shook his head, pulling out of that night.

"The cops didn't report your parents to child protective services?"

Brett dropped her hand and pushed away from the table, burying the sick feeling in his gut with the knowledge he was an adult now and could take care of himself.

"They weren't abusing me."

Alyssa tilted her head. "It sounds to me like they were."

"I had a roof over my head and food in my belly. They didn't hit me. Trust me, there are a lot of kids around here who have it worse than I did. Leave it alone."

He stepped toward the door.

"Let's write some more tomorrow night. I want to get more down about trainers and workout videos while I remember it could be an issue. If I have time, I'll try to write more of an outline. I don't want to forget anything then have to go back."

Alyssa adjusted her running t-shirt and slid off the table. She'd expanded her wardrobe, and not everything she wore had the Tower City Running Company logo on it now.

"I'm busy tomorrow night. I can't."

Brett frowned. "What are you doing?"

She'd never told him she was busy before.

"I have a date."

"Let me guess. With Tom?" Brett asked, stung. He'd just shared some of his shitty childhood with her, and now she was telling him she had a date.

Fuck.

"Yeah."

"Well, goddamn Alyssa, how much are you paying him?"

---

"THEN I ASKED her how much she was paying him, and she ran out crying."

Dane's jaw dropped and his eyes narrowed.

Brett didn't blame him. He felt like a total asshole. But he'd been so damned jealous, he totally lost it.

He had no idea why he'd been, still was, so fucking jealous. He had no claim on Alyssa and didn't want one. The only thing he could think of was he'd asked her to work on the book, and she said no.

That it was because she was going out with another man had nothing to do with it.

"Jesus Christ, Brett. You know you'll be lucky if she finishes the book after that."

"I know."

When Dane invited him for a run at Eagle Pass State Park, Brett accepted, gratefully. The crisp spring air slapped cool against his skin, and the warmth from the shining sun was welcome after spending so many hours inside. The snow was gone, and though the park hadn't greened up yet, the trails were dry.

It was a relief to get out of marathon headquarters for the morning and away from the prying eyes of the volunteers who wanted to know how Alyssa was doing with her training.

Five miles into the run, Brett spilled his guts to Dane; guilt and shame getting the better of him.

He expected Dane to treat him like a piece of shit on his shoe, and his friend didn't disappoint.

Brett sucked in a breath. "Do you think she'll go?"

"Of course she's going to fucking go," Dane said, stopping dead on the trail. "For fuck's sake, you practically pushed her into his arms. If you ever want to talk to her again, you're going to have to confess."

"Confess what? That I'm jealous? No fucking way."

"Then kiss your book goodbye. Why won't you admit it?"

"I can't be in a relationship. You know what happened between Marta and me."

Brett rubbed the back of his neck and paced, sticks and twigs snapping under his shoes.

He'd overdressed, and all he wanted to do was strip and jump into the Eagle Pass River. It wasn't deep enough to do anything but wade, but Brett bet the water was ice cold. Maybe the icy water would freeze some sense into his head.

"Actually, I don't, but if you want to remedy that, I'm all ears. Come on, we still have to run back." Dane slapped Brett's stomach and took off.

The bastard was more in shape than he was. The run/walking he'd been doing with Alyssa didn't compete with a ten-mile run at an eight-minute mile pace. That had been at his peak, and back then Marta had been able to run circles around him.

He purposely lagged behind because he didn't want Dane to question him anymore. It was his own fault he'd brought up Marta in the first place.

What could he say to make Alyssa forgive him?

Besides that. Anything but that.

---

"Then what did you do?" Nikki asked, her mouth hanging open, pressed against the table's edge where they were sitting in a booth at their favorite restaurant.

"I went home, ate a quart of butter pecan that I shouldn't have had in my freezer anyway, then threw it up. God, I've never felt so sick."

Alyssa pushed her grilled chicken salad around her plate. She called Nikki barely able to talk after crying all night.

Was she so undesirable, unlovable, people thought she had to pay for male companionship? The idea made her want to throw up again.

Brett thinking it made it worse. He'd been raised by parents who didn't care if their five-year-old ran away, yet had grown up to be a functioning, contributing member of society. What he did for the Tower City running community was invaluable.

What he did for himself was something else entirely.

Alyssa respected Brett for the man he'd grown into, and she sympathized with the little boy he still was.

How he could think so little of her tore her heart to shreds.

"Are you still going out with Tom tonight?" Nikki asked, then took a sip of coffee.

"Yeah. Why not? He's a nice guy, and if it makes Brett angry, so much the better."

"Don't do that. You'll hurt Tom like Brett hurt you."

Alyssa wiped her cheeks. Thinking about what Brett

said to her made the tears come again, and the fact Nikki was right made her feel bad, too.

"You're right, that was shitty. I said yes because being with him makes me feel good. Happy. Like he can see past the fat. Like you do."

"Being overweight isn't who you are. He sees how kind you are, probably loves your sense of humor as much as I do." She paused. "How does Brett make you feel?"

Alyssa took a gulp of her own coffee and remembered the feeling of Brett massaging her hand while he'd been deep in thought, back to when he was five, riding in a cop car in the middle of the night, when he should have been sleeping, secure in the knowledge his parents loved him.

"Hot and cold, but at the same time. When he looks at me, I feel like a bug under a microscope. My hands shake."

Nikki lowered her voice. "And you get wet." She giggled but sobered quickly. "I've told you to stay away from him. That he'd hurt you, and he did. But . . . Dane hurt me, and we got through it."

"You're suggesting I give him another chance."

"Not really. I'm just saying sometimes it's worth the risk, and sometimes it's not."

Pushing her plate away, Alyssa scoffed. "He hasn't said he wants anything other than to finish the book, and now he doesn't even have that. It doesn't matter what either of us wants."

"You're not going to finish?" Nikki raised her eyebrows.

"No, of course not. Why would I?"

"Professional integrity." Nikki ticked off the reasons on her fingers. "You start something, and you always finish. You're losing weight and feeling better. You're going to stop to spite him? The book will be a success, you told me that yourself. Those are the three big ones, but I could probably come up with reasons you don't care about, like you could punish Brett for being heartless, but to what end?"

"Fine. But I won't do anything until he apologizes. I didn't deserve anything that nasty. I don't say anything about who he dates, and a guy like that fucks around plenty, he's even said so."

"That's fair. Let me pay for lunch, then you go home and take a nap. Did Tom say where he was taking you?"

"No. He only said to dress in running gear."

Nikki grinned. "I know where you're going. You'll have a blast."

"Is this some kind of runners' secret?"

"Tom would be mad if I gave it away. But you'll have to tell me in the morning if I'm right. Better go home and sleep. You'll need the energy."

Nikki laughed when Alyssa narrowed her eyes. "You'll have fun, trust me."

---

Tom winked at Alyssa. "Trust me."

"Easy for you to say," Alyssa grumbled, staring out the passenger side window of Tom's car. She'd asked him to pick her up at Dane's store, not ready for him to know her address or see her loft.

Brett had hurt her, and Tom paid.

He'd seemed fine about it though, even going inside to say hi to Nikki before they left.

The secrecy made Alyssa suspicious, and her stomach rumbled; she hadn't eaten, expecting Tom to take her to dinner. "Was I naïve to think there would be food involved?"

"Yeah, but you have to earn it."

"I'm never going to want to see you again, am I?"

Tom grabbed her hand. "I hope not."

The city turned into a section of town Alyssa hadn't spent much time in—not that she had any reason to venture into Tower City's industrial park.

They drove by a huge parking lot full of bright yellow school buses. Several buildings boasted factories inside them, construction offices, or body shops. Alyssa thought they were going to drive through the industrial park alto-gether and come out on the north side of town, but Tom pulled into the lot of a warehouse-type building.

People, dressed in running gear as she was, came and went.

Alyssa's curiosity was piqued.

"Come on. You'll have fun. You've never been here before?"

"No. Never. What is this place?"

"You'll see." Tom held the door open but had to push her inside when she froze.

The warehouse was full of gymnastics equipment like trampolines, foam pits, and balance beams. A rock-climbing wall took up the entire back side of the building.

A rope jungle gym spread out in a corner, and Alyssa watched in fascination as one climber maneuvered the ropes, touching the ceiling when he reached the top. He hung like a playful monkey waving to his friends and looked so impossibly high, Alyssa's skin prickled. Her fear of heights kicked in, even though she was still safe on solid ground.

At the counter, Tom checked them in, and a tall black man high-fived him. "Tom! Haven't seen you around in a while."

"Hey, Gary. Been busy at the gym. I made reservations

for Alyssa and me. Only a couple hours." Tom gestured for Alyssa to join him at the counter, and she smiled timidly.

"She looks like a spooked rabbit." Gary guffawed, taking the two twenties Tom held out to him.

"It's her first time."

"You're in good hands," Gary said to Alyssa. "You can hang your coats over there, but first I need you to sign these waivers."

"Waivers?" Alyssa asked, pulling off her jacket.

A loud shriek pierced the air, and a woman who'd been climbing a rope let go and fell into the foam pit below.

There was no way in hell she was going to be able to do anything like that. Not only was she scared of heights, but she lacked the upper body strength, too.

"So if you die, you can't sue me," Gary said, pushing his silver-rimmed glasses farther up his nose. He adjusted his baseball cap as he grinned.

Tom patted her back. "Let me hang up your jacket. Don't listen to him. I won't let you die."

Alyssa wasn't so sure about that, but she handed her jacket to Tom and scrawled her name on the dotted line.

"Good luck," Gary said, laughing, before turning to another couple who were waiting in line.

Alyssa tried to ignore him, but her stomach twisted in knots.

Tom led her into the cavernous area. "What do you want to try first?"

"Uh." She scrambled for a way to tell Tom she didn't want to do any of it. She didn't want to disappoint him. He looked so proud he thought to bring her here, beaming as he took in the others having fun.

Tom laughed and took her hand. "Come on. We'll do the tramps to warm up."

"Do you come here a lot?" Alyssa followed him along the side wall so they wouldn't be in anyone's way.

"Sure. It's fun. One day when Gary brought his son to gymnastics class, he came up with the idea. He wanted to play, too, but the equipment was made for children. He opened this gym so adults could have fun, too. I had to make reservations. This place has a low capacity limit. It's the law, but it also makes the equipment more fun to play on. It's never crowded in here."

Tom led her to an empty trampoline and jumped on.

He waved at her to join him, but she watched him for a few minutes instead.

His blue eyes sparkled with fun, and he jumped into some small twists. He wore the clothes he usually did to train her at the fitness center—running pants and a t-shirt. The shirt fit him like a second skin, his pecs and biceps bulging, his stomach flatter than a pancake.

He was so different from Brett's long, lean frame. Tom lifted weights. A lot. Brett could run twenty-six miles without stopping. So unfamiliar with a man's body, Alyssa didn't know which type she preferred.

"Come on, Alyssa. Didn't you do this as a kid?"

Self-consciously, Alyssa shrugged. She didn't do much as a kid, always being a dreamer, a reader. An eater.

He did a few more twists, and Alyssa took off her shoes. She didn't want Tom's entry fee to go to waste, and after finding her groove, she started jumping in time with him.

Occasionally, he would drop on his ass then soar into the air only to land on his feet and keep jumping, never losing his rhythm.

Laughing, she tried it, startled when the trampoline boosted her back through the air with little effort.

They held hands like little kids while they bounced up and down.

Alyssa didn't care her boobs jiggled like huge water balloons, but she was relieved when they stopped. She needed to catch her breath.

"What do you want to do next?" Tom asked, wiping his forehead with the hem of his t-shirt.

The trampoline had been fun, but Alyssa's heart was pounding. Tom was sneaky—they were working out, but it certainly didn't feel like it.

Alyssa looked around. The rope tower looked like some crazy spider's web. She wasn't too keen to try it, but Tom caught her looking at it and dragged her across the floor.

The tower spread over a foam pit. If she lost her grip, she'd be perfectly safe. She would probably pee her pants in fear, but she'd land without a scratch.

"What do I get for a reward?" she asked as she started climbing. The ropes were tied into a fisherman's net, and she climbed as she would a ladder, the thick ropes bowing under her weight, swaying in the air.

"I'll think of something," Tom said close to her ear. He positioned himself behind her, and they climbed together, his hard chest pressed against her back.

His presence flustered her, and her foot slipped. "Holy shit," Alyssa hissed, her heart in her throat.

Shaking and trying to catch her breath, she gripped the net, and Tom steadied her, his hand resting on her stomach under her shirt.

"Even if you fell, you'd be safe."

Alyssa looked to the colorful foam bricks below them. People were flinging themselves into the pit, gleefully squealing as they fell through the air.

That was *not* the way she'd get down.

They were half way to the top when Alyssa stopped, unwilling to go any farther. She turned her head to look around the room, now having a birds-eye view.

"Having fun?" Tom asked.

Lightly, he pressed a kiss to her cheek.

Captured in his arms, pressed between his body and the rope, she couldn't pull away. Her heart pounded, and heat filled her face as Brett's accusation rang in her ears.

Tom liked spending time with her, and she couldn't think poorly of him until, *unless*, he did something to hurt her.

He wasn't like Brett, who'd insulted her two seconds after he met her.

Any woman with her head on straight would go for a man who valued her, rather than chase a man who treated her like a piece of trash.

Alyssa relaxed for a moment, Tom's body molded around her as they stood swaying on the rope. Other people who were climbing jiggled them, like ripples in the water, spreading out and out.

"This isn't so bad, but I'm climbing down. Don't expect me to drop into the pit."

"I'll go down with you," Tom said, pressing another kiss to her cheek. "Let's try the climbing wall, then I'll take you to dinner."

Alyssa stepped down, her heart skittering when her foot slid from the rope, but Tom steadied her every step of the way.

Even though she knew she couldn't get hurt, she still felt better when her feet were once again on solid ground.

She followed Tom to the climbing wall, watching a woman do cartwheels on a narrow gymnastics beam. The petite— and thin—woman miscalculated. Her hand slid off the beam, and she shrieked, only to be caught by the man watching her. Laughing, he swung her around in a circle, then took her mouth with his.

Alyssa pushed down the envy she felt for the woman. Never had Alyssa been in such a carefree relationship.

"Hey, are you okay?"

Alyssa jerked at the sound of Tom's voice. She'd lagged behind, and he stared at her from a few feet away, waiting for her to catch up.

"Yeah, sorry."

The rock climbing space was made up of a vast wall with brightly colored holds for toes and fingers.

She'd didn't want to try climbing the wall, but she didn't want to disappoint Tom. Through this whole process, the running, the dieting, the writing, now this, she was trying to be a good sport. Trying something new meant being flexible, having an open mind.

Alyssa had never been one to have an adventurous spirit, happy to have her safe routine in her loft in front of her computer.

But Tom looked so happy to share the gym with her. She didn't have the heart to tell him she wanted to sit this out, even if he probably would have been okay with it.

Tom shook hands with the two people who would control their harnesses. People, hell, they looked like kids, and Alyssa reluctantly shook hands with the young man who would be helping her.

It looked even worse than the spider's web, and she wouldn't have Tom's body to shield her. She'd be on her own.

Alyssa bit her lip. Maybe she should back out and just watch Tom.

Tom nudged her shoulder. "This is the last thing, I

promise."

"Okay."

Tom high-fived her. "Great!"

She let the young man fit her with a helmet and strap her into the harness, buckling it around her like a newborn in a car seat.

If only she felt as safe.

Tom gave her the thumbs up and started climbing.

It was slow going for Alyssa.

She had to carefully place each hand and foot onto a hold, steady herself, plan her next move, then slowly move her hands and feet into position.

Sometimes she misjudged, and she had to find the place she'd been anchored to before. It was like two steps forward, one step back. She hadn't made it to the middle of the wall by the time Tom made it to the top, slapping the ceiling in victory.

Sweat poured down her forehead into her eyes, and she wiped it away.

Tom chose that moment to let go, and the *swoosh* as he fell to the ground made her fingers slip from the brightly colored fiberglass.

With her heart in her throat, she scrabbled with the holds to save herself, trying in vain to find purchase.

When she landed on the padded floor, the impact sent a shock through her body, and her face slammed against a foothold jutting from the wall.

Pain made her cheek burst into flames, and she placed shaking hand to her skin. Her fingers came away bright with blood.

Tom ran to her. "Are you okay?"

She looked up to find a ring of people staring down at her, and she wished the ground would swallow her whole.

What a date this turned out to be.

---

TOM HELD HER hand as he drove her to her car.

Gary had pinched the skin of her cheek together with butterfly bandages, and Alyssa promised him she'd have it looked at by a doctor.

He also inspected the belay system to determine if it was an equipment problem or a staffing issue that had caused her fall.

The rope had tangled, and there would have been no way the young attendant could have helped her, even if he'd been paying attention instead of congratulating Tom on his climb.

That took some of the sting out of her fall, and she told Gary she would have been completely okay if she hadn't hit her head after she landed.

"I am so sorry," Tom said for at least the tenth time. "I just wanted you to have fun."

Alyssa tried to smile for Tom's benefit and said, "I did have a good time. I just need to lose some more weight first."

"But it wasn't—"

"I know."

Gary had made it very clear to Alyssa that men larger than her, heavier than Tom, climbed the wall all the time. It had been a freak accident and had absolutely nothing to do with her weight.

"I would feel more comfortable doing stuff like that if I were lighter, that's all."

"You'll have to let me make it up to you," Tom said, pulling into the parking lot of Dane's store.

Alyssa thought about Brett and his accusations, Nikki's

cautionary words at lunch.

She couldn't date Tom to spite Brett, but she could date Tom and hope it would turn into something more.

Turning in her seat, she asked, "What did you have in mind?"

Tom grinned and ran his finger over her bandage. "I'll need to think of something. I'm sorry for tonight."

Alyssa pressed a kiss to Tom's cheek. He sucked in a breath, and she smiled against his stubble. Maybe she was getting used to being touched.

"It's not your fault. I'll see you at the gym, okay?"

"Yeah. Are you sure you don't want dinner?"

"No, I just want to go home, but thanks. See you later." Alyssa climbed out of his car and leaned against hers.

God, she was so stupid. She'd just let the nicest man she'd ever met drive away.

---

AT MARATHON HEADQUARTERS, Brett hid in a small office. His head swam, and he didn't know where to turn.

He hadn't felt like this since his parents gave him five hundred dollars and told him to get the fuck out of their house. That had been his high school graduation present.

A feeling of abandonment washed over him. He hadn't heard anything from Alyssa, and he was too chickenshit to call her.

He'd blown it. There was no way he'd confess to being jealous of a trainer at their gym.

He wasn't boyfriend material, husband material, father material.

It was better things ended this way.

Misery radiated down to his bones.

Adding insult to injury, the shirts Nikki had been working on still hadn't come in, and he hadn't released the news there wouldn't be photographers at the expo or races.

Dane was busy at the store, giving Nikki a hand with the deluge of customers shopping before the race, and even Marta had been unusually quiet.

Brett felt very alone. Very much like the first night he'd slept away from his parents' house.

Displaced.

Unlovable.

What he wanted to do was go home and drink enough to black out, to forget everything, but he hadn't made it this far doing that. He just had to face facts that there were worse things than no shirts, no pictures, no book, and no Alyssa.

Though he didn't know what those things were.

To torture himself further, he wondered how her and Tom's date had gone the night before.

He'd spent the night in bed with a woman who'd called out of the blue whom he used to date way back when. They'd had dinner out, and dessert in. He'd slunk out of her house like a dirty alley cat around two in the morning and promised himself he'd never do it again.

A loud rap jerked him out of his self-pitying daydream.

Alyssa stood in the office's doorway dressed in a green dress and black blazer. A bandage was taped to her cheek and contempt blazed in her eyes. "Let's go."

"What are you doing here? And what happened to you?"

He bolted out of his seat and rushed to her. "Were you in a car accident?" he asked, shaking her shoulders, searching her eyes. They were hard, icy green chips, and slowly, he dropped his hands and stepped away.

"No. I had a . . . mishap last night. It's not a big deal. Let's go. I don't want to be late."

"Go where? Why are you dressed like that?"

"Do you want to fix your picture problem or not?" Without looking to see if he was following her, she started down the hallway.

Before racing after her, he patted himself checking for his phone, wallet, and keys.

He was glad Dane wasn't there to shoot him warning looks. On thin ice, he was damned lucky she was even there.

"Where are we going?" he tried again, trotting down the building's stairs.

He didn't know what picture problem she was referring to. The only problem he had was the shitstorm of that photography company going bankrupt, and there was nothing Alyssa could do about that.

She didn't answer, only climbed into her car, frowning impatiently while he rounded the tail end.

He settled into the passenger seat and studied her profile as she pulled out of the parking lot and onto the street. Her face was pinched, maybe because of the wound on her cheek, or maybe because she was with him.

A smart man would confess everything, but he remained quiet.

When they parked in the lot of the Tower City High School, all he could do was stare. He couldn't connect the dots between his marathon and the high school to draw a coherent picture.

Alyssa didn't speak, simply leading him into the building, her heels clicking against the marble as they crossed the school mascot, a large crow, that was laid into the floor.

"Hi, Kristy," Alyssa said, greeting a woman in the administration office who sat behind a large desk filled with stacks of paper. "Is David free? We're running a little late—we hit all the red lights."

"Oh, my God, what happened to you?" Kristy asked, standing from her chair.

"It's nothing," Alyssa said, giving the secretary a hug. "David's not giving some kid a hard time, is he?"

Kristy stepped out of Alyssa's embrace. "No. He's expecting you. You can go in."

Brett watched the exchange with interest. People knew Alyssa here. She was a writer, but she must do something else. And who was David?

"Come on," Alyssa said, pulling on his arm. "Stop daydreaming."

Brett followed her down the small hallway behind the main counter. He'd gone to school here, Dane too, but Brett hadn't started hanging out with him until college when they took the same business classes.

"Hey, David, hi, Claire, how are you? You know Brett Sommers."

Alyssa introduced them, and Brett shook the hand of the Tower City High School's principal, and a little blonde woman with hair so short she looked almost bald.

"Alyssa said you have a photography problem with the marathon," David McGraw said, leaning his hip against the front his desk.

How many kids sat here, sweating bullets, hoping the principal didn't call their parents, Brett wondered.

He'd never sat in the hot seat himself, knowing full well the only way he was going to get out of his parents' hair was to put his nose to the grindstone and work his ass off. He'd been too busy studying to get into trouble. He never studied at home though. Nope. By then he knew the score. He stayed out of his parents' way as much as he could. Leaving before they woke, and coming home only after Brett knew they'd gone to bed, they rarely crossed paths.

Alyssa sat next to him and crossed her legs. One of her black pumps slid from her foot and dangled from her toes.

". . . Yeah." He forced himself to focus. "The company I'd hired to take our photographs at the expo and along the route went out of business. We're not the only race affected, but that will be little consolation to the runners. I'm sorry. Alyssa didn't explain this. What exactly are we doing here?"

"That's where the school comes in," Claire said, speaking up from the side of the office. "Alyssa was thinking that maybe, if you agreed, my photography students could take your pictures. I have sixty seniors and just as many juniors who would be willing to stand along the routes and walk around the expo."

Claire nodded to Alyssa.

"Alyssa told us a little of what you need, but we didn't want to come to you until I spoke to the kids. They're pretty excited about helping out, and it's not a surprise that some of them have participated in the race in the past."

David rubbed his hands together. "We could make this into a community thing, you know? A 'Tower City pulls together to help their own,' kind of thing. It would be good publicity for the school."

Brett looked at Alyssa and tried to tamp down the emotional overload that threatened to drown him.

He'd treated her like shit since they met, yet when he told her how fucked he was, all she did was help him.

"How did you think of this?" he whispered.

Alyssa stared at her feet and didn't look at him.

"Alyssa subs here, English, of course. The kids love her," David said.

"The equipment . . . how would we access the pictures? These kids are minors, we would need permission slips, they would need rides to the routes." Brett's mind reeled.

"The high school owns cameras already. Probably not as good as what the company you hired would have used, but we're proud of our photography department. We could post the pictures on a site and maybe, if we can work it out, they could be free to download, but ask for a goodwill donation that would go to the school."

Brett nodded, and over the course of the next hour they hammered out the details that would save his ass.

"Why did you do that?" he asked when they were sitting in her car after the meeting.

Keeping her eyes on the road, Alyssa said, "I made the call the morning after you told me what happened. I was going to tell you about it the other night, but you interrupted me, and I forgot. I didn't want to cancel; it would have disappointed the kids. Claire called me and said they were pretty pumped to help you. To cancel because you were a dick to me would have been . . . I wouldn't have done that."

Pulling up in front of the building Brett rented for the marathon offices, she finally met his eyes. "Goodbye, Brett."

"Alyssa—" Brett said, his hand on the door handle. If she left him like this, he'd never see her again.

With her hands twisted in her lap, Alyssa looked away, but not before Brett saw the tears running down her cheeks.

He climbed out of her car and stood in the empty parking lot as she drove away.

---

ALYSSA TRIED NOT to cry on the way to her loft.

The reasons Nikki told her for not dumping Brett's book project ran through her mind, but none of it made up for the way Brett treated her.

He needed to have some professional courtesy too, dammit. He wouldn't treat Dane that way, or any of the marathon supporters, or the people who donated their time, money, and whatever else to his races.

Why should she be any different? She was volunteering her time, her expertise. She had every right to tell him to fuck off.

Despite what he thought, she could run on her own; she could lose weight on her own.

Nikki was right in that regard—she wouldn't let Brett take that away from her. He might have forced her to start, but she was the one doing the work; she was the one putting in the time.

In her bedroom, she kicked off her pumps and peeled the pantyhose from her legs. It had felt odd being dressed up, Brett seeing her that way. Well, he wouldn't be seeing her any way ever again.

When she'd said goodbye, she'd meant it.

She was done with the whole thing. She'd even tell Tom she wasn't up to the 5k run/walk, and she was relieved that she hadn't signed up to volunteer for anything during the race or expo.

The thought hollowed her out inside, and she dragged a hand through her hair. She pulled off her dress and threw on a robe. The old her would have dug into a bag of chips, pulled out her wine, but now all she had was sparkling water and cheese.

She was cutting her white cheddar bacon cheese into slices when a knock interrupted her.

Maybe Brett sent Nikki to check on her. He wasn't a

complete ass. But for some reason, he just couldn't treat her with any respect or kindness. She brought out his worst.

Alyssa opened the door and stepped back; she should have been used to finding Brett on her doorstep. He rushed to apologize every time he did something to hurt her. She was caught in a loop of abuse, and she had to stop it. "What do you want?"

"I came to say I'm sorry and to thank you for what you did."

He stood in her kitchen looking as out of place as he had the first day he'd wandered into her apartment.

"Well, it's not accepted, and you're welcome. We have nothing to say to each other."

"The book—"

Alyssa gasped, blood rushing in her ears. "It's always the book! The fucking book! I don't give a shit about your book, you know that? It's nothing compared to the way you treat me, the things you say to me. Why can't you treat me like a human being? Why can't you be nice to me?"

Her chin trembled and tears blurred her vision. Maybe she could get one truthful thing from him before he left for good.

"You've never had a kind word to say to me, never treated me like a person with feelings."

Hating herself for it, but couldn't stop herself, she said, "Tom treats me like a person, like a woman with a heart. And then you ask why I like to spend time with him. Why would you be so nasty to me?"

She met his eyes and was stunned to see him blinking back tears. His chest heaved, his hands fisted at his sides.

He backed her against the refrigerator, blocked her in with his arms. Leaning toward her, his breath feathering her cheeks he rasped, "Because I was jealous."

## CHAPTER FIVE

Make exercise part of your daily routine—Brett

Just get it out of the way then you can think about more pleasant things—Alyssa

---

H E CRUSHED HIS mouth onto hers and shoved his fingers into her hair, drawing her closer to him. Pulling back just for a moment, he repeated, "I was jealous," before pressing his lips against hers, loathe to break contact now that he finally had it.

He'd wanted it since the day he met her at Nikki's, but there was no way he would have admitted it then. He shouldn't be admitting it now, but goddamn it, when he watched her car drive away, he knew if he didn't do something, *anything*, it would be the last time he'd see her. Part of him died at the thought.

But now his chest loosened, he breathed easier. Alyssa was here, and she was letting him kiss her. He let his hand drift along the smooth curve of her neck, into her robe. She wasn't wearing anything under it, and his fingertips grazed her breast, his thumb tripping over her nipple as it pebbled under his touch.

She moaned.

"God, Alyssa. Let me make love to you, please. I want you so much."

Alyssa tore her lips from his.

He prepared for her to freak out, to order him out of her loft and to never come back, and he stiffened in surprise when she lifted a hand to his cheek. Tears he didn't know let fall wet her fingers, and he took her hand, pressing them to his lips.

There was something in her eyes he'd never seen before, something softening them, something that gave him hope.

"Alright."

Brett followed her into a part of her apartment he'd never seen before. A king-sized bed decorated in blushes and beiges was centered in the spacious room, the comforter twisted in a floral bundle in the middle of the mattress. "I thought for sure you would be the kind of woman to make your bed every day."

Alyssa smiled, then bit her lip. "There's a lot you don't know about me."

"Let me find out." Brett undid her robe's sash and let the material fall from her body. She stood in the middle of her bedroom, the sun streaming through her windows flirting with her skin.

Alyssa raised her arm to cover her breasts, and Brett stopped her, grabbing her hand. "I know I don't deserve to be here, I know I don't deserve what you're about to give me . . ." he looked away, ". . . and I can't promise that I have it in me to try to be a better man. Alyssa—"

She pushed up his t-shirt and ran her hands over his stomach. The lightness, the kindness in her touch, made him tremble, and he closed his eyes. Brett couldn't remember the last time he'd been with a woman who mattered. The women he'd had between Marta and Alyssa were just a blur of faces he couldn't name.

As she peppered kisses on his chest, he ran his fingers through her hair. Finally, he pulled off his shirt and shoved his warmup pants and briefs down to the floor.

"It's okay," Alyssa said, pulling on his hand, leading him toward the bed. "This doesn't have to mean anything."

But that was the problem; it was already meaning something to him.

He pushed her onto the mattress and gently covered her body with his. He was hard, and he was more than ready to push his cock inside her, to try to find the comfort that always seemed to elude him no matter where he looked for it.

"Wait."

Brett met her eyes, searched for a hint she was changing her mind, but she only ran her fingertips over his jaw covered in whiskers.

"I'm not on any birth control. I haven't been with a man for a long time."

Closing his eyes, he sighed. "I'm sorry. I wasn't thinking. I have a condom in my wallet."

This would have been the time to put on his clothes, run away before he made another huge mistake. But as he rolled the condom over his erection, he looked at her, her head resting on her pillow, knees bent, waiting, the comforter in a ball at her feet, he couldn't bring himself to leave her be.

She held out her hand, welcoming him to her. He

wished, just for a fleeting moment, that she was inviting him into more than just her arms, but he would have to make do with what she was willing to give him.

With the way he'd been treating her, it wouldn't be very much.

---

He didn't look at her like she was some fat blob on a bed. With reverence and awe shining on his face, he looked at her like she was heaven, and he was humbled he was given the chance to peek at it.

But there were shadows in his eyes that made Alyssa's stomach pitch, and he shivered under her touch.

He'd blown her mind when he said he was jealous of Tom. That he could admit it had shaken her, then he'd kissed her, and caught off guard by an admission she never thought she'd hear from him, she would have done anything he asked.

But this was what she wanted to give him. It didn't have to mean anything. To him, or to her.

He lay down next to her and covered her mouth with his. His latex-covered cock pushed into her hip, and she turned toward him, wanting him closer. Instead, his hand found the apex of her thighs, and she gasped when his fingertips grazed her sensitive skin. "Brett."

"You think I'm always using you, but I'm not."

Alyssa arched her hips, pressing against Brett's hand, increasing the pressure. She wanted to ask what he was doing then, if he wasn't using her to write the book, but this wasn't the time to call him out on his lie.

*Take what he's giving you*, she told herself as his tongue tangled with hers, as his fingers pushed inside her, his thumb slippery on her clit. It had been months, maybe years, since she'd made love, and it didn't take long for Brett to make her come.

Brett pushed his cock inside her, catching the last of her orgasm.

She gasped.

He was bigger than she guessed when she watched him slide on the condom, and he filled her as no man ever had.

As he stretched her, made her body accommodate him, she met him thrust for thrust, gripping his shoulders. He lasted longer than she thought he would, but he wasn't a monk. Not like she'd been a nun these past few years because she was tired of being hurt.

It was easier to be alone, and lonely, than to let someone poke and prod at her until she bled.

He shuddered in her arms and rested his forehead against hers.

When he pulled away, she turned her head so she couldn't see the regret that would be in his eyes after having sex with someone like her.

"I need to clean up. I'll be right back."

When he disappeared into the en suite bathroom and closed the door behind him, she hastily made the bed.

"You're welcome to stay if you'd like," she said when he stepped out of the bathroom, the toilet still running after he flushed it.

This was the part she hated. Her heroines were always so much more together with this kind of thing, though the men in her books *wanted* to be with the women they screwed.

Brett fucked her because he was jealous of Tom and the time he took her away from the book. She'd been naïve to think it was something more, and now she was offering Brett something he didn't want.

It took him only a second to prove her right.

He sat on the side of her bed and brushed his fingers over her bandage—she'd forgotten about her cheek. "I'm going to go. I have a lot to plan now with the kids doing the photos. Will you be free later?"

"To work on the book?" Alyssa asked, covering her breasts with the sheet.

"I— No, I mean, I want to keep working on it, if you're still willing to help me. I thought, maybe, but I guess it's better if we don't. Tomorrow, then."

She watched him dress, but she stayed in bed while he let himself out of her apartment.

She balled a pillow under her head and pushed her chin into the foam. This wasn't any better than two hours ago when she thought she'd never see him again.

All she knew for certain was she'd given her heart and body to a man who despised her and let her know it.

---

"You have no idea what you're doing," Dane said, leaning against the bar.

"That's been my whole life," Brett said. He drained his bottle of beer and reached for another that Ian set on a BB's coaster anticipating Brett's mood.

"What's he done now?" Ian asked Dane, wiping the bar with a white rag.

Brett looked up in surprise. It wasn't like Ian to horn in on their conversations, even if they were friends. "What do you mean? 'What's he done now?'"

"It's not like you've ever walked the straight and narrow

when it comes to women," Ian said, pouring shots of whiskey.

"I don't see you mailing out wedding invites," Brett grumbled.

He lifted the shot glass and in the lights shining above the bar, stared into the amber liquid before knocking it back.

The liquid burned smoothly down his throat, but it didn't take away the sting that he could have been at Alyssa's right now.

He'd been a fucked-up mess when he walked out of her loft. He'd wanted to stay, oh, God had he wanted to stay, going so far as to ask what she was doing later. When she'd pounced on the book—because why the fuck else would he want to spend time with her—he knew he was in trouble.

Running and writing were the last things on his mind.

"That's Dane and Nikki's job right now." Ian laughed. "I want in on the bachelor party you're going to plan, Brett."

"It's not until next year anyway, just cool it," Dane said, grabbing a handful of mini pretzels.

Ian scoffed. "Pretend you couldn't care less, but you love her, and we're happy for you. Let's get back to Brett. What apartment did you slink out of last night?"

Brett looked around Ian's bar. They were alone, again, and how Ian kept this place open was a mystery. An old Journey song played on the jukebox, and for once, he and Dane were sitting at the bar instead of at a table in the corner missing the dart board with dull-as-fuck darts.

"Nikki's friend, Alyssa, and it was this afternoon."

Brett glared at Dane for opening his big mouth.

Ian hooted. "I never thought I'd see that look on your face again," he said and shoved their shot glasses under the bar. "The only other time I saw it was when you were with Marta."

"What look? I don't look like anything. I don't do relationships."

"I've seen you with women, and you never look like that. You look at women like you would your dentist. A necessary evil. But when Dane said her name, Alyssa was it? You got some soft glowy thing in your eyes. Only for a second, but I'm a bartender. I can see these things."

"Fuck off. I've been so mean to her, I'd be lucky if she threw me a rope if I were drowning." He pointed at Ian. "And don't you ever mention Marta again. It's none of your fucking business."

Ian raised his hands and snapped a piece of gum between his teeth. "Sorry, man. I just thought you ran her out of town on a rail, that's all, and you never said anything about it to anyone."

Tension drifted around them.

Ian looked like he was enjoying the conversation, but there was a steely look in his eyes Brett didn't like.

"It's been eleven years. Who's Marta to you?"

"Nobody. Forget it."

Ian looked at the TV above the bar, and Brett tried to forget it like Ian said.

"Well, Alyssa saved my ass."

Both Dane and Ian leaned in to listen as he explained what she'd done for him and the race.

"That was some quick thinking," Dane said.

"Yeah, I know."

"You don't deserve her," Ian said, throwing his rag onto the bar top and stomping into the storage room, shoving the door so violently it slammed into the wall.

"What was that all about?" Brett asked when the swinging door settled. "He's never like that."

"You really don't know? Did you forget, or did no one

tell you?" Dane asked, setting an empty bottle of beer on top of a fifty-dollar bill.

"I have no fucking idea what you're talking about." Brett stood from the bar stool and stretched his arms over his head. He'd had a hell of an emotional rollercoaster day, and his body ached with fatigue.

"He had a thing for Marta. When you two broke up, he thought he had a chance, but then she hightailed it back to California. I thought you knew."

"I wasn't in a good place back then," Brett muttered, following Dane onto the sidewalk.

They'd met at the bar. He leaned against his car and took a deep breath of spring air. The aroma of coffee drifted to him from a coffee shop a couple blocks away. He shoved his hands into the pockets of his warm-up pants.

"You're not in a good place now," Dane said, leaning against the car beside him. "What's going on with you? Sleeping with Alyssa? She's not like that."

"I know. I know that. But you don't know how I felt watching her drive away. I knew deep down if I let her go, I would never see her again."

"The same way I felt when Nikki ran away. But this isn't the same thing. I was ready to commit, and you're not. You should have let her go."

Brett nodded.

It's exactly what he should have done.

But he didn't.

And now he didn't know what he was going to do.

---

"You went from deciding to never see him again to sleeping with him?"

Alyssa followed Nikki down a narrow aisle full of plastic covered wedding gowns in a bridal boutique called Desiree's Designs. Nikki was just starting to look for a wedding dress, this being her first trip to see what was available.

"Well, you know how it is."

Nikki huffed a laugh. "The sad part is, I do. And what happened to your cheek?" she asked, inspecting a white strapless covered in sequins. "What happened to my friend who spent all her time writing? I couldn't drag you out of your apartment for anything less than wine, a bag of chips, and homemade macaroni and cheese."

"It's your fault." Alyssa pushed back a row of dresses to make room to examine one more closely. "I like this one," she said, pulling the heavy wedding gown off the rack. "You introduced me to him in the first place."

Nikki snorted, taking the dress from her and checking the small pink tag for the size. "No wonder it's so cute, it's a two. I'd never be able to fit my ass into that." She hung it on the rack. "And you mixed like oil and water. There was no way you should have ended up in his bed."

Alyssa tore her eyes away from another dress, more pearls than she could count sewn down the bodice. "It was my bed."

"Ah-huh. Tell me from the beginning. How did your date with Tom go?"

Alyssa told her about Tom kissing her on the rope jungle gym and her mishap with the climbing wall.

"Well, it doesn't sound like you had much fun." Nikki pulled another dress from the rack. "Maybe I should go with cream instead of white. White makes me look so pale."

"You can tan. Or go to the spa and get one sprayed on. You'll probably want to do that anyway."

"Yeah, I guess you're right. But cream might look better with my hair color. I'll try on both, and you can tell me what you think."

"The gym was okay," Alyssa said, returning to the original thread of the conversation. "But I'll have a better time when I lose more weight."

"So, you're kissing Tom and sleeping with Brett. What about what Brett said to you?"

They drifted through the store looking at more dresses, tiaras, and veils.

A saleswoman dressed in a cream and beige business suit took the two dresses Nikki had chosen to try on and put them in a fitting room allowing Nikki to browse with free hands.

She told Nikki about the photography company closing, which Nikki had already known from Dane, and her idea to have the kids at the high school do it.

"After our meeting, I dropped him off fully intending never to talk to him again. I know what you told me at lunch, but professional courtesy goes both ways. He'd never treat anyone affiliated with the marathon the way he treated me that night."

Nikki sighed and held up two combs to the sides of her head, and the cubic zirconia glinted in the bright light of the boutique.

They looked out of place in contrast to Nikki's running gear. She'd just gotten off work and wore her running pants and Tower City Running Company polo shirt.

Alyssa had to admit, Nikki seemed happy engaged and working at Dane's store. An aura of peace surrounded her that she hadn't seen before Nikki started dating Dane.

"I was hoping you'd forgive him his rough edges."

"Apparently, I did," Alyssa said wryly, fingering an

intricate silver and pearl necklace. She looked at the price tag and sucked in a breath. Jesus. One too many zeroes.

She followed Nikki into a large fitting room.

Their conversation stalled when the boutique sales-person insisted on helping Nikki try on one of the dresses. She probably wanted the commission, and though they couldn't talk, it saved Alyssa from having to do the fifty-five tiny lace-covered buttons down the back of the dress Nikki had chosen.

When the salesperson led them to the viewing area, she left them alone to assist a mother-daughter couple who were also browsing dresses.

Alyssa's eyes softened as Nikki played with the volumi-nous lace skirt of the dress. She bound her hair in an elastic to create a makeshift updo at the back of her head. Her arms were covered in sheer white lace, and a sweetheart neckline discreetly showed off her cleavage.

Nikki was stunning.

Alyssa would never look like that. Even if she lost all the weight she wanted to lose.

"How did Brett end up in your bed?" Nikki asked, standing on her toes to give herself the illusion of high heels.

"He followed me to my loft and told me he acted like an asshole because he was jealous. Then he kissed me."

Nikki stared into the floor-to-ceiling mirror at Alyssa's reflection. "He said he was jealous of Tom?"

Sighing, Alyssa dropped her heavy black bag onto the pink-carpeted floor and sank into a wing-backed chair placed in front of the mirrors.

"I got swept up in it, but I realized it wasn't Tom he was jealous of. Brett blew up because I told him I was busy. The book means a lot to him, and I pissed him off when I told him I couldn't work on it. But he's an educated man, he's capable of writing parts of the book alone, and he should."

Nikki turned, the train of the dress twisting around her feet. "Brett chose you."

"What do you mean?" Alyssa shivered. She didn't like what Nikki was implying.

"Dane told him to ask me for help because he liked the way the handbook for the store turned out. But Brett always wanted you."

"Because he wanted me to be the guinea pig. He doesn't know any other fat women—I was his only choice."

"Don't call yourself that." Nikki frowned. "But I guess you're right."

"That's all it could be. He's disliked me from the start, just like you said."

"So now what?" Nikki turned back to the mirror.

"We keep working on the book. We finish it so we don't have to see each other again."

The idea made her sick inside.

He'd always wanted to use her, and he said after the book was done she could run with Nikki or not at all.

He didn't care.

Like all the other males in her life, he'd eventually leave her.

Brett wouldn't be any different.

---

She was making pretty damned good progress, if she did say so for herself.

Though her incline was set at zero, she was running at a decent pace and sweat poured down her body, dripping off her fingertips and elbows. While she decided she didn't want to weigh herself, her clothes were looser and her energy increasing.

Brett agreed her weight wouldn't be featured in the book, only her numbers to demonstrate she was improving her health. The book wasn't a diet guide, and her actual weight loss didn't matter.

"You've been holding out on me," Tom said, popping up by her side.

Startled, Alyssa lost her footing, and Tom slammed on the emergency stop button.

Alyssa clung to the treadmill's built-in handrail and tried to calm her racing heart. "Shit."

"Sorry," Tom said. "I didn't mean to startle you. I thought you saw me."

She'd been too lost in thought about Brett to notice Tom, and she blushed, hoping her face, red from exertion, would cover her embarrassment. "I was thinking about the book," she said, turning the treadmill back on, bumping up the incline and setting the speed.

"How's that going? How's your cheek?"

"Both are great. I didn't go to the doctor after all. Gary did a good job patching me up, and you can tell him the next time you see him. What's up? We didn't have a session today, did we?"

She'd only come to the gym because she needed to run but didn't want to go alone. She'd have to find music or listen to an audiobook. Minnesota was treating them to a beautiful spring day, and she should be outside, soaking up the vitamin D, not in the gym. Brett was right—she needed to learn to workout alone. And enjoy it.

"No, not today, but I was wondering if we could go out tomorrow night? I want to make the climbing wall up to you."

Alyssa looked over at him, holding onto the grips in front of her so the treadmill wouldn't spit her onto the floor.

Nikki's warning about using Tom rang in her head, but spending time with him wouldn't hurt if he knew they could only be friends.

She needed to break it to him before he asked her for something she couldn't give. She wished she could fall in love with Tom; he was sweet and kind. If only she'd met him before she'd met Brett.

The irony made her laugh. She'd met Tom because of Brett. "Tom, I'm not sure . . ."

She didn't want to lead him on, but she liked spending time with him and she felt like he understood her in ways other men hadn't before.

"Friends. Just as friends. I understand if you're not ready for more."

Legs burning, ass aching, Alyssa smiled at Tom's goofy grin and bright eyes. "Okay, just as friends."

Tom leaned over the treadmill's handrail and gave her a smacking kiss on her uninjured cheek. "Fabulous. I'll text you."

Alyssa finished her workout feeling out of sorts.

Tom knew she didn't want more, but it didn't seem to deter him much.

Brett was only using her, and he didn't try to hide it, either.

Men were a pain in the ass. No wonder she avoided them.

---

BRETT TROTTED UP Alyssa's sidewalk more nervous than hell.

He hadn't seen or spoken to her since he'd pulled the condom off his cock in her bathroom and took off.

It wasn't one of his finest moments, but they needed to work on the book, so he'd have to face the consequences like a grown-up.

Like he had before.

Yeah, right.

Throwing a hissy fit because Alyssa was spending time with another man and accusing her of paying him for company was really mature.

He tapped on the door, and it swung open.

"Come in. I have egg bake in the oven. Did you want to eat dinner?"

She was dressed in cotton capris leggings and a large sweat-shirt decorated with the Victoria's Secret logo. It intrigued Brett to think of Alyssa shopping for bras and panties. He wondered what kind of lingerie she wore under her clothes.

"Yeah, I guess."

He felt out of place, and he stood in front of her sliding glass doors and looked into the park, his hands shoved into the pockets of his warmup pants.

Alyssa handed him a beer.

"Alyssa, I—"

"It's probably best we don't talk about it, huh?" she asked, crossing her arms over her chest, making her breasts swell.

She'd been so soft and supple under his touch, so tight, hot, wet.

It hadn't been the best sex he'd ever had. No, sex with Alyssa had been fueled by jealousy and rage, but thinking of the look in her bright green eyes when he'd made her come made him hard all over again.

"If that's what you want."

He should have been relieved. They weren't going to have "the talk." He wasn't going to have to break up with her when the book was done because they wouldn't be together. She'd be with . . . Tom.

Angrily, he pushed that thought down and took a swig of his beer. It was his favorite; she'd started keeping it in her fridge.

"Brett, we both agreed it didn't mean anything, didn't we? What more do you want?"

"No, you're right. I should be thankful you're being such a good sport. Not every woman would be."

Her green eyes were flat, the sparkle missing.

He hated it.

"It's fine. Whatever, you know?"

Brett relaxed as they ate, and they talked about where the book was heading and Alyssa's progress.

Her cheeks were rosy, her hair glossy. She was slimming down, and he wanted to know how much, but he'd never ask. Her emerging collar bones were sexy, the curve of her shoulder, the soft white of her skin made him want.

"We haven't run together for a while. Did you want to go tomorrow?"

"Yeah, sure," Alyssa said, forking up a bite of cheese, bacon, and mushroom egg bake.

"We can go to Eagle Pass State Park. Have you been out there?"

Alyssa shook her head. "That's Nikki's thing. I'm more of an inside kind of gal."

"I was out with Dane recently. It's a good time of year because the temperature is mild, but the bugs haven't started to come out yet."

"Sounds fine. I'll clean this up later. Let's get some work

done. Did you write out the outline like you said you were going to? I was thinking about women's running groups, and there's a couple in Tower City formed by mothers and working women. They meet in the evenings."

Following her up the stairs to her loft, Brett winced.

He couldn't see her face, but he was sure her pouty lips were twisted in a frown. The last time he'd spoke of the book's outline was the night he'd accused her of paying Tom for company. He tried to focus on the topic at hand instead of wondering how many times she'd seen Tom since then.

Dane accused him of pushing Alyssa straight into Tom's arms with his jealousy and anger, and he was afraid Dane was right.

"That's a good idea. Dane's store holds a weekly run, and you can participate for free. We can include looking up local running groups for moral support."

They worked on the book, Alyssa typing, Brett lounging in her giant bean bag chair. He didn't feel at ease like he normally did, didn't enjoy being with her as he had in the past. There was a formality between them now, an invisible wall, and he didn't know how to get past it, or if he should try.

"Thanks again for what you did at the school. I've talked to Claire a couple times, and like you said, the kids are excited to help. I don't know how happy they'll be on the course at seven in the morning, but I guess we'll find out."

Brett spoke to Alyssa's back, and her shoulders stiffened at the mention of Claire's name. He tried it again to test a hunch. "Claire said she'd be there that morning to help wrangle the kids."

Alyssa turned around in her swivel chair. Her eyes were flat, her lips puckered into a scowl.

Hmmm. Maybe he wasn't the only one with a case of the green-eyed monster. It made him feel somewhat better that he wasn't the only one resentful of the time they spent with other people.

Dane's warning rang in his head.

*You should have let her go.*

Walking out to his car after giving Alyssa a hasty peck on her cheek in goodbye, he wondered if it was a little too late for that.

———

BRETT DIDN'T LIKE the way last night had gone, and he stewed about it on the way to Alyssa's the next morning. He only had himself to blame, and he felt sick inside knowing they'd grown apart because of him.

But it wasn't like he was ready for a relationship, and he'd used women before. Alyssa was different though, and his face still heated in shame when he thought about what he'd accused her of.

Paying for a running buddy was a valid concern, and Brett congratulated himself for blaming his actions on the book. It was all about the book, and now that it seemed like Alyssa would finish it, he shouldn't have anything to worry about.

He should try to be friends with her. Good old-fashioned friends.

They would be thrown together often enough with wedding things, and he didn't want to ruin Dane and Nikki's celebration because the best man and maid of honor hated each other's guts.

As friends, they could move on. He could find another

woman to fuck, just like the good old days, and Alyssa could date Tom until her heart's content.

They would both have what they wanted.

The end.

"Are you okay?" Alyssa asked, pushing her bag to the floorboard.

"Sure. Why wouldn't I be?"

"You just look like you're in a pissy mood, that's all."

"I always am." He pulled onto the highway that led to the state park.

"That's true," she said, adjusting the sunglasses resting on the top of her head. "You just seem more so lately."

"I haven't heard from Marta in a while."

Alyssa's shoulders slumped, and she looked out her window. "You talk to her a lot?"

Brett didn't know why he said anything, but he hadn't realized it was bothering him until the words flew out of his mouth.

He'd been calling her, but every time he called, he reached her voicemail. Her cell and at her office. It was like she was avoiding him, and that wasn't like her. She still remained in contact with him, and at the beginning, that had surprised the hell out of him, but he liked knowing she was happy and living a good life despite what he'd done to her.

"She usually calls me," Brett said, watching the trees as he drove along the two-lane highway. They were beginning to green, the grass in the ditches losing their brown muddy look.

Spring was finally coming to Minnesota. It was a beautiful day, and he would enjoy showing Alyssa around the park. "But I've been calling to say hi, and nothing."

"Maybe Dane knows something."

Brett grunted in surprise. "You talk like you know who she is."

Alyssa laughed, finally looked his way. "What? You think Nikki hasn't warned me off you? She told me what she could, which wasn't much. I know you hurt Marta somehow and made her run home to California. It's not such a big secret."

Brett swore under his breath. He should have known Nikki would tell her best friend what an asshole he was and how poorly he treated women.

Looking Nikki in the face would be impossible now; Alyssa and Nikki probably told each other everything.

Well, no one knew why Marta left. It was between the two of them and always would be. He didn't have to worry about that.

"It's none of your business," he muttered, turning onto the gravel road that led into the park.

Alyssa smirked, some of her attitude resurfacing.

She'd gotten all doe-eyed since they'd gotten closer and the steely glint was welcome. "You brought her up, dumbass. I've told you—I don't want to hear about you and all your women."

Brett drove past the office. He didn't need to stop for a parking pass—the park gave him one every year for helping organize a small trail race held every September. He would be busy in the fall helping with that race, then showing Nikki the ropes in October for the first annual women's run.

He liked being busy; it tamped down how miserable he was.

"Well, I don't like you telling me about all the time you spend with Tom," Brett said, turning into a parking space, but taking up two spots.

The park was quiet—they were the only ones in the lot.

The sun shone brightly through the window blinding him, and he pushed his sunglasses onto his face and jerked the key out of the ignition.

Alyssa shoved out of the car. "I don't tell you anything. I could have seen him a million times since yesterday. He could have spent the night," she lifted her chin, "and ran out the back as you came up the front. How do you like that?"

Brett slammed his own door, the sound echoing through the trees. He backed her against the car. "Did he?"

He was close enough to her to smell mouthwash.

"Fuck off."

They stared at each other for a moment, then she laughed.

The tension broke, and he rolled his eyes. "You're incorrigible."

She grinned. "Incorrigible? No one says a word like that out loud."

Brett rested his forearms on the hood of his car, trapping her. "You're probably the first woman I've dated who knows what it means."

And because the idea pleased him and turned him on, he kissed her.

## CHAPTER SIX

There's going to be setbacks—you have to work through them—Brett

If you're discouraged, remember why you started—Alyssa

---

A LYSSA MOANED AND held his face in her hands, his cheeks and jaw smooth from his morning shave.

His lips moved slowly over hers, his tongue teasing, asking her to open, which she did, willingly.

She didn't like he'd been trying to call Marta, but she'd come to a conclusion while she was shopping with Nikki.

It would be better to be friends with Brett than nothing.

She'd always wondered why her heroines chose that route, and she finally understood. It was better to be friends, take what you could get, and be happy with that, than not have anything at all.

Listening to him talk about other women would be difficult. She'd been jealous last night when Brett brought up Claire. Little pixie Claire who probably weighed ninety pounds soaking wet.

Brett rubbed his hand along her breast, and it made her wet, her panties uncomfortably damp in her tight capris leggings.

She wanted him to slip his hand into her running pants, into her panties, and rub her until she went over the edge.

Hoping to give him the hint she was willing and able, Alyssa ground against him.

"You wanna fuck?" Brett asked against her mouth.

Though inwardly she flinched at his choice of words, she nodded because there was nothing she wanted more. And it's what they'd be doing anyway, she forced herself to admit.

There was no love involved.

Brett pulled on her hand, and she followed him off a trail. She walked with him until she thought by the time they'd get there he wouldn't want her anymore, but he turned to her near a grassy clearing by the Eagle Pass River and guided her hand to his cock. "Sure?"

Alyssa's muscles clenched, wanting him inside her.

A fallen tree lay next to the riverbank, and Brett led her to it. "Get on your knees."

She knelt, unnerved she couldn't see his eyes. He sounded angry, but maybe that was lust. She hoped that's what it was; that he wanted her as much as she wanted him.

Alyssa faced the log and leaned against it, thankful the ground was dry. He peeled the leggings over her hips without a problem; he'd probably done that a million times.

She closed her eyes, pushing back the shame. She was an active participant in this, her damp panties proof.

Brett pulled her shoes off, and Alyssa lifted each knee so he could finish undressing her. The fresh air felt oddly sensual against her ass—she'd never had sex outside before, but she didn't think much more than that because Brett nudged her thighs apart and pushed his fingers inside her.

Alyssa whimpered. His fingers felt so good.

"Jesus, Alyssa, you're so fucking wet. I want to be inside you."

"Yes, please." She panted into her arm propped on the log. Only his cock would feel better than his fingers.

He pushed inside her, then stilled as he reached around her hips to her clit. "Come on my cock, baby. I want to feel you come."

"Brett," she cried.

"You're so wet," he murmured, "you want me." He pulled completely out of her, then rammed back inside her, the tip of his cock crashing into her center. "Can you play with yourself, sweetheart? I want to move, but I can't touch you at the same time."

"Okay," she said. She took up where he left off, and as he banged into her from behind, she made herself come, pushing on her nub that had swollen to an enormous size.

She convulsed around him, her knees shaking.

Grunting with every thrust, he came, and warmth spread through her.

He gripped her to him, breathing heavily in her ear.

He nibbled the back of her neck. "God, Alyssa, you feel so good. I could stay inside you forever." He took her earlobe into his mouth and sucked.

The hot tip of his tongue sent shivers down her spine.

He pulled out, and his semen ran out of her, wetting the insides of her thighs.

He hadn't remembered they needed birth control, and

she'd wanted him too much to care. She closed her eyes and rubbed her cheek with the back of her hand.

Pasting a smile on her face, she twisted around to face him.

Brett pushed his sunglasses to the top of his head. His hazel eyes were clear and sparkling. He took the hand she used to get herself off and smelled her fingers before slipping them into his mouth. "You taste so good. I want to eat you out. Will you let me one day?"

Speechless, she nodded.

"Good. I'm going to hold you to that."

He released her hand, and easily tucked his cock into his running pants.

Alyssa gritted her teeth in annoyance. Men had it so easy.

She was literally dripping wet and would have to pull skin-tight running leggings over damp panties. It wasn't fair.

Still on his knees, Brett kissed her, and she tasted herself along with a hint of coffee. "I have some water bottles in the car. Meet me back there?"

"Okay."

At least he was a gentleman and wouldn't stand around while she dressed. It was bad enough she had to watch herself do it, though she'd lost enough weight the capris she wore were a different size than the ones Nikki had chosen for her in Dane's store.

He walked away, twigs crunching under his running shoes. Shoes he hadn't needed to take off, she noted, scowling.

Alyssa grabbed her running leggings and panties and untangled them. After pulling them on, she sat on the log and pushed her shoes onto her feet. The Eagle Pass River trickled in a shallow stream beside her, and the silence helped calm her furiously beating heart.

Chugging a bottle of water, Brett was leaning against his car when she stepped from the trees. He looked so sexy in baggy running pants and a white Tower City Marathon t-shirt. Sweat glistened on his skin, and the breeze ruffled his blond hair.

He held out his arms, and like a child in need of a hug, she stepped into his embrace.

"I don't want to fight, Alyssa," he said, his chilly palm cupping the nape of her neck. Her ponytail had come loose, and it drooped, resting on the back of his hand.

"I know," she mumbled into his chest. So he wasn't the only one who felt sick inside when they didn't get along. "I don't either."

"Good. Are you ready to do some running?" he asked, nudging her shoulder to look into her eyes.

She could see this as a form of a truce, maybe a friends-with-benefits thing, though those never ended well. She'd written enough of them to know someone would always end up wanting more, and that someone would be her. "Yeah. Sure."

They ran for a while, and she hoped she impressed him with her increasing stamina. She was nowhere near running a half marathon, but she crept closer every day, something she didn't think would ever happen.

He slowed them down after mile four, and they hiked some of the trail, stopping to look over the brown expanse of the prairie. The flowers were starting to bloom, adding splashes of color. She'd never seen such a wide-open space —unless she counted looking over the ocean when she visited her parents in Florida.

"So, what's your story?" Brett asked, sliding his sunglasses over his eyes.

She missed being able to look at them, but she did the same. "What do you mean?" she asked, walking down the trail, her arm brushing his.

"Did you grow up here? How do you know the principal and the teachers at the high school?"

Alyssa pulled at a dead . . . she didn't know what it was. The grass looked similar to wheat, but she didn't think that's what it was.

"I grew up here. I went to the high school. I don't remember you, though. I've hung out with Nikki since second grade. She slapped some kid who was making fun of me, and we've been friends ever since."

"Was the kid making fun of your weight?"

She jerked a shoulder. "I've always been a big girl."

Brett kicked at a stick, and they started up a steep incline. "Are you an only child? Did you eat for company?"

Alyssa pricked with discomfort. She didn't want to tell him it was the only thing that made her feel better while she listened to her mother cry. "My mom was a poor single mother, and we didn't have access to healthy food. I lived on hot dogs and macaroni and cheese."

He shuddered, and Alyssa bumped into him. "It's a common problem, Brett. Do you see what people donate to food shelves? Ramen noodles and boxed macaroni and cheese. What did you give them out of my pantry? All my Oreos. It's how it starts."

"How do you know the school staff?" he asked again, rubbing the back of his neck.

Alyssa didn't mean to make him feel bad, but rather than apologize for speaking the truth, she let him change the subject.

"I have a teaching degree. Sometimes I substitute teach. I've even subbed in the photography department. You're going to have some really talented kids helping you."

"You didn't like teaching?"

Alyssa studied the bridge that ran across the shallow river.

She didn't recognize where they were, and she hoped Brett was leading them back to his car. If she'd been alone, she would be lost.

"I wasn't able to command the room the way a teacher should. The kids ran all over me. Of course, that was over ten years ago, and I don't have that problem now, but back then, I still felt like a kid myself. I liked English, but I felt lost career-wise, so I decided to try and write a book. That worked out pretty well, and I don't have to deal with kids, either."

She tried to laugh, but the humiliation of being told by the principal to think of another line of work came up front and center and cut her to the quick.

She stopped in the middle of the bridge and propped her arms on the wooden rail. If she'd wanted to take her shoes and socks off, she could have waded across the shallow river.

Brett stepped behind her and rested his chin on her head. She thought maybe he wanted to have sex with her again, but his cock was soft against her ass. He was simply holding her, and she swallowed against a lump lodged in the back of her throat.

"Thanks for telling me," he said.

"Yeah. Nikki could have told you if you would've asked her. She's been there every step of the way."

"You don't see her much anymore though, huh?"

Alyssa sighed.

Here was some common ground. Brave in her sympathy, Alyssa pushed a kiss to Brett's forearm, and he tightened his hold on her.

"Not much. She told me Dane's lease is due soon, and they've been going through their stuff. Now with the race coming up, the one she's planning, and the store, no, I don't see her much at all anymore. But you have the same thing going on with Dane, don't you? He's with Nikki all the time?"

"I see him at marathon headquarters. He helps me out there quite a bit."

"That's nice for you." She'd forgotten about that.

"You're plenty busy, Alyssa," Brett said. "You work out a lot, you're learning how to cook, and you see Tom."

He stiffened against her when he said Tom's name. Brett wasn't happy she was seeing her personal trainer, but besides telling her to stop using him as a running buddy, Brett hadn't told her to stop seeing him completely.

Not so eager to make a claim on her himself, she thought bitterly.

The old hostility she felt from Brett's accusation came back and to needle him, she said, "Yeah, I do. I'm seeing him tonight, in fact."

She turned in his arms to watch his reaction, prepared for him to yell at her, but instead, his eyes chilled, his mouth drooped, and he dropped his arms to his sides.

She felt two feet tall.

Just as she was about to apologize, offer to break the date and ask if he wanted to come to the loft for dinner, a whimper came from the ground.

A dirty, mangy, brown-haired dog approached them cautiously, hobbling along as if every joint ached.

"Jesus Christ," Alyssa said, horrified. "That poor dog."

"He was either dumped here, or he ran off when his family was camping, and they couldn't find him and had to leave him behind. My cell is in the car. I'll call the cops."

Alyssa pushed him away, appalled. "No! He's sick, and they'll bring him to the pound to be put down."

"He needs it," Brett muttered.

Alyssa ignored him, and she knelt on the wooden bridge and held out her hand.

The mangy dog sniffed it, then carefully moved closer. Alyssa rubbed the side of its head.

"He needs care," Brett said, grumbling, but bending down, too.

"What do you think he is? I'm not good with breeds."

"He looks half mutt and half German Shepherd. Let me call the cops. I can't take care of him."

"No. Let's bring him into town. I'll pay his vet bills." Alyssa looked into the dog's deep brown eyes and felt a kinship with the dog she'd never felt with another living soul. All her pain and hurt and humiliation of abandonment were mirrored in the dog's eyes. "I won't leave this dog. He's mine now."

"You're going to keep him?"

"Yes," Alyssa said, rubbing the dog's neck, the fur matted with dirt. "I was thinking of getting a cat, but a dog would be better. He'll keep my butt moving for walks, and if he's half German Shepherd, he'll run with me too. I own my loft, I can have pets if I want."

Brett sighed. "He's going to make a mess in my car."

"Your piece of junk is already a mess. If you don't want him in your car, go get mine, but I won't leave him here."

Her eyes filled with tears, and she grabbed his hand.

Brett had to feel something for her. He wouldn't force her to leave the dog behind. It would run away before she could come back for him herself.

"Fine, but he won't make it to the car. He can barely stand."

She was going to repeat she wouldn't leave the dog behind when Brett gathered the dirty dog in his arms.

Her heart constricted. If she hadn't already fallen in love with him, she would have right then. The way he carefully pulled the dog to his chest and stood, trying not to jostle it too much, melted her heart.

That the dog tucked his head under Brett's chin made a tear slip down her cheek.

"Do you know a good vet?" Alyssa asked on the way into town.

"I've heard good things about the one on Ventura Boulevard. Lots of runners have dogs, and almost everyone I know uses them," Brett said, looking at the backseat in the review mirror where the dog lay on the seat, whimpering.

"You can drop us off there, then."

"Okay, but I can't stay with you. The race is only a few days away. I have a shit-ton of crap to do at headquarters. Dane is probably wondering where I am right now, and I'm surprised he hasn't texted to bitch me out."

"It's okay. I'll stay with him and find another way home. I'll Uber if I have to."

They drove in silence back to Tower City, and Brett carried the dog into the vet's office.

Alyssa liked the look of the place and relaxed as a friendly technician instructed Brett to bring the dog to the back.

"You can go," Alyssa said, rubbing the dog as two techs and the vet surrounded the exam table.

"Are you sure?"

She wrapped her arms around Brett's waist, ignoring the amused glances of the vet techs. "Yeah. Thanks for bringing us here. I don't want to leave him alone. He needs me."

As Brett stepped back, Alyssa studied his eyes. A veil that usually hid what he was feeling lifted, and she sucked in a breath at the vulnerability he revealed before his eyes flattened into vacant spheres.

Brett needed her, too.

---

AFTER THE DOG was bathed and fed, they placed him in a kennel with a heated blanket. He was too thin, and even in the mild spring weather, the poor thing shook until he began to warm. He nuzzled Alyssa's hand as his eyelids closed in sleep, and she sat for hours, petting him as the vet staff bustled around behind her attending to clinic patients.

The veterinarian saw everything from sick mice that wouldn't eat to birds that ate too much and provided daily routine appointments in between.

She called Tom to cancel their date, explaining the circumstances. She was torn between seeing him again and breaking things off. He liked her, and he showed her he did. He treated her with kindness, like she was a person.

Brett used her for her writing skills and, more recently, for sex. He might need her—in ways she didn't know, and probably never would, unless he explained them to her—but he'd never let himself take anything she wanted to give him.

She'd hand Brett her heart on a silver platter if she thought he'd take it.

Tom would take it and treat it like it was made of glass.

But she didn't want him to have it. She'd have to tell him she couldn't see him anymore. She hoped they could stay friends because she didn't want to find a new trainer at the gym. They worked well together, and she trusted him.

Alyssa rested her head against the black-wired side of the kennel.

"Would you like to take him out to potty? He might have something in his system now. Then he can have more food when you come back."

"That sounds good," Alyssa said, standing from the tiled floor.

The dog looked up in alarm, but calmed when Alyssa cooed, "Let's go outside baby, okay?"

The tech buckled a blue color around the dog's neck and handed Alyssa a leash. "We have a large grassy area in the back. I guess we'll have to give this guy a name, huh?"

She winked at Alyssa before turning her attention to a wall of cages that house two sick cats.

Alyssa was running dogs' names through her head when her cell phone rang. Her dog, yeah, her dog, looked up at her from sniffing the greening grass. He was shivering again. She couldn't keep him out there long, though even just after a bath, a small meal, and a long nap, he looked better.

Digging the phone out of her pocket, she gently tugged on the leash to lead the dog toward the door of the building.

"Hey, Nikki," Alyssa said, relieved Nikki called her. She'd forgotten she was stranded at the vet's office and needed to find her own way home.

"Have you heard?"

Holding the door open, Alyssa watched the dog shakily pad into the building and make his way to the kennel. He lowered himself onto the blanket and closed his eyes. The short excursion exhausted him.

"Heard what? I've been at the vet's office all day. I even canceled my date with Tom. Brett and I—"

"Lyss, listen. Brett got a call at headquarters before he went home for the night. His parents are dead."

## CHAPTER SEVEN

Sometimes you have to cut your losses. Not everything works for everyone—Brett

If you have a support system in place, you can make it through anything—Alyssa

---

B RETT LEANED BACK in his chair. Things were going his way for a change. The shirts Nikki had been working on *finally* came in, looking fantastic, too, and his photography problem was taken care of.

The Tower City Journal was going to do a write-up about it for the Lifestyles page. He needed to remember to tell Alyssa and arrange a time when she could be at the interview with him.

Brett wanted to give Alyssa the credit she deserved.

"Hey, you're almost smiling," Dane said, placing a cup of coffee on Brett's desk.

"Can't complain," Brett said, gratefully grabbing the

Tower City Marathon mug. He took a sip, burning his tongue. Caffeine deprived, it didn't stop him from taking another gulp of the strong black liquid.

"Did you work out with Alyssa this morning?" Dane asked, sitting in a swivel chair next to him.

Past dinner time, headquarters was empty except for Dane, but Brett had nowhere to go.

If Alyssa hadn't told him she was seeing Tom tonight, he would have asked if she wanted to do dinner. He wouldn't object to finding his way into her bed again, either. She'd been so wet this morning, so willing, her clit huge and slippery under his fingers. He wanted to put his mouth there, make her moan his name.

His cock twitched.

"Yeah. I took her out to the park, and we found a half-starved mutt that must have gotten dumped alongside the road."

He twisted his face in disgust. People shouldn't have pets if they didn't want to take care of them. It made him sick. The dog was lucky Alyssa found it—she'd take good care of it.

He remembered she didn't have a ride home, but she hadn't seemed bothered by the fact when he dropped her off.

She'd probably call Tom to pick her up. In fact, they were probably already on their date.

"That sucks," Dane said. "What'd you do with it? Bring it to the pound?"

Brett scoffed. "No. I wanted to, let them put it out of its misery, but Alyssa made me bring her to a vet's office. I left her there with the dog this afternoon."

"Having a dog isn't a bad idea. I wouldn't mind if I didn't live in an apartment that only allowed cats. Well, I guess I'm heading home. Do we need to do anything last minute?"

"Nope, not as long as the water comes tomorrow."

"They promised. They said it was on the truck, en route."

"That's the best we can do then."

"Seeing Alyssa later?"

Brett shook his head.

He'd be spending the night at home, alone. He could always call a woman, get drunk to take the edge off, but the idea didn't feel right anymore.

Even if Alyssa was with Tom. That was her prerogative. He didn't ask for exclusivity. Fuck, they weren't even dating.

Though she made him food more often than not. Maybe she'd enjoy going out. He could take her to an Italian place downtown. He was a sucker for lasagna. "Nope. For once I'm just going home. Maybe even to bed early."

"You should. The next couple of weeks—"

The rotary phone sitting on Brett's desk rang, and he frowned. It was technically after business hours.

The marathon voicemail relayed his email address and cell phone number, but since he was sitting right there, he answered it. "Tower City Marathon, Brett speaking."

"Do you want me to stay?" Dane asked, but Brett waved him off. He could take care of this last-minute thing.

"Is this Brett Sommers?" a soft, professional-sounding voice asked.

"Yeah. What can I do for you?"

Brett propped his feet up on his desk. It was too late to sponsor the race or for an entry fee to be returned. They never gave back fees; either the runners forfeited the money when they skipped the race, or they made arrangements for the fee to be carried over to the next year.

"This is Lucille from the Pine View Senior Living Community."

"Can I do something for you, ma'am?" Brett asked, uninterested. The name didn't sound familiar and watching Dane walk to the door, he wanted to head home, too.

Tears made the older woman's voice tremble. "We've had a fire here at the facility—"

Oh, now it clicked. "I'm sorry, the marathon doesn't provide charity of that nature."

Dane pushed the doors open and gave Brett a look over his shoulder.

"No, sir, Mr. Sommers, we're calling to let you know there's been a fire at the facility, and it affected the wing your parents were living in . . ."

Brett stood in a rush, and Dane looked over his shoulder and frowned as his chair rolled into the wall.

". . . I'm sorry to inform you they didn't survive. We need you to come to the office as soon as you can."

"My parents didn't survive?" Brett asked, making eye contact with Dane who hurried to stand next too Brett's desk. "What do you mean? They're dead?"

Lucille's voice squeaked with sorrow. "It happened early this morning. The fire department reported that a resident didn't turn off his stove before going to bed. A cat may have knocked a roll of paper towels onto the burner, and it caught fire. Bits of the burning paper landed on the floor, igniting a pile of newspapers. It was a tragic accident."

The woman burst into sobs.

Brett's mind blanked. His parents were dead. Just like that. No goodbye, no hope of some kind of absolution. No explanation.

Dane rested a hand on Brett's shoulder, but he shook it off.

"It was an accident," the woman repeated, sounding just as old as the people who lived in the senior community.

"What should I do?" The words scratched his throat.

"Please Come to the office. There was no mention of you in your parent's file. Finally, one of their friends told me how to contact you."

Brett wasn't surprised. "Okay."

Numbly, he placed the handset on the base, not saying goodbye.

"Let me drive you," Dane said.

"Yeah."

Brett grabbed his keys, wallet, and phone and followed Dane to his truck.

"You'll have to give me directions," Dane said as he pulled onto the street.

"I . . . can't. I have no idea where it is. I never visited them there."

Since he turned eighteen, he hadn't seen his parents anywhere.

Dane didn't comment, only pulled his phone from his pocket and looked up the address. "It's on the other side of the city. It will take a while to get there."

Brett rested his head against the back of the seat. His temples pounded with a headache. He thought about calling Alyssa, knowing her presence would help, but she wouldn't appreciate him interrupting her date.

She'd accuse him of being jealous, of not wanting her to see Tom. Both of which were true.

The kicker was, he couldn't have her for himself.

They spoke with the senior community director,

Lucille, and she was more in control of herself than she'd been over the phone.

"We have the attorney's number on file your parents hired to write their will. We can give that to you, and you can plan . . ."

Brett tuned her out.

While Lucille rambled, he took in the plants that crowded every available surface, the filing cabinets lining the walls, the watercolor landscapes that hung behind her desk.

"I can't help with this, ma'am," Brett said when she took a break to breathe. "I didn't know my parents, haven't spoken with them in years."

"Then we can handle what you can't."

Brett stood and shook her hand. There was nothing he could do. Nothing he *wanted* to do. What he wanted as an explanation, some maybe an apology for the way they'd treated him all his life.

He wanted to look into his mother's eyes, his fathers, and ask how two people could treat an innocent child the way they'd treated him.

They were dead, and he couldn't, and he'd have to find a way to move on without that closure.

"Thank you for telling me this, but it's best you continue on as if my parents didn't have a child. They didn't, not really, and I should't have come. Have a nice evening."

"I'll take you home," Dane said when they reached the parking lot. "You're in no shape to drive. Nikki and I can drive your car back to you."

"Thanks," Brett said, but he didn't care about that. He didn't care about any of it.

So many years wasted, only for his whole life to come to this moment.

Dane dropped him at his apartment and offered to stay, but Brett declined.

Dane probably felt he owed him for the way he'd stood by him when Dane and Nikki had their fight last year, but he didn't need his friend's support.

He didn't need anything.

Brett let himself into his studio, and the stale air hit him like a brick wall.

He cracked open a small window and fell onto his futon, only rolling over to pull his cell phone out of his pocket. He threw it onto the floor where it landed with a thud on the worn carpet. He bunched up his comforter and shoved it under his head.

He wished Alyssa was with him. No, scratch that. He wished he was at her place. She was always cooking now, always feeding him. But it wasn't his stomach she fed when she was with him, she fed his heart, his soul, and boy, was he hungry.

Her loft felt like home—such an alien concept when he felt like he hadn't belonged in his own house growing up.

Now that mangy mutt would be sharing her bed instead of him.

His phone lit up, and Brett looked over the edge of the futon. Dane's number glowed on the screen. He turned away. Let Dane think he was already sleeping—or drunk.

Grabbing the bottle of Jack he kept under his futon so he never had to move when he wanted a drink, he sipped from the bottle and stared at SportsCenter until he couldn't keep his eyes open anymore.

"HE HASN'T BEEN at headquarters for the past few days," Nikki murmured as they walked behind Alyssa's building.

Alyssa shrugged. "Is he alive?"

Nikki pushed on her arm. "Alyssa!"

"Sorry, I didn't think. I'm sure he's okay."

She was more concerned than she let on, but what Brett did was none of her business.

Busy with Hunter, she visited the vet whenever she could, and they said he could go home with her soon.

She'd restarted the book she'd tried to write in November, wrote as much of the running book as she could without Brett's input, and of course, she ran.

She didn't have time to babysit Brett. He'd just found out his parents passed away. She was giving him space. At least, that's what she told herself.

"The race is in a week, and Dane has had to make a lot of decisions he's never had to before. Brett won't answer his phone to answer a simple question."

"He'll be okay—he's grieving, and that's to be expected. Dane's helped Brett put together a ton of races. Go see him if you're that worried."

"I can't." Nikki bit her lip and looked over the trail.

It twisted around a playground and a man-made pond. Ducks floated on the water, enjoying the spring day.

The sincere misery in Nikki's voice caught Alyssa off-guard. Nikki's bright blue eyes glinted with tears, and she rubbed her hands over her cheeks.

"I need to work at the store later, and Dane can't leave headquarters, there's just too much going on. It would mean a lot to both of us if you would go over there. Just poke your head into his apartment, make sure he didn't die of alcohol poisoning. Maybe bring him some food?" she asked hopefully.

Alyssa groaned. When Nikki asked her to do something, she was powerless to say no. "Fine," she grumbled.

She wasn't that put out, but she didn't want to appear like she missed him, or she was nosy about how he was doing. Brett didn't ask her to go over there.

"I'll need his address, and I'll do it when we get back."

Nikki hugged her, and Alyssa returned it, wrapping her arms around the taller woman. It was nice to have friends, and she did say she'd rather be friends with Brett than nothing.

A friend would check on a friend, bring him a meal.

His parents just died. Now she felt dumb not visiting him sooner.

She couldn't win.

<hr />

When she pulled alongside Brett's apartment complex, parking her car on the street full of potholes, Alyssa's lips curled in disgust at the dumpy building that was just down the street from where she grew up. Stepping out of her car, she winced as a train rumbled by, its whistle nearly deafening her.

Trash littered the parking lot, cars were parked wherever their drivers chose to leave them.

She did see Brett's junker on the street down the block, so at least she knew he was home.

The apartment didn't have a security entrance, and mailboxes were missing doors; or locks dangled from being pried loose.

She hoped Brett didn't receive important mail there.

Juggling the bags of food she brought, she let herself into the building and quickly trotted up the stairs.

Nikki said he lived in 215. The building smelled of cigarette smoke and urine. It wasn't a pleasant combination.

She knocked on his door, looking around as she waited. She felt like she was in a trashy movie and could be shot down any moment only to bleed out on the brown dingy carpeting in the hallway.

When he didn't answer, she tried his doorknob, and it turned without resistance. She let herself in, and the smell of booze and body odor overtook the sour smells in the hallway.

His apartment consisted of two rooms: the main room and a tiny bathroom.

Brett lay on an old futon barely covered by a ratty comforter that, Alyssa guessed, used to be blue.

The TV, an enormous old thing that sat on the floor, played ESPN, the picture a sickly yellow, the sound off.

Setting the grocery bags on a card table that had seen better days, she said, "Brett?"

His foot twitched, and he mumbled something she couldn't understand.

"Hey," she said, kneeling in front of the futon and putting a hand to his unshaven cheek. His skin was ashen, and he reeked of alcohol and sweat. His cheeks were sunken, and even though all he'd probably done was lay there for the past three days, he looked exhausted.

Like she did when she had one of her nightmares. She hadn't had one in a while.

Not since she started running.

Not since she started spending time with Brett.

"Fuck off," he muttered and turned away.

He wasn't wearing anything besides an old pair of black boxer briefs, and the expanse of his back beckoned her. She ran her hand along his skin, from his neck down to his hip.

The two times they'd made love there hadn't been time to appreciate how he felt in her arms, or the strength of his body against hers. He hadn't given her the chance, but she wanted one. She wanted to hold him, to kiss him. To tell him she loved him while he moved inside her.

"Brett."

He rolled onto his back, and this time there were tears in his unfocused eyes. "My parents are gone."

"I know, honey," she whispered, wiping a tear that trickled from one of his eyes.

"I'll never be able to tell them how much they hurt me."

She leaned against the futon's metal frame. "They didn't deserve you. You're a good man."

"I'm a bastard. I hurt people. I hurt you."

With an unsteady hand, he tried to touch her face, but she flinched away, afraid he'd poke her in the eye.

She grabbed it with both of hers instead and squeezed. "Not as much as you think."

"Then kiss me, Lyss. Please."

Her heart sputtered when he used Nikki's nickname for her. She pressed her lips to his, and he pulled his hand from her grasp to fork his fingers through her hair.

"I'm sorry, so sorry."

He was drunk, had probably been in a booze-induced coma for the past three days, and she had no idea what he was apologizing for, or what he'd been thinking about while drowning in despair.

"It's okay," she said. And because he was drunk and she knew he wouldn't remember, she said, "I love you, Brett. It's going to be okay."

"Show me," he mumbled against her lips.

Alyssa pulled off her top and exercise bra; she never changed after her walk with Nikki.

He pushed down his briefs, and his cock sprang free.

With the amount of alcohol in his system, she was surprised he could get it up at all.

She kicked off her shoes and dragged her running capris over her legs. The futon was already spread out and Brett scooted to the middle of the thin mattress. She lay down next to him, and the bars of the frame pushed into her bones.

Alyssa wanted to enjoy this. The other two times were so rushed, and tonight Brett wouldn't know the difference if she took her time.

He propped himself up onto his elbow. "You're so beautiful."

Brett's admission made Alyssa want to roll off the futon, throw her clothes on, and run.

No one had told her that before. That she *could be*, with work, was always implied, but never had she flat-out been told she was beautiful without qualifiers.

But the night wasn't about her.

"Brett," she said on a sigh.

He kissed her slowly, his tongue invading her mouth.

She ran her fingers over his chest, his neck, through his hair.

He kissed his way down her neck, pausing to flick his tongue in the hollow of her throat. His fingers trailed down her belly and found her clit. Her hips lifted of their own volition, and he pushed his fingers inside her.

"You feel so good," Brett mumbled. "Let me taste you. You said I could."

Alyssa stilled.

Just because he remembered through his drunken haze something from last week, that didn't mean he would remember what she said to him tonight.

He was too drunk, tired, mired in misery to recall something she'd so desperately needed to say, but too scared to admit when he was sober.

"Okay," she whispered, and she shivered as he kissed his way down her belly.

His hot mouth covered her, and she moaned, slipping her fingers through his soft blond hair, pushing him closer.

Brett's tongue slid over her clit, and the stirrings of an orgasm began to slither between her legs.

"Stop," she said, gasping, "or I'll come."

"That's the idea, baby," he said, but stopped, kissing the inside of her thigh.

"But this night is for you. Please, Brett."

He smoothed his lanky body over hers, nudging his cock inside her. She came as soon as he was sheathed fully inside her, and as she floated down from the high, she thanked God he'd forgotten birth control again.

She wanted to give him a family. A little girl with blonde pigtails, a little boy with hazel eyes. They would be his family. She would be the family he never had.

After he came, he rested his head against her shoulder, and she cradled him in her arms. It didn't matter alcohol oozed from his pores; it didn't matter he smelled like he hadn't showered in a month.

That was what misery smelled like, and she would rescue him from it.

"Thank you for coming over."

Alyssa kissed his cheek. "I did better than that. I brought food."

Taking his time, Brett kissed her, then rubbed his jaw along her cheek. She loved the feel of his whiskers against her skin. "Thank you."

He slipped out of her, and she sighed. "Why don't you shower? I'll try to make some dinner."

Brett brushed her hair from her face, and the tender way he looked at her stole her breath.

"Good luck," he said, pressing a kiss to her forehead before rolling off her.

Naked, he walked across the small room and into the bathroom. The water started running.

She padded into the kitchen and cleaned up with a damp paper towel. After she dressed, she unpacked the steaks and potatoes she brought.

Humming, she fixed dinner while Brett showered.

---

LIKE CLOCKWORK, THE hot water ran out five minutes into his shower. It was enough to clear the cobwebs from his mind and rinse the smell from his skin.

Alyssa was brave touching him the way he'd stank.

He washed his hair and took the time to shave. If he felt like something the cat dragged in, he probably looked it, too.

Stepping out of the bathroom feeling a million times better, a towel wrapped around his waist, the scent of beef frying wafted to him across the small expanse of his apartment.

"Smells good."

Alyssa stood in his kitchen area, poking at two steaks with a fork.

"Your kitchen leaves a lot to be desired," she said with an eyebrow raised.

Brett stopped digging in his dresser drawer to look at her. "So does my whole life."

He frowned when someone knocked on his door, but

before he could walk the twenty feet to answer it, the door flew open and a short brunette burst into the room and into his arms.

"Marta?" he asked, frozen in place.

As Marta clung to him, he looked over her shoulder to Alyssa.

Her face went paper white. Her hands trembled as she turned off the burner under the steaks and pressed Stop on the microwave.

He couldn't stop her from gathering her purse off the card table and walking out of his apartment because Marta was pushing her lips to his and there was nothing to say.

---

SHE COULD HAVE handled that better, but watching Marta fling herself into Brett's arms was more than she could tolerate.

At least she'd turned off the steaks and stopped the potatoes. He could finish making them for Marta if he wanted.

Alyssa sat in her car, her hands shaking on the wheel. Taking a deep, watery breath, she started the car. The sun was just beginning to set, the days finally longer as winter slipped away.

Out of curiosity, Alyssa drove the two short blocks to where she'd grown up. Brett lived in this neighborhood because he didn't care; she'd had to because her mother couldn't afford anything else.

Marta came back.

And from what Alyssa knew, Brett loved her. Had loved her.

She didn't know what he felt for Marta now. They'd

stayed in touch all these years—mainly because she called him. Probably because she wanted him back.

Any woman with eyes and a brain would want him back.

She was glad Brett was too drunk to remember what she told him because she regretted saying it now.

The expo was a week away. She would go, make notes of her impressions for the book.

She planned to finish it quickly. She could run five miles now without stopping. It was a slow five miles but an accomplishment nonetheless. After wrapping it up, she would turn it over to Brett. He could add whatever he wanted to. Then it would be done.

All of it.

Alyssa stared at the dumpy building where she'd spent her childhood in a small, dingy apartment. Her father's words not meant for her ears echoed through her mind, her little four-year-old heart shattering as her father let himself out the door.

They hadn't lived here. Not then.

She'd had to give up her back yard. Her dog.

And she'd turned to food.

Alyssa wiped her cheeks.

There hadn't been a time she wanted to go through Dairy Queen's drive-thru more than she did now.

Eating didn't help. If she'd learned anything from this whole running manual fiasco was that eating made things a hell of a lot worse.

After digging her cell out of her purse, she checked the time. She groaned in disappointment. It was too late to visit Hunter. She wanted to bring him home soon. Even after just a few days at the clinic, he looked healthier, and his excited yips when he saw her always made her heart turn over.

For now, she'd need to settle for a shower. Sticky with come and tears, she felt dirty, and Brett's body odor coated her skin.

She hoped Marta could help him.

Someone needed to.

---

JERKING ON A pair of basketball shorts and a Tower City Marathon tank top, Brett scrubbed his hair with his towel. It'd been a little over ten years since he'd seen Marta. Ten years since he'd held her in his arms. Ten years since he broke her heart.

She sat on his black futon now, the same one they'd made love on before, the same one Alyssa had just told him—

He'd had women tell him that before.

It never made a difference.

It was never true.

"What are you doing here?"

She didn't look like she'd been traveling, instead she looked perky—her hair in two little pigtails along the sides of her head, a pink tint coloring her cheeks.

Her running clothes were still smooth though she'd been folded into an airplane seat for the better part of the day.

"I signed up for the race," she said, her brown eyes dewy with compassion, yet a little guarded. "Did I interrupt something? She didn't have to go." Marta tucked her hands between her knees.

"It's probably a good thing she did," he muttered,

stomping into his kitchen. The steaks were starting to congeal in the pan, and he scraped them into the garbage.

Alyssa had tried to hide it, but she'd been crying when she snuck out the door. That thought pissed him off, too.

She had no right to cry.

He'd made goddamn sure he hadn't made her any promises.

The fact that through his booze-soaked misery she looked like his angel of salvation had nothing to do with it.

Let her run to Tom after fucking him.

She was good at that.

Brett pulled the potatoes from the microwave and lobbed them into the trash as well.

"Dane told me about your parents," Marta said, watching him clean his kitchen.

Pulling a beer from his fridge, Brett said, "Nothing will change."

He didn't need any more booze, but he didn't stop himself from popping off the cap and taking a long draw.

"But—"

"Nothing will change, Marta. You know that. Hell, it's a relief. It was stupid to live in the same fucking city and not have any contact with them. Now I have a real excuse."

He narrowed his eyes. "Where are you staying?"

He hoped she didn't think she could stay with him. Those days were long gone.

"Dane's. He's at Nikki's all the time, and he said I could stay at his apartment. He wanted to pick me up at the airport, but I came straight here to see you."

"I'm fine."

"Who was that, Brett? You didn't tell me you were seeing anyone."

"I'm not. We're working on a book—a running manual

for beginners—and she's helping me, that's it. Besides, I tried calling you a couple times. You never answered, so I don't think you should be on my ass about not knowing."

"I wanted my visit to be a surprise," Marta murmured, looking at the floor.

"Mission accomplished."

Brett rubbed a hand over his face. "Look, I'm sorry. It will be nice to have you here for a while. Staying at Dane's is a good idea. Let me bring you over there. I need to talk to him, anyway. I've left him holding the bag at headquarters for long enough. Where's your luggage?"

"In the hallway."

"You'll be lucky if they're not stolen," he said, gritting his teeth and palming his car keys.

"Are you alright to drive?" Marta asked frowning, following him to the door.

"Alyssa woke me up."

"Is that her name? Who really is she to you?"

Brett hefted Marta's duffle bag to walk it down to his car.

He glanced at her out of the corner of his eye.

She looked the same: small, slim. Her brown eyes bright with energy, her hair done like a little girl's. What would their life be like now, had they stayed together? How many kids would they have had if he'd let her—

Brett shook his head. "Nobody."

---

ALYSSA DIDN'T SEE anyone the week of the race. The store kept Nikki busy, and Dane worked at headquarters from sun up to sun down.

Brett didn't text or call.

She worked on the book and ran.

Tom tried to talk her into running the Saturday morning 10k race with him, but she promised she would visit his booth at the expo instead.

Alyssa was used to race week—at least, she was used to Nikki being busy. But now that she'd been spending time with Nikki, Dane, and Brett, she felt abandoned by everyone.

Everyone except Hunter. He'd bounced back with amazing speed, and Friday morning before she stopped by the community center to visit the running expo, she drove by the vet's office.

He'd become the vet's mascot, and they let him wander around the office, his nails scratching the white and grey tile.

When Alyssa stepped inside, he was right there waiting for her.

"Hey, sweetheart," she said, dropping to her haunches to scratch his ears and accept an enthusiastic lick to her cheek.

"Alyssa," the receptionist greeted her warmly. "He's been watching for you."

"He's a love," Alyssa said, standing. "He looks ready to go home."

The blonde receptionist nodded. "The vet has some good news on that front."

After a quick meeting with the vet to schedule Hunter's follow-up appointment for the end of the month, Alyssa led Hunter to her car.

She hadn't expected to be able to bring him home, and she hoped the community center wouldn't mind her bringing the dog into the building. It seemed cruel to pick up Hunter only to drop him off at her loft, leaving him alone in a strange place for most of the day.

Cars filled the huge parking lot, and people came and went toting bright yellow and blue string bags.

When she stood on a deck overlooking the expo, she was amazed again at all Brett did to put the marathon together.

Over the intercom, an announcement sounded, alerting runners of a speaker who would begin in ten minutes.

Hunter looked around with curiosity, and Alyssa was relieved he wasn't scared of all the activity.

No one had stopped her when she walked through the turnstile into the center, but Hunter had gotten plenty of glances and pats on the head. Alyssa explained numerous times she'd rescued the abandoned dog from Eagle Pass State Park.

Dressed in her workout gear and holding Hunter's leash, she chatted with runners picking up their bags and bibs or registering last minute for a race. It made her feel like she belonged.

Spotting the booth Nikki was manning to promote the women's race, Alyssa started toward it, weaving her way through the crowd. Maybe she would run that race next year.

If she was still running.

Or she could help Nikki. Or not.

She and Brett would never work out. If she were honest with herself, she knew their chances were slim to none, and she didn't want to be tied to the running community in a way where she'd have to see him all the time. If she volunteered, he would be her boss of sorts, and she didn't care for that idea.

Nikki spotted her and waved, and she brought Hunter over to meet her.

"So this is the sweet boy," Nikki squealed, running from behind the table to pet the dog. "It'll be fun to take him running with us. I wish I could get a dog."

"He bounced back surprisingly fast," Alyssa said, looking at all the booths and people milling around the grey concrete floor. She'd never been to an expo before, though Nikki had invited her along several times.

The expo was open to the public whether they signed up for a race or not, and many booths advertised products for everyone, not just runners.

"He's lucky you and Brett found him."

"How's Brett doing?" Alyssa asked, trying to sound like she didn't care.

"Busy with this, though there haven't been any emergencies that have come up, thank God." Nikki lowered her voice. "He won't talk about his mom and dad. Not to Dane, anyway. Marta on the other hand . . ." Nikki held up her hands and shrugged.

Alyssa's heart dropped to her feet.

Of course he'd tell Marta everything. Well, she should be glad he had someone. Remembering the misery in his eyes when she'd looked in on him brought tears to hers, and Hunter must have felt her distress because he rubbed his head against her thigh and whined.

Nikki's smile strained. "Are you sure you don't want to run something tomorrow? Or the 5k tonight?"

"No." Alyssa shook her head. "I'm going to walk around a little then go home. I only came because I promised Brett I would write about my impressions in the book."

"Lyss . . ." Nikki trailed off uncertainly. "I told you a long time ago not to get involved with him."

Resting her hand on Hunter's muzzle to soothe him, Alyssa said, "Yeah, you did. I just couldn't help it, you know?"

Nikki sighed. "I know. Hurting men are too much to resist."

She tried to speak around the lump in her throat, but she couldn't manage anything other than a squeak.

Squeezing her shoulder in goodbye, Nikki turned away to answer a question about the women's race.

Alyssa hoped she'd run into Brett, but at the same time, she hoped she wouldn't. She didn't want to see Marta hanging on him. Nikki hadn't said they were back together, so that was something.

She didn't know why she was holding out hope. He wasn't in any frame of mind to be in a relationship.

Love only did so much.

"Alyssa!"

Tom's voice cut through the crowd.

Flanked by two large banners displaying the benefits of joining the Tower City Fitness Center, he was sitting behind a table littered with brochures and what looked to be a sign-up sheet.

"Hey."

She stopped scanning the expo to focus on Tom, who looked handsome dressed in khaki pants and a light blue polo shirt stitched with the Tower City Fitness Center logo.

"So, this is the guy who took you away from me," Tom said, laughing, bending down to pet the dog. "He looks good."

"Yeah," she agreed, rubbing Hunter's neck. "Even after just a few days, he looks a lot better. Still on the thin side, though."

"You'll fix him up," Tom said, standing, then leaned against his table.

"I hope so. You should've seen the vet bill. They told me since I'm adopting him, the Humane Society would pay it."

Tom whistled. "That was lucky." He held out his arms. "Come here. I've missed you."

Alyssa stepped into the V of his thighs and let him rest his forearms on her shoulders.

"Your cheek is healing."

"Yeah. I don't think it will scar."

Tom brushed the side of her face with the pad of his thumb.

Alyssa wished she could feel something for him. He was so sweet. He'd treated her with respect from the beginning, but she'd never be able to be in a relationship with him, or anyone.

Not with the way she felt about Brett.

She couldn't use Tom that way.

Uncomfortable with his attention, she looked away, and her skin prickled when she met Brett's eyes across the crowded floor.

He was talking into his cell phone, holding a clipboard, and even from that distance, she could see his eyes ice over.

Alyssa stiffened and fought the urge to pull away, but Tom noticed.

"So, that's how it is, huh?"

Alyssa broke eye contact with Brett. "I don't know what you're talking about."

"You and Brett."

"There's nothing between us."

Tom laughed and yanked on the ends of Alyssa's hair. "Like hell there isn't. If looks could kill, you'd be scraping me off the floor."

"He doesn't want anything like that," Alyssa said, looking into Tom's eyes.

"Then let me help."

Alyssa tamped back a smile. "What can you do?"

"Make him jealous."

Tom pulled her into his arms and kissed her.

## CHAPTER EIGHT

When you work with someone toward a common goal, it makes things easier—Alyssa

Figuring out those goals before you start is a good idea. In other words, don't ambush
your partner—Brett

You can't help it if things evolve—Alyssa

At least give a guy some warning—Brett

———

"Y ou could just admit you want more," Dane said, amused, watching Brett scowl.

Brett slid his cell phone into the pocket of his running pants. "And just why in the hell would I do that?"

"Because you do. Are you still sleeping with her? You know she's not like your other women. You always make sure they know the score."

Brett trudged across the expo floor. Things were going off without a hitch. The volunteers for the booths had shown up, all the speakers were in attendance. The youth race the night before had gone well and boasted the most kids participating to date.

The 5k was set for that evening, and the weather was holding in their favor.

Having Nikki, Dane, and Marta there had been a tremendous help. It made things a lot easier for him.

Alyssa was only at the expo to write down her experiences for the book, but he should have insisted she run a race. She could handle the 10k just fine, but he didn't want to push. Not all runners raced, though sooner or later most caught the bug. If Alyssa kept running after the book was completed, he'd bet a year's salary Nikki would convince her.

"Alyssa knows the score. Why do you think she's still hanging around that guy from the gym? I've made it plain enough I'm not interested in a relationship."

He opened the door to a small office the community center cleaned out for his use. He needed a breather. There were too many people around, and they all wanted a piece of him.

"Then why does it look like you want to murder the guy she's talking to? Is the book done yet?" Dane followed him into the cramped office and shut the door.

Silence enveloped them, and Brett sagged in relief.

His phone buzzed in his pocket, but he ignored it.

Marta was around somewhere, and everyone knew Nikki. They could ask her for help as well.

"I don't know where we are with the book. We haven't worked on it for a while. I've been busy with my parents and the race."

If busy meant getting drunk and wallowing, then yeah, he'd been busy. And in no mood to write.

"She's been running," Dane said, opening a bottle of water.

"Yeah, she's holding up her end of the deal." Brett had been impressed with her on the trail.

Dane raised his eyebrows. "Then isn't it time to hold up yours?"

---

DANE DIDN'T KNOW what the fuck he was talking about, Brett grumbled to himself as he walked up the front sidewalk to Alyssa's loft. There was no bargain for him to keep. He would have his book; she would lose weight. Which was what she was doing.

She looked good, he thought, letting himself into her building, and it made jealousy roll in his gut whenever he thought about her and whatever the fuck his name was.

It's not like Alyssa seeing Gym Guy was a crime, though Brett hadn't seen anyone for a while.

He didn't need much in way of companionship or sex, and what he required he'd been getting from Alyssa whether she was fucking both him and Tom at the same time or not.

Like hell he was going to ask if she was sleeping with the guy. It wasn't any of his business, and she'd never asked him if he was sleeping with other women, though she probably assumed he was sleeping with Marta since she'd come back.

As he waited for Alyssa to open her door, he groaned. He didn't know why Marta was still hanging around. The race was over, but she was having a fine time staying at

Dane's and hanging out with all of them. She even suggested having a small engagement party for Dane and Nikki at Ian's bar.

That was part of the reason he was at Alyssa's tonight. To invite her to the engagement party, to work on the book, and something else.

What Dane said at the expo bothered him.

Alyssa was doing him an enormous favor, and now he felt like he owed her for helping him.

He didn't like it.

Hair messed up and barefoot, Alyssa opened the door wearing black leggings and a Tower City Marathon t-shirt she must have purchased at the expo. She looked adorable, and her apartment smelled like fish. Brett mentally rolled his eyes. Those two thoughts did not belong together.

As it always did when he stepped over her threshold, tension drained from his body. She was making him dinner. They would eat, work on the book, and he would go home, just like when they first started.

He hadn't realized how soothing that routine had become.

And how much he'd come to depend on it.

"Hey, you look cute," he greeted her, stepping into her loft.

"Thanks. Nikki talked me into the shirt. How did the expo go? We're having fish, rice, and vegetables, by the way."

"It was fine. The races went fine. It was a good year. The kids had a blast taking pictures. That whole deal worked incredibly well. It makes me wonder if we can't do it every year, though the race is paid a chunk of the picture sales. I would have to make up that difference in sponsorships. I'm going to ask Dane to help me crunch the numbers, but for now, we have a photography company scheduled for next year."

Brett took a seat on her couch and pet Hunter, who had made himself at home. "So, this is the dog, huh? He doesn't even look like the same mutt."

With that, Hunter crawled into Brett's lap and tucked his head under Brett's chin, the same way he had that day in the park.

Alyssa smiled. "He remembers you."

Brett rubbed the dog's neck and grimaced when the dog's wet nose touched his skin. "Is he okay? What did you name him?"

That he didn't know made him sad. He wasn't a part of Alyssa's life at all. She'd rescued the dog weeks ago, but they had talked so little he didn't know what she named her dog.

He bet Tom knew. The thought rankled, and he gritted his teeth.

"Hunter. He's a good dog. Surprisingly healthy. Hunter, come."

The dog reluctantly crawled off Brett's lap and with a sad look in his dark brown eyes, slunk to a corner where Alyssa had laid out a huge cushion-like pillow.

"Sometimes he'll sleep there, but he's a lonely guy, probably missing his previous family, and mostly he sleeps in bed with me at night. I shouldn't let him do it but . . ." Alyssa's smile faded. "Are you hungry?"

"Yeah."

He was a lonely guy too, and he wanted someone to sleep with. Silently, Brett grunted with disgust. Now he was jealous of her dog.

He needed to get a grip.

Over dinner, they talked about the expo, the races, and

he filled her in on the wonderful job the high school photography department did.

"How's Marta?" Alyssa asked, clearing the table after their meal.

"Okay."

He didn't want to talk about Marta, but her question was a good lead-in for the engagement party invitation.

"She's hanging out with Dane and Nikki. They've been taking her around the city. She wanted to see how it's changed since she moved to California."

"She's lucky she's able to stay in Dane's apartment, though she probably would have stayed with you, right?"

She turned away so he couldn't see her eyes, but her jealousy both pleased and pissed him off. She had no right to be jealous when she dangled Tom in his face.

But with the need to explain, to make her understand that he and Marta were over, he placed his hands on her shoulders and drew her close.

Washing the frying pan she'd used to cook the fish, her hands stilled under the running water.

"She never lived with me," he murmured into her hair. "She stayed in the dorms on campus."

"Okay."

Alyssa finished rinsing the pan and turned the water off.

Brett pressed into her while she dried her hands. "We're only friends."

He made her face him, and he searched her bright green eyes. There were shadows in them, disbelief, and fear. But there was love in them too, and he didn't doubt what she said to him that night in his apartment.

"Brett, I—"

He shook his head. "Things are okay? Things are good?"

Alyssa nodded. "Yeah, no problem. We're going to work on the book some more, right?"

"Yeah."

"Hunter," Alyssa called, and the dog bounded up the stairs full of joy because he hadn't been forgotten.

They followed, and when they reached Alyssa's office, Brett laughed. "He's in my spot."

The dog had made himself comfortable on her large bean bag chair.

"That's his favorite spot to sleep when I'm up here writing."

They went through the parts of the book Alyssa had written on her own when he'd been busy. Alyssa's commitment astounded him, and he cleared his throat, impressed with all she'd done without him having to ask.

"Thank you," he murmured, sitting in the chair she'd pulled out of the closet for him.

She tucked a piece of hair behind her ear. "You're welcome. I did what I could, but I wasn't sure where you wanted to go with this. I believe in this project. Nikki was right. Running gives me something. A satisfaction. A . . . I'm not sure. I feel better." Her mouth quirked. "I'm starting to look better."

Brett ran his fingers over the soft skin of her jaw, chagrined by the way he'd treated her before he'd gotten to know her.

"You were fine, before, Alyssa. Only a fool couldn't see it."

Blushing, she looked away.

"Marta's planning a small engagement party for Dane and Nikki. Will you go with me?" He frowned. Caught up in their intimate moment, he'd forgotten, or wanted to forget, she was seeing Tom.

"Unless you want to invite Tom to go with you."

———

ALYSSA LOOKED AT her twisted fingers resting on her black wrist pad. She had to put a stop to this. She would never earn Brett's trust if she continued to let him believe she and Tom were a couple.

"Tom and I aren't seeing each other."

"He kissed you at the expo. I saw him."

"When you walked by, and you saw us standing there, I stepped back and Tom noticed. He only wanted to make you jealous, give you a push, he said. I tried to tell him there wasn't anything going on between you and me, but the way you were glaring at us, he didn't believe it."

Brett blew out a breath. "He's right. There *is* something between us, and he did make me jealous. He has all along."

Blinking in amazement, Alyssa's mouth dropped open. But before she could ask if he'd gone crazy, he kissed her.

"I don't want there to be anything. I've tried to fight it, but I can't," Brett mumbled, smoothing the pad of his thumb over her trembling lips. "I'm not . . . I'm not good at relationships, Alyssa. I don't have anything to give."

Alyssa didn't believe that for a minute. He had a lot to give; he was just afraid to be shot down.

He'd tried to give his parents love only to be turned away time and time again. They'd taught him he was unlovable, and now when someone told him they loved him, he didn't believe it.

She was glad he was too drunk that night to remember

that she'd told him that as well. He wouldn't have believed her.

"Will you make love to me, Brett?" she asked, her breath feathering his thumb. She said it like that to counteract the way he'd asked her at Eagle Pass State Park. He might be fucking her, but she was making love to him.

He smiled. "Here?"

Rubbing her fingers over his stubbly jaw, she smiled, too. "Probably not here. We don't need an audience."

"Sounds good."

Nervously, she led Brett down the stairs and into her bedroom. They'd made love three times, but this felt like the first time to her.

Her heart hammered, thumping against her ribs; she hoped he couldn't hear it.

"This color looks good on you," Brett complimented, tugging at the hem of her lavender-colored shirt before pulling it over her head.

"Nikki picked it out. She's such a girlie-girl." Alyssa laughed, shoving her hands under his Tower City marathon shirt and grazing his nipples with her fingernails.

On a ragged breath, Brett replied, "So are you. You just haven't felt like it."

Alyssa didn't take offense.

Overweight, it was difficult to feel girlie when she couldn't fit into anything cute or pretty.

Oh, companies made things for women her size, but it didn't look the same.

"Come on, admit it," she said, watching him pull his t-shirt over his head. "All you saw when you looked at me at Thanksgiving was a dumpy broad chugging champagne."

Brett dropped to his knees and pulled her running leggings down her legs, kissing up her thighs as he did so.

Laughing, Alyssa lifted her feet so he could pull the tight material over them. "That's not true," he said, grabbing onto her panties and sliding them over her ass.

While he undressed her bottom half, she finished the top, unclasping her bra and throwing it to the floor. Her breasts ached for his touch; her nipples tingled. As Brett knelt before her, she wondered if he could smell her arousal.

When he stood, she returned the favor, drawing the running pants he lived in over his strong legs.

She rested on her knees in front of him, his erection eye-level. She hadn't taken his briefs off yet, and through the cotton, she pressed her mouth to his cock and puffed a hot breath onto his hard shaft.

"Jesus Christ, Alyssa," Brett muttered.

She laughed. "Is that good or bad?"

He groaned.

Running her hands along the backs of his thighs, she pressed her mouth to his cock and did it again.

A shiver ran along his body. "Get up here," he said, "before I blow in my briefs."

He pulled his underwear off and kicked them aside.

She'd never had fun while she had sex. Always so ashamed of her body, it had been lights out and under the covers. But it was summer in Minnesota now, and sunlight still streamed through her bedroom window.

Sex in the light was a new feeling for her, but she never thought once about covering up. Not when Brett licked his lips as his eyes roamed her body. Not when he advanced on her, backing her across the room to the bed she hadn't made that morning. Not when he tackled her, throwing her onto the mattress and suckling her nipple as he rammed his fingers inside her.

It was her turn to moan.

"Like to tease me, huh?" he asked before nipping at the sensitive skin of her breast. "Two can play at that game."

"Be inside me, Brett. Please," Alyssa said, running her fingers through his hair.

He wiggled his fingers. "I am."

"Not like that."

"Impatient," he said but did as she asked, pushing his cock inside her as he claimed her mouth with his.

She'd never felt so fulfilled. Sex had never felt so right.

Alyssa prayed to any god who would listen that her love for him would blossom into something more that night.

There was nothing she wanted more than to give him a family. A family who would love him unconditionally, like his parents never had. She wanted to take care of him. Love him for the rest of their lives.

She spread her legs as wide as she could, and when he levered himself over her, she reached between their bodies to her clit.

"I'm going to come," Brett said, a deep moan coming from the back of his throat.

"Yes, please."

Her own orgasm began when Brett finished, and his cock twitched as her muscles clutched around him. As he covered her with his sweat-drenched body, she moaned, and she ran her fingertips lightly over his slick back.

"Hmmm. You feel so good," he mumbled into her neck.

"So do you." She paused. "I've never had sex the way I've had it with you."

Brett pushed up. He didn't slip his cock out of her, only pulled away enough to look into her flushed face. "What do you mean?"

"So . . ." She faded, searching for the correct word, ". . . uninhibited. In the light. With my exes, we did it in the dark. For me, because I was ashamed of my body. For the men I dated, because they said they couldn't get hard looking at me."

Tears sprang to her eyes.

"Oh, God. Alyssa, look at me, honey."

Brett's face blurred from her tears. She didn't know why she confessed a stupid thing like that. Her last boyfriend had been a long time ago, but he'd been especially cruel, and the wounds felt like they'd been inflicted on her only yesterday.

Gently, he wiped her tears from her cheeks and ran his wet fingertips over her lips. Her tongue darted out to taste his skin, his musk, and her tears.

"Not one of those men deserved you," Brett whispered, cradling her.

"When you look how I do—did—and you're always being treated like that, you start to believe they're right."

She wanted to tell him about her father, her biological father, but she didn't want to make this about her. He'd had a rough few weeks, too.

"I'm sorry about your parents."

They hadn't talked about them. According to Nikki, Brett didn't talk to anyone. It wasn't healthy—the silence.

Brett flopped onto his back and covered his eyes with his arm.

Immediately, Alyssa regretted bringing them up. But rather than rescind her question, she smoothed the top sheet over them. "You didn't have a funeral?"

Several seconds went by before he spoke. "No. The woman at the living community gave me the name of my parents' attorney. He told me they named one of their friends as the executor of their estate and left all their money to their church."

Alyssa shuddered at the hypocrisy. They'd gone to church, claimed to be God-fearing people, yet emotionally, and maybe physically, abused their son all his life.

"I'm sorry."

She couldn't think of anything adequate to tell him. She moved closer, but he cringed away, and she slid back to her own pillow.

An idea exploded in her mind. He felt exactly like she did. Dirty, tainted. Unloved. Blame. Shame. The men she'd dated made her feel like that.

Brett's parents made him feel like that.

Maybe they weren't so different after all.

"I don't need their fucking money."

"No," she said, "But you needed them to love you. Why didn't they put you up for adoption, or . . . or . . ." She choked on the words, "why didn't your mom have an abortion?"

She couldn't imagine anyone wanting or needing to do that, but surely it was better than neglecting a child his whole life.

His face red, Brett rolled off the mattress and grabbed his shirt off the floor. "What the hell kind of fucked up question is that?"

Baffled, Alyssa watched as he yanked his clothes on. "I just—"

"Well, it's fucked up. Jesus Christ."

Alyssa blinked at the wall in shock as Brett slammed out of her loft.

She didn't understand what just happened, and her stomach heaved.

Alyssa barely made it to the bathroom before she threw up.

SIMMERING IN his rage, Brett pulled into his apartment building parking lot.

He hadn't meant to fly off the handle like that. Quite honestly, it was a valid question. Besides his parents being religious zealots, there wasn't a valid reason why they hadn't given him up or why his mother hadn't gotten an abortion.

It wasn't like she'd had mixed feelings, or that she had to give him up because she didn't have the resources to take care of him.

No, it would have made them look bad in the eyes of God and the church congregation.

That was all.

They'd put a roof over his head, food in his belly, and clothes on his back. They'd done their duty toward him as well as they thought they should.

Brett flexed his fingers on the steering wheel then shifted his car into Park before he forgot.

Nowhere in the Bible did God command parents to love their children. He thought he vaguely recalled a verse encouraging parents to spank their kids or something, and he should probably be glad they didn't use that as an excuse to beat the shit out of him.

But that would have meant they saw him, and whenever either one of his parents looked his way, they stared right through him.

He bit back a string of profanities when he found Marta waiting for him in his apartment.

She looked ready to run.

Not run like she had when she moved back to California after graduation, but *run*. Like he hadn't done since his last with Alyssa, and that had been a measly five miles.

Maybe he wouldn't feel so shitty if he'd fall back into a serious running routine.

Maybe running the marathon he organized every year.

It'd be a good idea to let Marta pound the shit out of him.

He couldn't imagine what Alyssa was thinking the way he slammed his way out of her apartment. He deserved what Marta could dish out.

"What the hell are you doing here?" he asked, kicking his door shut.

"Well, nice to see you, too," she said, but her smile faded as he glared. "What's wrong?"

"Nothing."

"Where were you?"

"Working on the book with Alyssa."

Brett grabbed a beer out of his fridge then thought better of it, trading it for a bottle of water he bought in bulk from Walmart.

"How's that going?"

"Fine. What are you doing here?"

"I thought maybe you would want to go for a run. It's been a long time."

It *had* been a long time. Over ten years. He remembered them running their long runs only to come back here and shower, fall onto his futon and make love with all the abandon only kids could have.

Brett studied the little speed demon. Her hands were braced on her hips, her foot tapping in impatience.

Her hair was pulled back into a ponytail the best it could be, but Brett knew by the end of their run it would look like she hadn't done anything with it at all.

Her face was clean of makeup, and her running clothes, a Tower City Marathon racerback tank and matching racing skirt, looked brand new. A GPS watch was buckled to her wrist, and a black racing belt that probably held her phone encircled her waist.

She looked like she could kick his ass.

He wanted to let her for being such a dumbass.

"Fine. Do you want to go out to the park? We have a couple hours of sunlight left."

Marta brightened. "Sure! I haven't been trail running in a while."

Brett changed into shorts and his own tank, not giving a fuck Marta watched. She'd seen it all before. Many times.

At this time of evening they'd need to be dosed liberally with bug spray, but being out of the city would help.

Soothe his nerves.

Calm his heart.

Because holy crap, he was thinking he was doing something he didn't want to do.

They drove in silence, and in the parking lot, they sprayed down with bug repellent.

The sky clouded over, and the breeze picked up, but rather than make him cold, it would keep him cool and the bugs away.

He knew the trails well enough he could keep Marta away from the path where he'd screwed Alyssa. He didn't need to think about taking her from behind—Jesus. He just said not to think about it.

His cock twitched.

Fuck.

"How long are we going?" He started at a trot.

"How far can you go?" Marta asked, tongue in cheek, rubbing his arm with hers.

"I don't know. The last long run I went on was with Dane a few months ago. I have no idea how far I can go."

Marta shrugged. "Then we'll play it by ear. Slow down, stop trying to impress me. You'll burn out by mile four."

Brett adjusted his stride and tried to save some of his ego by telling himself it was for Marta because she was so short.

"When are you going home?"

Marta stuck her tongue out at him. "Tired of me already?"

"No. Yes."

"Well, you're going to have to get used to it. I might stay."

Brett groaned. "Are you serious? What about California?"

"It's not about California. It's about Tower City. The university has asked me to coach their track team. It's not the direction I thought I would go, but I'm in talks with them."

Brett grinned. "That's great. You've been keeping it a secret?"

"I didn't know how you'd feel if I stayed here. It's not like things ended well between us, and we never talk about it."

"Nothing to talk about."

"You're wrong."

Brett knew he was. He was all kinds of wrong. Wrong for Marta, wrong for Alyssa.

He focused on the woods, the fresh air filling his lungs. It would storm tonight. He could feel the wet in the air, the cool breeze as it blew through the trees and over the prairie making the plants dance.

"I never blamed you, you know." Marta's words were almost lost in their footfalls and the rattle of new leaves in the trees. "It was my choice, too."

"Do you ever think about what we would be like now?"

"Of course I do," Marta said, looking at him from the sides of her eyes. "But I doubt I'd be where I am professionally. At least I know I did my best. Coaching at the university would be a big deal."

Brett didn't think it was enough for what Marta had given up all those years ago.

"But you need to move on. Why are you still alone because of a choice we made eleven years ago? Don't you want to get married and start a family? You're in a better place now."

Brett's laugh was full of bitterness. "No, I'm not. Things haven't changed. In fact, they're worse. I was never able to ask my parents why. Why they treated me like that, why they didn't give me away." He wouldn't bring up the other option Alyssa asked him about.

"Surely by now you've realized it was them and not you."

While Brett's leg muscles and lungs burned from the exertion he was unaccustomed to, he thought about Alyssa crying over the way men treated her.

He'd told her it had been those assholes, and that it didn't have anything to do with her. But that wasn't true. If she'd been slimmer, prettier, smarter, taller, whatever the fuck, they wouldn't have treated her that way.

Maybe his parents wouldn't have treated him the way they'd had if he'd been smarter, better looking, maybe even a girl. It was them, but it was also him.

That's just the way it was.

"They're dead, Marta. I'll never know what they were thinking. I'll never have that closure."

"They're dead," Marta said, running her hand across her forehead. The gesture broke her stride, and she stumbled over the path's uneven terrain. "So it doesn't matter why. They took over thirty years of your life. Will you let them take the next thirty?"

"I'm fine."

"Why were you so mad when you came home tonight? Did you and Alyssa have a fight?"

"No. She asked me about my parents, and I didn't want to talk to her about it. She put me in a bad mood."

"I saw her at the expo. Nikki pointed her out to me. She's pretty. Her eyes are sensational." Marta sucked in a breath.

Brett marveled he still knew every nuance of Marta's face, her mannerisms. She was going to say something that would piss him off.

"It's okay if you like her, Brett. Hell, I hope you do. I want you to get close to someone, fall in love, have some rugrats that won't leave you alone."

"I don't want kids, Marta. Things haven't changed that much I would subject some poor kid to a man like me for a dad."

"Then there is nothing going on between you and Alyssa?"

Brett glanced at his GPS watch. They'd only been running for four miles. It felt like forty—emotionally and physically.

"No."

"I don't believe you."

"I don't care."

"Yes, you do. Think about where we could have been. Think about what our family could have been like. You weren't ready. I wasn't either. We were kids. We could have ended up like Dane and Liz. But we aren't those kids anymore who don't know what they're doing. You're an adult who puts together a huge marathon every year." She paused to draw in a wheezy breath.

Brett smirked. Maybe Marta was losing some stamina in her old age.

"We're not the same people. No one has caught your eye in all these years like Alyssa has. Life usually doesn't give you second chances. Don't blow this one."

"Hell, Marta, even if I could be honest and admit I have feelings for her, I've been a prick since the moment we met. She probably doesn't even want me."

Marta stopped dead in her tracks, her hair a wet tangled halo around her head. Shoving her hands on her hips.

"Then you're going to have to ask yourself some hard questions. Do you want her? If she wants you, do you want her? If yes, then it's time to start being nice."

---

"THAT WAS A pretty rude question," Nikki said as they walked the paths behind Alyssa's loft.

Nikki brought them coffees, black with cream.

Alyssa's days of sipping double mocha lattes were over.

But even without the chocolate, she was enjoying the early morning walk with Nikki and Hunter.

Nikki didn't need to put in so much time at the store as she had before the race, and that made Alyssa happy. Falling back into their regular walking schedule would be welcome.

With every passing day, Hunter looked better and better.

He missed Brett. The poor dog had whimpered for hours after Brett slammed out of her apartment.

She thought the dog would have preferred to leave with

Brett rather than stay with her, but he seemed happy now, sniffing along the trail at the dandelions popping up along the concrete and eyeing the ducks when they passed the pond.

"Well, I think if you've been sleeping with someone, you have a few rights, and that includes asking questions."

She'd told Nikki about Brett's behavior the night before, and Nikki's reprimanding her put her back up.

Nikki laughed, and the happy sound of a woman in love sounded over the park. "I suppose that's true. Don't you guys work on the book anymore? It sounds like all you do is fight and have sex."

"Well, this was after we worked on the book."

Alyssa tugged on Hunter's leash to urge him to move along from a park bench he coated liberally with urine.

Frowning, she said, "Well, I've been working on the book, and I showed him what I'd gotten done while he was busy with the marathon and his parents' death."

"When will you be done?"

Uneasily, Alyssa shrugged. When the book was finished, she wouldn't see Brett anymore.

The coffee turned bitter in her stomach, and she threw her full coffee cup into a trash bin as they walked by.

"We can be done anytime. I can run five miles without stopping. I'm technically not a beginner anymore. I had a checkup at my doctor's the other day, and my numbers are improving. I don't know what else he wants me to put in it."

"What's next then?" Nikki asked, frowning when Alyssa threw her coffee away. It wasn't like her not to enjoy a coffee.

"Then we polish it up, have a few people read it, like you, or Dane. Brett probably knows a million runners who would look at it for him. He can have Marta look at it. Oh," she caught herself, "she's leaving. She probably won't have time for that."

"Actually, she might stay here. She was offered a coaching position at the university. I guess that's a big deal. She'd be taking over for the coach she moved here to train with in the first place." Nikki kicked a rock across the sidewalk that Hunter, straining against his leash, attempted to chase.

That was it then.

Alyssa tried to swallow around the burn in her throat, but it was impossible. She hadn't realized she'd been waiting for Marta to go back to California to give her and Brett breathing room to figure things out until Nikki said Marta wasn't going.

"So, what does that mean?" she murmured.

"I don't know. I don't talk to Brett much. You know him better than I do now, being you've been sleeping together." Nikki elbowed her. "I doubt they'll get back together. But if they do, wouldn't you be happy for him? He needs something. Someone."

It was too much to ask that someone be her, Alyssa thought. But Nikki made a good point. She'd rather Brett be happy with Marta than with no one. Because Nikki was right—all she and Brett did was fuck and fight. And a couple couldn't build a relationship on that.

He and Marta had history, and that trumped desire.

"Will you come to the engagement party Marta is throwing us at Ian's bar?"

Alyssa was grateful Nikki changed the subject, but she knew sooner or later Marta's name was going to start to piss her off.

Annoyed, she turned away, petting Hunter who was

gazing up at her with a concerned look. That was, if dogs could look worried about their owners.

Planning an engagement party was supposed to be *her* job.

She'd been irked when Nikki asked her, but *she* was the maid of honor. She felt stupid she hadn't thought of throwing them one but with the marathon and writing the book, a party hadn't crossed her mind.

"Are you mad?"

Nikki rested a hand on Alyssa's shoulder, and she fought like hell not to shrug it off like a spoiled brat. Nikki wasn't a traitor being friends with Marta. If Marta stayed, and it sounded like she was going to, Nikki would be part of a foursome—Nikki and Dane, and Brett and Marta.

Alyssa would be the outsider, just like she'd been all her life.

"I just thought that was my job." She tried not to sound sullen about it, but she didn't succeed.

"Actually . . ."

"What?"

"Well . . . Dane's mom somehow heard about the party. See, the problem is, Marta's planning a friends-only thing. There's quite a few of our high school friends and their university classmates still around, and Marta wanted, well" —she backtracked— "maybe she didn't mean for it to happen, but it's kind of turned into a class reunion. Anyway, so Dane's mother was hoping we'd have something . . . classier for family and friends."

"And that's what I would plan?"

"If you're feeling up to it. I gave Peg and my mom your phone number."

Dammit. *Be careful what you wish for; you just might*

*get it.* It made her feel a weird combination of put-upon and included.

"When's Marta's party?"

"This weekend. Ian's going to keep his bar open Sunday night. He usually closes at six, but we'll take it over. It sounds fun. Have you been there?"

Schmoozing with Brett's and Dane's buddies from the university didn't sound fun and seeing people from high school sounded close to torture, but she *was* maid of honor. She knew she'd be doing shit like this when she told Nikki she'd do it. "No, but I guess I will."

Alyssa wouldn't have imagined in a million years that her life would change so drastically when Nikki was hired to manage Dane's store.

Lucky her.

## CHAPTER NINE

Working out will force you to face your
fears—Alyssa

Or make you ache until you can't think about anything
except how much you hurt—Brett

Isn't that the same thing?—Alyssa

---

MARTA'S WORDS RANG in Brett's ears as he jabbed at
his phone to call Alyssa. Start being nice, Marta
said. Didn't she know how difficult it was for him to be nice
to anyone? If he was suddenly nice to Alyssa, she'd probably
have a heart attack.

"Hello?" she answered, sniffling.

Brett stopped pacing his little apartment. "What the
fuck is wrong with you?"

*That wasn't being nice.* "I mean, what's wrong?"

"Oh," she sighed. A rustling sound came over the phone

like she was using a tissue to wipe her nose. "I just wrote a lovely scene. This book is coming together better than I thought it would."

"Our book is making you cry?" Brett asked.

"No. I'm writing something else. What do you want? You're ruining a sweet moment between me, and Sara and Blake."

"Who the hell are they? Do you have visitors?" He didn't understand what was going on.

"No, I said the book I'm writing. What do you want?"

"What about our book? Why aren't you working on that?"

"Why would I work on that? My part is done, and the last time you were over, you yelled at me and slammed out of here. I'm starting to think that it might not be a good idea for us to spend time together anymore."

Brett didn't like the sound of that. And it wasn't just to finish the book. The book *was* almost done, so if he wanted to keep seeing her, he would have to think of something else.

"Are you going to Dane and Nikki's engagement party? You never said the last time I asked."

"I have to go." The irritation in her voice came through loud and clear. "I would look like a bitch if I skipped it. Plus, now I got conned into throwing a different party for Dane's and Nikki's families to go to. Apparently, they don't want to, or they weren't invited, to Ian's."

Brett clung to the topic like a drowning man hanging onto a life raft. "We should talk about this over dinner tomorrow night."

"What for? We're talking now."

Brett sighed. She was going to make him say it. "Well, I

thought it would be nice if we dressed up and maybe went on a date."

"A date?"

Brett heard a shuffling, then a dull thud. "Alyssa?"

"Sorry, I dropped the phone in shock. What do you mean, 'a date?'"

"You know. Food? Conversation? Wine?"

He'd heard a saying that things that came easily weren't worth it in the end. He didn't think whoever came up with that sparkling piece of advice knew what they were talking about.

"Well . . . I did want to tell you that I'm sorry about what I said the other night—"

"I overreacted," Brett interrupted before she could apologize further. She didn't need to; he'd been the one who lost his cool. "We can talk about it over dinner."

She groaned, and the low moan made him hard. That's exactly how she sounded when he was so deep inside her he couldn't think straight.

"Fine. I don't know what this is about. You've been happy enough coming over here, eating my cooking, then screwing me after. Why do we need to go out?"

"Because. Someone told me I needed to start being nice. So, this is me, being nice, to you. I'll take you to dinner, we'll talk like regular human beings about our friends getting married. We'll talk about the book over dessert, and then if we haven't killed each other, maybe we can still fuck."

He frowned.

That's probably not what Marta meant.

"Fuck off."

"Wear something nice!" he said before she hung up.

She was so goddamn contrary.

He grinned and threw his phone onto his futon.

He loved it.

---

AFTER SHE'D HUNG up on him, Brett texted her the time he'd pick her up.

She hadn't responded, so he wondered if she'd be ready. She was probably writing and eating ice cream.

No, she wouldn't be eating ice cream, she'd changed her eating habits and stuck by them, which impressed him.

Changing to a healthier diet when someone wanted to lose weight was something many people grappled with, but not Alyssa. After Brett gave her a list of foods she could eat, she never had a problem sticking to the plan.

He slammed out of his car feeling awkward in his olive dress pants, cream-colored shirt, and olive and cream striped tie.

The last time he'd had to dress up like this was a few years ago when he'd been invited to a banquet celebrating the top influencers of Tower City. The mayor had given him a plaque, that now, if he remembered correctly, was buried under a stack of towels in his linen closet.

Brett knocked on her door not knowing what to expect. He hoped she took his invitation seriously because they did have things they needed to discuss.

Dane hadn't asked him to be his best man, but he'd been when Dane married Liz, and he didn't think he'd be replaced this time.

"Come in!"

When her holler filtered through her door, Brett let himself into her apartment. Hunter greeted him enthusiastically, and Brett hunkered down to pet the dog, digging his fingers into his thick fur for a brisk rub.

"Hey, buddy," Brett said, turning his face away so he wouldn't be welcomed with a mouth full of tongue. Tonight, the only tongue he wanted in his mouth was Alyssa's.

"You didn't say where we were going, so I hope this is okay," Alyssa said, coming from around the corner where her bathroom was located down the hall.

Brett looked up from Hunter's watery brown eyes, and all thought left his brain as his gaze traveled from her dark green pumps, up her bare legs, to the green flared skirt of her dress that stopped just below her knee. The waist of the dress cinched in, giving her a spectacular hour-glass figure. A cowl-neckline framed a silver and emerald necklace.

She wore little makeup, only something that sparkled on her lips, and black eyeliner and mascara that made her eyes stand out. She'd done nothing new to her hair, but it shined more than normal, and the curls were more defined, yet still tousled. One of his favorite things about her, her hair always gave her the look like she'd just been truly fucked, in a very, very good way.

"I thought we'd go to Grill, or someplace downtown, but you look good enough for Glass House," Brett said, standing, brushing the dog hair off his pants.

"Here. Sorry." Alyssa offered him a lint roller which he took gratefully. The mutt sure did shed.

As if he heard Brett's insult, Hunter whined.

"He knows we're leaving without him," Alyssa said, nudging Hunter into the living room.

"Will he be okay alone?"

"Nikki's going to take him for a run with Dane later, and I took him out before I got dressed. He'll be fine for a little bit." Alyssa raised an eyebrow. "Glass House? Can you afford that?"

Opening the door for her as she grabbed her purse and keys, Brett scowled. "Of course I can. Well, I couldn't every week, but this is special."

He waited as she locked her apartment door and shoved her keys into her purse. It wasn't the humungous black bag she usually carried. She'd traded in that monstrosity for something small and black, with a slim silver chain for a strap.

"You look amazing. Really."

"Thank you. I had to go shopping. All the dresses I own are too big. I couldn't go crazy because I want to lose more weight, but I bought a couple things since I'm going to need to dress up for Nikki and Dane's parties."

In the car, Brett settled behind the wheel, and with a sigh, he watched Alyssa fuss with her seatbelt. She didn't belong in his car.

Or with him.

"What are we celebrating?"

Her question brought him back to earth, and he shifted his car into gear.

Glass House would be empty at this time of day. It was too early to eat dinner. The people who traveled in the social circles that ate at Glass House chose to dine around nine or ten o'clock.

But that was okay, too. Brett would never object to having Alyssa to himself.

"Well, you said the book was done, pretty much. The marathon went off without a hitch. I mean, with something like that, it could always be worse. You can look at this as a thank you meal. Thank you for helping me with the book, thank you for putting me in touch with the high school and bailing me out of that photography fiasco. I appreciate it." He took her hand and kissed her knuckles.

Alyssa's jaw dropped, and Brett laughed as he stopped for a red light.

Glass House was empty, just like he guessed, but they chose to sit in the bar first. He ordered a beer, and she ordered a chocolate martini.

Brett shook his head and ran his finger along the rim, smearing a drop of chocolate. He licked it off his fingertip.

"What? I starved myself today to give myself the calories to eat out. You said we're celebrating, so I am."

He couldn't complain when she took a sip and smoothed her tongue over her lips.

"You've never met Ian, have you?" Brett asked, leaning back in his chair and resting an ankle on his knee. He needed to get his mind off her tongue.

"Nope. Nikki said something about him going to school with you."

"We were all in the same business classes together. That's how we got to know each other. Dane went into banking after graduation, then opened his store when he realized he didn't like it. I did some management-type positions before I took over a franchise of workout gyms. I guess I felt like Dane. It was boring. We'd all been in the track program, you know that, and we were all pulled into that direction—running—eventually. Marta tried out for the Olympics, but she didn't make it. She gave up and started planning running retreats."

"And the marathon?" Alyssa asked, smiling at the waiter as he brought her another martini.

"We'd participated in some, back then. But you had to travel to get to them—not every town hosted their own like most cities do today. When I brought it up to the mayor, he didn't care one way or the other. He didn't understand how big of a coup it would be if you could get something like that off the ground. It took me . . . seven, eight years, to make the race grow to this size. The ten-year anniversary isn't next summer, but the year after. We're going to have to make it an extra-special race."

"That could be about the time your book comes out."

Brett brightened. "You think?"

"Yeah. We could tell them about the anniversary, that it would help sales if they coordinated the release around that date. We'll have to start reaching out to publishers and agents soon. Write a proposal. It shouldn't take too long for it to get picked up. It's a good book."

Brett reached for her hand. "It's good because of you. Without you, the book would have been nothing."

Alyssa blushed, setting her cheeks an adorable shade of pink that shimmered in the candlelight.

After they finished their drinks, they moved to a table in the dining room for dinner. Brett looked around as the waiter filled their water goblets and asked if they wanted an appetizer. Alyssa ordered crab-stuffed mushrooms, and his stomach slid around as she sighed. She was always doing something to turn him on.

"It's nice in here. I haven't been for a long time," she said.

The restaurant was decorated in silver, bluish-grey, and black. Blue-grey painted walls shimmered in silver light that glittered from crystal chandeliers. Their table was a pitch black coated in lacquer that shined, even though the lights were dim.

"I never have."

He'd never cared to eat at the fanciest restaurant in Tower City. But this was a special occasion, perhaps even a starting point for Alyssa and him.

He needed to make a decision about his relationship with her.

Her green eyes sparkled with the candlelight, and he knew which way his heart was leaning toward.

His brain told him something else entirely.

"So, what did you want to talk about? Dane and Nikki's party? Are you going to help me plan it or what?"

With friendly conversation, they passed the evening chatting about the two engagement parties, and where they thought Dane's and Nikki's mothers wanted the fancier party to take place.

He offered some venue ideas, and so did she, and she saved the suggestions in her phone.

"Do you want me to pay for half?" Alyssa asked after the waiter discreetly placed the bill on their table and slunk away.

"Nah, I can get it." He looked at her and smiled. "You have a smudge of chocolate . . ."

Alyssa rubbed her lips with her napkin. "Did I get it?"

Brett shook his head. "No. Here." He reached across the table and brushed a spot of chocolate at the corner of her mouth. Their eyes met as his skin touched hers.

"Thanks," she whispered.

He cleared his throat and scooted his chair from the table. Smoothing his tie, he stood. "You're welcome. Let's go."

With his hand resting on her lower back, Brett led Alyssa to the door. As they were stepping out, another couple stepped inside.

"Whoa. Is that you, Alyssa?"

A blond man dressed in a three-piece navy suit with a young brunette woman clinging to his arm spoke to Alyssa, and she acted as if she hadn't heard.

"Alyssa," he barked.

Brett's lips curled in disgust.

Reluctantly, Alyssa turned toward him.

Brett narrowed his eyes at the change in her. Her cheeks had gone white, her eyes had lost their shine.

"Parker," she greeted him softly.

Parker whistled. "Look at you, doll. You've changed since we dated."

Alyssa looked at the floor, and her hands gripped her purse until her knuckles turned white.

He shook the brunette off his arm and leaned toward Alyssa, trapping her between his body and the frosted glass door.

"You couldn't do this for me, huh?" he muttered, running his finger down her neck and over one of her breasts.

She started to tremble, and he tensed, waiting to see what she would do. He didn't know who this man was to her, and he didn't want to interfere if it was going to cause her trouble.

Parker continued to graze her breast with his fingertips, over the silky material of her dress.

Suddenly, he gripped her chin in his hand, digging his fingers into her cheeks. "You fucking bitch. After all the money I spent on you, after all the time I wasted on you . . . all I asked is that you fucking lose some weight. You couldn't do that for me, but you could do it for him? You fucking whore."

"Parker!" his date squealed.

The shriek jolted Brett from his trance, and he pulled Parker away from Alyssa who stood frozen in shock against the door.

He clutched the asshole's shirt in his fist.

"Don't you know that's not the way you treat a lady?" Brett asked, shoving at Parker against the wall.

He didn't care who was watching.

"She's no lady," Parker said, and wiped his mouth with the back of his hand.

Unable to stop himself, Brett punched him, his fist connecting neatly with Parker's jaw.

He savored the satisfaction of watching the prick stagger and slide to the floor.

Screaming, his date rushed to his side, her heels clicking against the tile.

Shaking out his hand, though it hadn't hurt much bringing that loser down, Brett nodded to Alyssa.

"Don't think I won't press charges, you fuck," Parker yelled, propped up on one elbow, holding his jaw with his other hand. "I know who you are, Brett Sommers, and you'll fucking pay for this."

Brett knelt and grabbed the hair at the back of Parker's head. "I want to see you try, asshole. Then Alyssa can press charges, too. The hostess saw what you did to her. You think you'd get away with manhandling a woman like that, you miserable piece of shit?"

He pushed Parker back to the floor, where this time the man stayed, resting his cheek against the tile, groaning.

Looking at Parker's date, Brett ran his hand through his hair. "You better cut and run honey, before you end up on the wrong side of his fist later tonight. He's the type of scumbag who will make someone pay for this. Don't let it be you."

The brunette nodded dumbly, her hair swirling around her shoulders.

Holding the door open for Alyssa, he said, "Come on, sweetheart, I'll take you home."

As they walked across the parking lot he tried to put his arm around her, but she cringed away. In his car, she cowered against the door, quietly crying, sitting as far away from him as she possibly could.

It pissed him off. "Those are the kinds of men you dated?" he asked in disgust.

"They were the only ones who would."

He barely understood what she said through her tears, but he had, and it made him want to throw up.

After the long ride in silence, he parked on the street in front of her building, and Alyssa stepped out before he could turn off the car.

"Hey!"

Alyssa was already pulling the keys out of her purse as she rushed through the door of her building.

"Alyssa, wait."

"No, please. Go home, okay? I'll be fine, I just need . . . I just need . . ." She choked back her sobs.

She stumbled up the stairs in her heels, and Brett stayed close behind her in case she fell. After reaching her loft, she attempted to slide the key into her door's lock, but her hand was shaking too badly to make them connect.

"Alyssa," he whispered, gently closing his hand over hers. "Sweetheart."

The word sounded foreign coming from his mouth. He hadn't called anyone sweetheart since Marta. No one had meant that much to him that he bothered with endearments.

"Will you look at me?"

Slowly, she turned her gaze from their joined hands to look at him. Her face was streaked with tears, her skin pink from where the bastard had gripped her chin.

He pulled his hand from hers and wrapped his arms around her.

As she cried, he was brought back to the day she'd visited him at headquarters, when he'd taken her down to the storage area.

She'd cried into his shirt, and it was the same keening as now.

Defeat.

The disbelief things could get better.

He knew the sound. It echoed in his brain with the tears he refused to let fall. But he felt those things just the same.

They were alike, in so many ways, and every hour, every minute he spent with her, he realized just how true that was.

Taking the keys from her, he kissed the top of her head. "Come on, it's not that late, but it's been a long day."

Hunter sat on the other side of the door wagging his tail, waiting for them. He whined when he picked up their tension, but Brett ignored him and led Alyssa to her bedroom.

He turned her around and reached for the zipper of her dress. "I've been waiting to do this all night," he said, and was rewarded when she sniffled a laugh.

"You don't have to stay. I don't feel like . . . you know."

Brett wanted to take offense, but he couldn't.

He hadn't been treating Alyssa with any more respect or kindness than that other guy. He might not have been so blatant about it, oh, who was he kidding? Yes, he had. There'd been times during their months of working together he'd been downright mean.

He could stop, though. Stop being mean to her, and just admit he was in love with her.

Only, admitting something like that was pointless.

"That's okay." He slid the dress from her body and held her hand as she wobbled on her heels.

She wore a black bra and panty set, and the sight of her standing there in nothing but lingerie and a necklace took his breath away.

"Get into bed," he said and started to undo the knot in his tie. Without a suit coat, he hadn't been appropriately dressed to dine at Glass House. He was lucky it was almost summer, and they relaxed their attire rules.

"I said, I'm not—" she protested as she climbed into her messy bed.

"There are some days we've spent together and haven't had sex," he said, unbuttoning his shirt.

"Yeah. We spent those days fighting."

"That's not true."

He unbuckled his belt and undid the button of his dress pants.

"Name one day we didn't have sex *or* argue," she demanded, fixing the sheet on her bed. She drew the bedding up to her face, and her eyes peeked from the edge of her comforter.

At a loss, he frowned. There had to be a time when they'd acted like normal people.

Hunter padded into the room and jumped onto the bed.

"Ha! The day we found Hunter. We went for a run and talked. That's all we did."

He climbed into bed, and while she giggled, the dog blocked Alyssa in on her other side.

"That's is so not true! You did me from behind against a log." Her soft belly jiggled slightly under his arm as she laughed.

"Dammit," he grumbled into her hair as he settled in,

tightening his arms around her. "You got me there. But it was a good day."

She met his eyes. "Yeah. That was a good day. Thanks for dinner and beating up Parker. It was nice."

"You're welcome. It was the least I could do. Let's go to sleep. I'll wake you up early for a morning run."

"Like hell you will. You don't even have running clothes here."

Brett nuzzled her cheek with his nose. "You're right. I guess we'll sleep in, and I'll let you make me breakfast in bed."

"That I can do. Goodnight, Brett."

"Goodnight, sweetheart."

---

SHE KNEW SHE was dreaming, but she couldn't help herself from calling out. "Daddy!"

"I'm sorry, Allie. I don't want you . . ." he mumbled, before shutting the door behind him.

Sobbing, her mother begged a man who was no longer there not to go. Patrice rushed past her, up the stairs to her bedroom, where little Alyssa could still hear her mother's cries.

Her daddy didn't want her.

"Alyssa, you're dreaming. Wake up."

Gasping for breath, Alyssa sprung forward, clutching the sheet to her breasts.

Brett rested a hand on her neck, rubbing his thumb back and forth across her damp skin.

"Shh, shh. It's okay, I'm right here."

She'd had her dream again. The dream she'd had for twenty-seven years. She would never be able to stop having nightmares about the night her father left them. Left her behind.

"Sorry," she whispered, lying back. She tucked herself into Brett's side. Of all the nights to have her nightmare, while Brett was in her bed.

"What were you dreaming about?"

Her room was pitch black. Making eerie clicking sounds, Hunter's nails tapped on the hardwood flooring somewhere in her loft. She slid over to give Brett room now that the big dog wasn't taking up half the bed, but he followed her.

"My father. When I was a little girl, he left my mom, and I watched him go. My mother tried to stop him, but it didn't help."

"Do you know why he left? Did your mother ever say?"

His soft voice weaved a comforting spell around her. For once, her father's abandonment didn't hurt as much as it used to because she was with a man who understood what it was like.

"I heard him say he didn't want me. He looked right at me and told me he didn't want me. I've always known he took off because he didn't want kids, and my mother never told me any different."

"I'm sorry."

"It's okay. It's why I ate."

"It's why I started running."

"You never told me that before."

"I've never told anyone. The first year it was offered, I started running after school because I never wanted to go home. But I realized I was good at it—I made friends. Running was a haven for a kid with no family. My coach was all I had until I met Dane. We didn't start hanging out until college because in high school he was a popular kid, and I was a nobody."

"I would have been a nobody without Nikki." Alyssa rested her head on Brett's shoulder. "Thank you for what you did at Glass House, for punching Parker. He had it coming, and you don't have to worry about him pressing charges. He's too cowardly for that."

"I wasn't worried." He pressed a kissed to the top of her head, and the gesture made her heart constrict.

She loved this man; she wished he would let her show him.

"You could do the same in retaliation. I'm sorry I didn't pull him off you sooner."

"I should have fought back. I'm not very good at that."

Brett reversed their positions. "You seem to hold your own with me just fine," he murmured into her neck.

Biting her lip, Alyssa hoped telling the truth wouldn't bite her in the ass. "Because I knew you were worth it. I tried harder to whip you into shape."

Brett moved over her, and Alyssa spread her legs, inviting him in. As he pushed into her, the dregs of her nightmare floated away into the dark. Wrapping her arms around him, she welcomed him to her.

"I want to be worth it to you," he said, tipping his head to take one of her nipples into his mouth.

She arched her back, enjoying the tender way he held her. They were finally moving forward. Slowly, but they were moving forward. Maybe there was hope for them. "Let's take things one step at a time."

"Does that include my breakfast in bed?" Brett yanked her hips up, and Alyssa groaned as he thrust.

"How do you like your eggs?"

AN OLD REBA McIntyre song boomed from the ancient jukebox sitting in the back of the room. The song threatened to make Brett's ears bleed; he hated country music.

Nursing a beer, he sat at the bar.

Late, he'd walked through the door not two minutes before. He'd been at Alyssa's, and they'd been walking Hunter along the paths behind her building. Neither one of them wanted to be here tonight, but he'd taken longer than she had to change and make the drive downtown.

She was already seated and sipping a drink, holding court at a high-top table in the center of the room, looking spectacular in a black form-fitting lace dress. The neckline exposed her collarbone and the tops of her shoulders, and she'd pulled her hair back into some kind of twist. Diamonds twinkled at her ears, and Brett's eyes hungrily followed the graceful curve of her neck.

He wasn't the only one to notice, and she shared her table with three other men admiring her just as he was. Only, they were with her, and Brett was across the room. That wasn't the way it was supposed to go.

He frowned.

"Stop scowling," Dane said, shoving another bottle of beer in his hand. "You're supposed to be celebrating that I found the love of my life."

Brett held back an impolite snort. He was happy for Dane, but this was the first party of many, and he wasn't as enthusiastic.

Still, he had a part to play. "Yeah, man. I'm happy for you," he said, clinking the neck of his beer bottle with Dane's in toast.

His eyes slid back to Alyssa, and he glowered.

One of the men scooted his chair closer to her and was tracing the lines of her palm in a lame attempt to read her fortune. It was all a ruse to touch her, and he didn't blame the bastard one bit.

"So, you and Alyssa?" Dane leaned against the bar and took a swig of his beer. "The way you acted when you met her, I never would have guessed. But then, it wasn't too long after that you started talking about her and the book. I think you fell for her right away, and you've been denying it all this time."

"Not everyone is like you and Nikki," Brett muttered.

"You're right. The second I saw her, I fell like a ton of bricks. Are you sure it wasn't the same for you and Alyssa?"

No, he was sure.

With Alyssa, it had been a slow burn. Spending time with her, running, cooking meals together. They'd opened up to each other, and over time, he'd realized how spectacular she was. How smart, kind, and tenacious she was. The night he punched Parker had sealed the deal as far as he was concerned.

But that didn't mean he knew what he was going to do. He'd spent the past ten years after Marta slipping and sliding from one relationship to the next because of his unwillingness to commit.

Alyssa knew this about him, too, and she never told him she loved him again. She was afraid to say it while he was sober, or she hadn't meant it at all.

Brett refused to believe she lied that day. The look in her eyes, the way she'd made love to him the day she checked on him after his parents' death, that had been more than just sympathy.

That had been love.

The pain that had radiated from her when Marta ran into his arms, that had been heartbreak.

They never talked about his relationship with Marta, or what he'd done to her.

Marta flitted around the bar, chatting with everyone, connecting with old friends.

No, he and Alyssa never talked about Marta, though Nikki must have told Alyssa Marta was thinking of staying here.

Alyssa never asked what that would mean for them, so maybe she didn't want more than what they were doing, or she didn't care.

Dane watched Nikki try her luck at the dartboard, and just for a moment, Brett was envious his friend had passed the difficult part in his relationship and had only good times to look forward to.

"You're a lucky guy. I'm happy for you, but you know that. Nikki's a good woman. She won't bail."

Dane smoothed his hot pink tie that matched the hearts decorating Nikki's cocktail dress. "No, she won't bail. We still go to therapy once a week. She's in it for life. She saved me."

Brett could hardly hear him over the music, his friend's voice pitched low in awe he found a woman who would truly be there through sickness and health, for better and poorer.

"You would have saved yourself."

"I'm not so sure about that. I might have ended up married to Holly, then twenty years and three kids later realized how miserable I was. Nikki healed me in other ways. Listen, Brett—Alyssa is a good woman, too. If you love her, if you want a life with her, don't let how your parents treated you push her away."

Brett wasn't ready for a conversation like this. All he knew was that he was tired of watching friends from high school and his old college buddies fall all over themselves for a chance to talk to her and bring her drinks.

"Hey," Marta said near his elbow, and she slipped her tiny body between his and Dane's.

She stood on the gold rail that ran along the bar, and it gave her the few inches she needed to look Dane and Brett in their eyes.

"Hey. Thanks for organizing this—it's great to see the old gang," Dane said.

Marta beamed. "You're welcome. It's nice to see everyone. I can't believe how many of us still run—except this guy here." She elbowed Brett. "It's quite the oxymoron that the marathon director doesn't run his own race. We went out to the park the other day, and I kicked his ass."

"That's not true," Brett said, grabbing Marta around her waist and hauling her into his lap, tickling her.

As she howled in laughter, she wrapped an arm around his neck to steady herself.

Brett rarely saw Marta dressed up and tonight she wore a navy dress with silver flats. Her hair was still a mess, and she never wore makeup. Not that he could tell. She usually smelled like sunscreen or bug spray, but tonight he caught a whiff of perfume.

"Can I get you another drink?" Ian's gruff voice put a halt to Marta's joyful shrieking.

Someone wasn't happy Marta had her arm around his neck. Brett smirked.

Ian glared at both of them and waited for their order. While Marta gave Ian her request for a glass of wine, he sought out Alyssa to see if she was still having her fortune told, or whatever the fuck.

Instead, he met her gaze.

Her eyes had filled with tears; her lips trembled.

Dammit.

He couldn't imagine what Marta clinging to him looked like.

Nothing good.

Without breaking eye contact, Alyssa pulled her purse from the back of the chair and slid to the floor, pausing for a moment to find balance on her heels.

In an attempt to smile, she turned up the corners of her mouth. She nodded at him, almost as if she were telling him it was okay, and before he could pull away from Marta's embrace, Alyssa wove her way through the crowded bar and slipped out the door.

"Fuck."

"What? Have another beer. You're the biggest stick in the mud I've ever met," Marta said, pushing a cold bottle of beer toward him.

"No. Alyssa saw us, and she just took off. I need to go after her."

"Shit. I'm sorry. I didn't mean—I'll go talk to her. I've been wanting to anyway."

That sounded like the worse idea in the world, but before he could stand up and stop her, in flats, Marta was halfway across the room.

## CHAPTER TEN

Training is like climbing a mountain—once you reach the top, it's all downhill from there—Brett

Just don't break your neck on the way down—Alyssa

---

"ALYSSA, WAIT. STOP."

Alyssa's heels clicked a sharp staccato beat along the sidewalk as she headed toward her car. She was glad she'd driven herself on the off-chance Brett would want to stay longer than she did. After all, they were his friends, and gatherings like that exhausted her.

She had a year of parties and wedding duties to attend, and she didn't want to stay longer than necessary, though she should have said goodbye to Nikki.

"Alyssa!"

She ignored Marta running behind her. She didn't need to hear that she was back together with Brett.

The way Brett's eyes looked while he tickled Marta tore at her heart.

She'd never seen him that happy.

Nikki was right.

He deserved a love like that; someone who would make him happy.

"Alyssa, please," Marta said, grabbing her arm attempting to stop her.

She'd almost made it to her car. It had been a bad move to let Brett see she was leaving. She should have made for the ladies' room and snuck out the back. Then she wouldn't be standing on the sidewalk at eleven o'clock at night with a woman just her height but half her weight. Well, maybe not half. Not anymore.

She was still losing weight at a steady pace.

Sometimes she wouldn't have time to snip the tags off her new clothes before having to exchange them for a smaller size.

The thought thrilled her. But she'd never look like the tiny dynamo standing in front of her with the pleading look in her eyes.

"I'm going home," Alyssa said, taking a hopeful step toward her car.

"Brett wanted to come after you, but I asked him to let me. I've wanted to talk to you for a while now. Do you mind?"

Hell yes, she minded.

But fuck if she could say she did.

"Come on," Marta said, tugging on Alyssa's arm she still gripped in a tight fist, not taking the slightest chance Alyssa would bolt.

Smart woman.

Marta led her to a coffee shop doing a surprising amount of business so late at night.

At the counter, she stood awkwardly with the woman whom she hadn't officially met, and Marta paid for their plain coffees.

If she was going to sit through this torture, she might as well enjoy it, and she took the few seconds she needed to fill her cup to the brim with cream.

Marta made a beeline for an empty loveseat, and Alyssa sank into it gratefully. She wasn't used to heels, and the bottoms of her feet burned. After she kicked them off, she tucked a foot under her ass.

She looked everywhere but Marta, but the other woman didn't give her a choice when she leaned forward, invading her personal space.

"Alyssa, it's not what you think."

"You don't know what I think."

No, Marta had no idea.

"Brett and I aren't together. We're only friends."

"Marta, it's fine. Brett . . . he's lonely. I think he has been for a long time. I barely know him, and if he's happy with you, I'm woman enough to step aside and be happy for him."

She set her coffee on the squat table covered in local magazines advertising things to do in Tower City. She slipped her pumps onto her feet, gathered her purse, and stood unsteadily.

"I was pregnant, once."

Alyssa's eyes slammed to Marta's.

She'd been pregnant. She and Brett had a child together. "Then you two belong together. I can't get in the way of that."

"We don't have a kid," Marta said impatiently. "Will you sit down and listen?"

Alyssa sank into the leather loveseat, her hands wound around the strap of her purse, the chain biting into her skin. "What happened?" She needed to know.

"Brett and I were in college—at the university. We were careless, and I got pregnant." She paused and a took a sip of coffee. "You know about his parents?"

"How they treated him, you mean?" It was too hot in the café, and under her dress, sweat dripped down the sides of her ribs.

"Yeah. It was neglect. Emotional neglect, but still neglect. Anyway, you know I was in track—I wanted to make it big. Long story short, I was pregnant and neither of us were in a good place for a baby. We were practically kids ourselves. Brett thought he'd be a shitty dad, and I'm saddened to find out that hasn't changed."

With a shaking hand, Alyssa covered her belly. She hadn't gotten her period yet for the month, but her mind was spinning too out of control to figure out when she would, if she did.

"What happened?"

Marta took a sip of her coffee. "I thought about keeping it, you know? But a baby would have taken away my running scholarship, and I was training hard to make it into the Olympics. Brett didn't want kids at all, so he was no help there. Wouldn't even talk about the possibility of keeping it. I would have been on my own. We were young, he was pressuring me to get an abortion, so that's what I did."

Tears filled her eyes, and Marta looked at the ceiling to keep them from running down her face.

Alyssa bit her lip and waited for Marta to continue.

"After it was over, Brett was wracked with guilt, and we had a huge fight. I told him he couldn't have it both ways. I did what he wanted me to do. What I wanted to do, too, but I wasn't going to be blamed for his guilt. We broke up, and after graduation, I went home."

Marta met her eyes.

"He's blamed himself ever since. If you love him, you've got a long road ahead of you. His parents made him feel unwanted, then he didn't want his own kid. The abortion was my choice too, but I never told him that if he'd wanted our baby, had given me any kind of support, it wouldn't have taken much persuasion to convince me to keep it. He already felt bad enough, and I couldn't add to it. Even if it was the truth."

Alyssa blinked.

She'd been having unprotected sex with him, thinking a baby would rescue him. Anchor him to her.

She was so stupid. All it would do is push him away. Probably for good.

"You've kept in touch," Alyssa murmured, running her thumb along the cardboard sleeve of her disposable cup.

"Yeah. I wanted to be sure he wasn't going to hurt himself somehow. But all he did was bury himself in work. I think that's why he started the marathon—it took up every second of his life. For a long time, the marathon was all he had, besides Dane. Before he met you, he used women for sex and nothing else. I've never heard him talk about someone the way he talks about you, and I've kept tabs on him for over ten years."

"We fight more than we do anything."

"But he always comes back, doesn't he?" Marta whispered. "He always comes back. When I left for California, he never came for me. He chases you—don't run too fast."

With nothing more she could say, Marta stood and walked away, dropping her coffee into the garbage container on her way out the door.

---

ALYSSA NEVER CAME back. Neither did Marta. And Brett tried like hell to figure out what that meant. If Marta told Alyssa what he thought she had, Alyssa would never want to speak to him again.

"How much do we owe you?" Brett asked Ian as he and Dane helped clean up after the party.

"Nothing. Marta paid in full."

Brett placed a chair upside down on a table so Ian could mop. "That's crazy. There was an open bar."

"It's paid. Take it up with her if you don't like it."

Brett glared at Dane who was gathering empties from tables along the back wall near the jukebox and dart board.

"Don't worry about it," Dane said, carrying an armful of empty beer bottles to the bar for Ian to recycle. "Nikki and I will talk to her. We don't expect her to spring for the whole thing. Where'd she go, anyway?"

Brett's eyes slid to Ian. "Do you need anything else?"

"I'll mop in the morning. Thanks for staying."

Dane shook Ian's hand. "Thanks for letting us have the party here. It was cool seeing everyone again."

Brett only nodded at Ian in thanks.

The man wanted nothing to do with him because he'd treated Marta poorly in the past.

Ian was defending Marta in his own way, and that was something Brett understood and appreciated, so he kept his distance.

Marta and Ian would have to work that out between

them, and Brett had no interest in being in the middle or defending his actions from so long ago.

"Think Alyssa is all right?" Brett couldn't help but ask Dane when they were outside.

"Why wouldn't she be? You and Marta were only goofing around. Where did she and Marta run off to, anyway? Nikki was upset Alyssa didn't come back, and she didn't say goodbye to anyone."

The sidewalk was empty but for a few stragglers making their way home after bar-hopping. A drunk couple leaned against a building near the parking lot laughing and making out.

Brett never knew that carefree freedom. His parents had always weighed on his mind, then the way he'd treated Marta added to it. He envied the couple who could laugh and worry about nothing but being hungover the next morning.

Hands on his hips, Dane snapped, "Will you talk to me?"

"When Alyssa ran off, Marta followed her to explain. That's all. Thanks for asking Nikki to check on her."

He'd kept Marta's abortion from everyone. Marta had too, as far as he knew.

It's not something someone wanted to toss around, even in these days of women's rights. It was a private matter and he wanted to keep it that way, but he wasn't going to be able to anymore.

Brett's old beater and Dane's truck were the only vehicles in the parking lot besides a car so old it didn't look like it had been moved in the past one-hundred years.

"What aren't you telling me? What could Marta say to Alyssa that would keep either of them from coming back to the party? They ran out before midnight and it's going on three in the morning." Dane leaned his back against the tailgate.

Bret blew out a breath and rested his ass against the truck's bumper.

"When Marta left after school? That was because of me. I knocked her up when we were a year from graduation. I wasn't ready for a kid, neither was she. She wanted to run, and she needed her scholarship. We decided she'd get an abortion. Things weren't the same between us after that, and she went home. Now you know our big secret, and I think that's what she told Alyssa. Alyssa ran out because she probably thought Marta and I were getting back together, and Marta told her we never would. I mean, why would Marta want me back? She looks at me and sees the family we didn't have." His voice sounded too loud in the still night.

"If Alyssa loves you, she'll forgive you that," Dane murmured.

Brett scoffed. "I'm not sure Marta has."

"She wouldn't have stayed in touch with you if she hasn't forgiven you. Marta cares about you. We all do. Including Alyssa. Especially Alyssa. You need to make up your mind about her."

"I've been waiting for us to finish the book."

"It's not about the book anymore," Dane said, pulling his keys out of his pocket. "Drive safe."

Brett crept through the downtown streets and into the newer part of Tower City to Alyssa's loft. He couldn't see her windows; her loft faced the park behind her building. He knew what Nikki drove, and she wasn't there.

He wanted to go inside and talk to her, but he was a coward. Asking Marta what she said to Alyssa to prepare himself sounded too much like high school, and he refused to do it.

Dane was right to call him on his shit. He either needed to tell Alyssa that he loved her too, or let her go.

He pulled away from the curb.

It wasn't about the book.

It never had been.

---

By the time Nikki knocked on her door, Alyssa was already in her pajamas. With Hunter keeping her company, she sat in her loft and sipped coffee, looking over the book she'd been writing. The middle of the night was always a good time for her to write, and her melancholy mood put her in a perfect frame of mind to plot out the sad scenes she needed.

"You should go home and get some sleep," Alyssa said, closing the door.

"I don't work at the store tomorrow, so it's fine. Where did you take off to?" Nikki dumped her purse onto the kitchen counter and made herself at home as she always did, helping herself to a mug of coffee. "You know, I really miss that flavored creamer you used to buy. This plain cream stuff is boring."

"Brett would kill me if he found that in my fridge," Alyssa said, refilling her mug.

"Is he the reason you ran out?" Nikki sat at the table and toed off her high heels. She started taking the pins out of her updo.

"Kind of. I knew Marta's been hanging around spending time with Brett, but I didn't want to watch it. They look so comfortable together, so natural. She can get him to smile, she can make him relax. If they would have been strangers to me, after watching them, I would have guessed that they'd been together for years and years."

"They aren't though," Nikki said, running her fingers through her hair.

"I know. Marta told me."

"Where'd you go?"

"I wanted to go home, but she followed me out. I saw Brett tickling her, and I just . . . if he wanted to be with her, I would step out of the way. When you asked me that one day if I would rather see him happy with Marta or miserable alone . . . Tonight I understood what you meant. He was happy with her. But Marta said that's not what's going on, that he talks about me in a way he hasn't talked about any other woman."

"What *is* going on with them? Did she tell you?"

Alyssa nodded. "It's very . . . personal, something I don't feel right knowing because it wasn't Brett who told me. Anyway, Marta says they're only friends, but I don't know what that means for him and me. Even if he feels something for me that he hasn't felt for another woman since Marta, it doesn't do me much good if he won't do anything about it."

"Even though he loves me, Dane had to deal with things from his own past that made him put distance between us. This sounds similar. Hang in there, show him you can wait for him, and if you're lucky, things will pan out."

Wrinkling her nose, Alyssa said, "I've never been that lucky."

Nikki placed her mug in the sink and leaned over to hug her. She was taller than Alyssa, but in heels, Nikki towered over her. On tip-toes, Alyssa returned her hug the best she could.

"Well, I'm glad you're okay. I need to go home; it's late.

Dane stayed behind to help Ian and Brett clean up. Let's go for a run tomorrow. After all the booze tonight, we'll need it."

"That sounds good. Talk to you in the morning."

Nikki had given Dane space, and it worked in their favor, though Alyssa hadn't understood Nikki's reasons at the time.

Because she'd committed to the book, she wouldn't disappear out of Brett's life, but she could stop running with him.

To keep herself from calling him, she worked out at the gym, taking classes and doing floor work with Tom.

She was relieved Tom never gave her a hard time for the way things ended, and her cheek healed so perfectly she never thought about their first, and only, date.

She wondered how fast she could climb that rock wall now. Maybe one day she'd try again. It would be nice if Brett were there to catch her if she fell.

Whichever way she could, she would make this work because she wanted to be there to catch him, too.

---

ALYSSA FILLED IN the empty hours with running, Hunter, and her book. She sent it off to her editor who was head over heels as she hadn't expected a new book from Alyssa for months.

She worried about giving Brett space as it felt more like abandonment rather than courtesy, and she hoped she wasn't giving him the excuse he was looking for to move closer to Marta.

After all, he'd never told Alyssa what he was thinking,

but if actions spoke louder than words, he had to feel something for her.

Yeah, she supposed punching Parker was something he could have done on his own to make him feel like a man, but Marta was right in a way, too.

Brett always did come back, but it'd been a week of no communication and she thought at least he would have reached out to make sure she'd made it home after Nikki and Dane's party.

She tried to push dumb thoughts like that out of her head, and she was cleaning her bathroom, listening to a publishing news podcast when a text from him came through.

*Are you mad at me?*

She washed her hands before she answered. The text made her smile and gave her hope.

*No, I'm not mad. What makes you say that?* she texted in reply.

It took a while for him to answer, so Alyssa finished cleaning, and she was shutting the light off when her phone chimed.

*We haven't talked in a while. Do you want to bring Hunter for a run?*

She wanted to see Brett desperately, and without thinking she almost typed *yes!* though she wasn't sure if she'd let enough time go by.

Well, she wanted to see him, had missed him this past week, and if that made her pathetic, so be it.

*Sure. Come over whenever you'd like.* Her fingers trembled while she typed.

Again, it took him forever to reply. Maybe he was rethinking inviting her for a run but didn't know how to rescind his invitation.

She'd let him squirm. By the time he responded, she was naked and letting the water warm up for a shower.

*I'll be over later in the afternoon. About 4.*

She responded with a smiley face and shut off her phone.

He wouldn't text her back, unless he decided to back out, but she had a few hours before that happened and as she stood in the shower she planned what she would make them for dinner.

A run, dinner, and falling into her bed to make love was a routine she wouldn't mind carrying out for the rest of her life.

---

BRETT TEXTED ALYSSA when he couldn't stand her silence anymore. He'd carried through with the promise that he wouldn't ask Marta what she told Alyssa.

In fact, the day after Dane and Nikki's party, Marta flew back to California. She had a large running retreat to plan before she could move to Minnesota permanently, but she'd be back in a few weeks to find a place to live. Staying in Dane's apartment had been a money-saver, but his lease was up soon, and Dane offered to ask his landlord if Marta could move in.

Maybe Brett needed to move onto that street, too. Looking around his dumpy apartment, he thought he should finally move somewhere else. Anywhere else. Staying wasn't necessary. He'd been doing it because he felt he didn't deserve better. That was a mental hurdle he still needed to jump over.

He shaved to look presentable. With Marta gone, Alyssa not speaking to him, and the marathon finished, he hadn't had a reason to shower, much less dress or shave. He'd been bumming around his apartment stewing, playing video games, and drinking beer. A lot like he had before Alyssa and the book started taking up all his free time.

It wouldn't be terrible if he and Alyssa worked out. He used to go on double dates with Dane and Liz, with Marta, back in school. He missed being part of a group. Being invited to Nikki's last year for Thanksgiving had reminded him of that.

On his way to Alyssa's, Brett's heart pounded, and his palms dampened.

If she wasn't mad, then why the silence?

He'd quickly become used to running with her, or working on the book.

Alyssa had squirmed into his life, and she filled a void he hadn't wanted her to fill. She had anyway, and fuck, imagining her not being around made his stomach churn.

"All set?" Brett asked when she opened the door.

She always cooked on the days he came over to work on the book or run, and her kitchen smelled like soup. Trying to see through the condensation gathered on the lid, he leaned over the slow cooker.

She nudged him aside. "It's turkey chili. We can eat when we get back. If I feed you now, we won't go." Alyssa regarded him critically, one eyebrow lifted, and he fought against the red that stained his cheeks. "When was the last time you ran?"

Brett cleared his throat.

"Ah-huh."

"You don't go every day," Brett said defensively, stepping into the hallway with Hunter.

She handed him the leash and locked her door, shoving

her keys into the thin running belt cinched around her waist.

It was warm enough outside for her to wear running shorts and a baggy racerback tank over an exercise bra. Her shoes looked brand new. She must have visited Nikki at Dane's store recently. Although, once Dane and Nikki married, it would belong to both of them.

He pet Hunter on the head earning him a whimper and a cold nose to his palm. The dog wanted more, which put Brett at a loss; he didn't have anything to give to anyone.

"Yes, I do. It was hard at first, to want to go, but I had the book and my sessions at the gym to keep me accountable. After I got used to it, I started to enjoy it, and it didn't feel so shitty anymore. Then I brought Hunter home, and now I have to go. A long time ago you said I would like to get outside by myself, and I do."

Hunter tugged on his leash, and Brett followed the dog outside.

They walked in silence for a few minutes, and he took the time to appreciate the weather.

The sun was shining, and big puffy clouds floated in the sky. A light breeze blew, and the grass sparkled a brilliant shade of green.

The park maintenance hadn't been out yet to mow, and colorful yellow dandelions dotted the yard.

After being inside for almost a week, the colors hurt his eyes, and he pushed his sunglasses onto his face.

Alyssa did the same, and he regretted not being able to look into the intense green of her irises.

He started running, a light jog with Hunter by his side, and Alyssa followed suit. They ran for a few minutes in silence until Alyssa asked, "Is there any news about your parents?"

"Like what?" Brett puffed. He had to take it slow. They hadn't talked about how long they would run, and he had absolutely no idea how far Alyssa could go. He'd lost track of her.

"I don't know. Like, they left you absolutely nothing? Not even a note? Did the people who took over their estate ask you if you wanted anything of theirs? Don't you have baby pictures you wanted? Your parents died of smoke inhalation, right? If it was only smoke damage, almost everything should have been salvageable."

"My parents taking pictures of me would've implied they were happy to have me, that they were proud of me. I was on my own from the day I was born. If I had a school play, they would drop me off and come back. Sometimes. When I was in second grade, they forgot I was at the school, and my teacher brought me home."

Days like that, school activities, field trips, he used to fear, he used to loathe, until one day he saw them as excuses, reasons, for not having to be at home. And if his parents forgot to pick him up, well, so much the longer he was away from them.

She fell silent, and Hunter broke her stride for a moment when he tried to veer off after a bee. "So, there's nothing?"

"Nope. The woman at the senior living facility passed my name along to my parents' friends, and a woman called to tell me they were going to have a sprinkling of the ashes ceremony if I wanted to go. She could barely speak, she sounded like she had a stick so far up her ass. I think someone forced her to call. I thanked her and declined. I don't even know where the ceremony was. It's supposed to be where people liked to spend their time, right? I don't know what my parents liked to do.

After I moved out after high school, I never saw them again."

"Their death changed nothing for you?"

"You saw me. I wish . . . yeah, I wish I would have had the balls to ask them why. But I didn't, so now I'll never know. It's okay."

He wanted it to be okay. It didn't matter why they treated him the way they did, it only mattered that he didn't let it define him as a person, but he hadn't done a very good job of that so far and he struggled with it every day.

"Do you . . . do you think you would have treated your own child like that?" Alyssa's eyes focused on the path in front of them.

"You only know what you know."

Was that harsh enough? Fair enough? Truthful enough? He didn't know how to love a child because he hadn't been loved while he was growing up.

"Marta told you, then."

"Yeah, she did."

"And you don't think I'm some gigantic prick for asking her to do that?"

"It's not for me to judge you. Maybe it's better you did that than realize when he was four years old you didn't want to be a parent anymore and decide to leave."

Glancing at her out of the corner of his eye, he asked, "Like your dad did to you?"

"Yeah. That pain, that shame you're not enough, not wanted, stays with you all your life. But I don't need to tell you that."

"No, you don't."

"Will you ever want kids?"

"I don't know. I wanted to talk to you about what we were doing, where we were going. I, ah, missed you this week, and I didn't know if you hated me for what Marta told you, and changed your mind about us, or . . . I guess I don't know what I was thinking. I don't want to hurt you, but I don't know what I'm doing and if you decide to stick with me, it's going to take some work." Brett stopped and wiped his forehead with his arm. "What do you say?"

---

ALYSSA STOPPED, TOO, and wished she had a bottle of water. Minnesota summer hadn't fully kicked in yet, but running made her hot and thirsty, and this conversation made her mouth dry as it was.

There was no way she could start a relationship, a real relationship like the one she wanted to be in with him, on a lie.

It *was* a lie, after what Marta told her. A lie of omission was still a lie.

"It's not going to matter what I say after I tell you this." She didn't want to say anything because she knew he would walk away, but she deserved it.

"What? What's going on?"

Alyssa paced in a small circle one hand on her hip, the other on her forehead. She felt like she was going to throw up. "Do you remember the first time we made love?"

That hadn't been what they had done, not the first time, but she refused to boil down what they had together into a handful of filthy words.

Brett nodded.

"I stopped you because I'm not on birth control."

Brett pulled his sunglasses from his face and narrowed his eyes. "But you took care of that, right? You never said anything else about it, so I assumed you took care of it."

"No, I never did—"

"Fuck!"

"Brett, the time at the park surprised me, okay? I thought the time in my loft was a one-time thing. Then you wanted to at the park and I just, I just wanted to be close to you, so I didn't stop it. I wanted you inside me, I wanted . . . I went to see you after your parents died, and by then I was in love with you." She pushed her sunglasses to the top of her head and wiped at her eyes. "I had the dumb idea that if I got pregnant we would be a family."

"That wasn't your decision to make."

"I know," she said bitterly. Boy, did she know. "That was before I talked to Marta, before I knew how you felt about children."

Tipping his head back, Brett blew out a breath. "Have you gotten your period?"

"Yes, last month and the month before."

Glaring at her he accused, "But not this month."

"No. Not yet."

"So you could be pregnant because we fucked the morning after Glass House."

There he was going back to sounding like what they did was just rutting, like thoughts and feelings weren't involved, like they were animals acting on their primal urges.

It was more than that for her, and it had been for a long time.

"Maybe."

Suddenly the anger was gone from his face, and it was replaced by something that Alyssa feared more: sadness. Despair. Hopelessness.

"I can't do this, Alyssa. I can't be in a relationship with someone who would betray me like this. I can't be a father; I don't want to be a dad. If you're pregnant, you're on your own. I don't want any part of it." He handed Hunter's leash to her and took a step back. "I'm sorry."

Alyssa believed he was, but it didn't stop her heart from cracking. She'd tried her best to love him, to help him, but he'd always been too far away.

The blank look on his face, the way he looked at her, but not *at* her, made her want to hurt him as much as he'd just hurt her.

Never mind that he was already hurting and had been all his life. She wanted to pay him back for making her fall in love with him, for making her want a family with him.

As he turned to leave, as she knew he would, abandoning her on the sidewalk just as her father had abandoned her in their house that one horrid morning, the words flew out of her mouth. "She would have kept it, you know."

He stopped dead, not a muscle moved in the whole frame of his body. "What do you mean?"

"Marta. She would have kept it."

"It was her decision, too."

He still wasn't looking at her which made what she had to say that much sweeter to deliver.

"She said that to make you feel better, but Marta would have kept your baby. She loved you, she loved that baby, and you made her throw it away."

The tears gathering on his eyelashes sparkled in the sunlight, and one fell, falling, falling, onto the cement.

Alyssa tugged on Hunter's leash, urging him to his feet, then she was running as fast as she could away from the heart she'd just broken, the way he'd broken hers.

CHAPTER ELEVEN

After training smart for so long you'll feel like you won't
need anyone—Alyssa

But you will—Brett

———

A FTER A GOOD round of crying, she bought a plane
ticket to see her parents. Her mother would be
thrilled; she was always asking Alyssa to visit or move near
them.

Florida was home to too many bugs for her to make a
full-time move, but her parents lived in a condo near the
beach, and right now time near the ocean was what her
heart needed.

She'd never loved a man before. She thought she'd been
in love; she thought one or two of the men she'd dated had
been The One, but she'd never felt anything the way she
felt when she looked in Brett Sommers' hazel eyes.

Alyssa was packing a suitcase when someone knocked

on her door. She wiped at her cheeks to dry them. It seemed no matter how hard she tried to stop crying, the tears still came, still slid unbidden down her face.

And it wasn't because Brett had cast her aside.

She'd expected that.

Deep down inside she knew they'd end this way.

No, it was because of what she'd said to him.

Marta had told her that information in private, and she'd expected Alyssa to keep it that way, not fling it at Brett the first chance presented to her.

The look on his face would haunt her for the rest of her life. How dare she, what right did she have, to hurt him with a choice he'd made so long ago? He already regretted it, and she'd done more than pour salt in his wounds.

"Hey!" Nikki said, bouncing into her loft. "I haven't seen you forever, I thought we could go get—" She stopped abruptly when she noticed Alyssa's splotchy face. "What's wrong? What happened?"

"Nothing happened," she muttered, leading the way to her bedroom so she could finish packing. She didn't know how long she was staying and she packed enough clothes for a few weeks. Being she could do laundry at her parents' place would help her panty situation.

"Then where are you going?" Nikki asked, tilting her head at Alyssa's suitcase open on her unmade bed.

"I'm going to visit my parents for a while. My mom's been badgering me to fly down, and since Brett's book is done, and I sent my editor the one I started back in November, I'm in the clear."

She contemplated a gauzy aqua and pink shirt from her closet. The blouse would look nice paired with white shorts or capris pants if her mother wanted to go for dinner.

"What about Brett?" Nikki asked as she sat in a chair placed under Alyssa's window.

"What about him? I didn't ask him to go, if that's what you mean." But the mention of Brett's name brought the tears back, and she could barely speak.

"Will you tell me what happened?"

The understanding and sympathy along with the compassion in Nikki's voice were Alyssa's undoing, and she sank onto the edge of her bed and sobbed into the balled-up shirt clutched in her hands.

Nikki let her cry it out, and when Alyssa finally came up for air, she held out a wad of tissues.

Gratefully, she blew her nose.

"We're not together anymore. Not that we ever really were. But we're completely over now; we had a big fight yesterday and he said he didn't want to see me ever again."

Alyssa thought back to Marta's words. *He's chasing you.*

He wasn't chasing her anymore.

"Maybe you should start at the beginning," Nikki said.

"Yeah, you're right."

Alyssa met Nikki's eyes. "Do you know now, Marta and Brett's big secret? What made Marta move back to California?"

Nikki shook her head. "No. If Dane knows, he didn't say anything."

"Okay, well, when they were in college, Marta got pregnant, and she had an abortion. She told Brett it was for the best because she was trying for the Olympics, they were young . . ."

Alyssa waved her shirt in the air to imply other reasons young people didn't want a baby.

"I didn't know any of that, and I, well . . ."

Ashamed, she looked away. She couldn't believe she

was so stupid. Trapping a man with a baby. "We've been having sex, and I'm not on anything."

Nikki swallowed. "You're pregnant?"

"I don't feel like I am, and I'm not late. It could go either way at this point. But, I didn't know Brett and Marta's past, and I thought having a baby would be giving him the family he needed. I love him, Nikki, and I wanted to give him the world."

"But he's not ready?"

"He's more than not ready. He flat out doesn't want it. Yesterday, on our run, when I told him we've been having sex without birth control, he flipped out. He told me if I'm pregnant I'm on my own—he'd want no part of it."

"Things sound messy, but not . . . irreparable. Especially if you're not pregnant. That would give you two time to work things out—if you still wanted to."

"There's more."

Nikki asked, "How could there be more? Isn't what you told me enough?"

"More than enough. But you know when Marta and I talked during your party, when I ran off thinking she and Brett were together, and she came after me?"

Nikki nodded.

"Marta told me in confidence that if Brett would have asked her to keep it, she would have. That she would have made a family with him."

"Most women would, I think," Nikki said, then bit her lip. "Marta was what? Twenty-three, maybe? It would have been scary not having support—especially from your baby's daddy."

"I know, but she didn't tell *him* that, she told me. When Brett and I fought yesterday, all I wanted to do was hurt him, the way I was hurting. I told him that Marta would have kept it had he asked. He looked like death warmed over."

"Oh, Alyssa," Nikki murmured.

She cried into her shirt. "I know, I know. Marta told me her secret, and the first thing I did was fling it in Brett's face. It wasn't my secret to share, but I did it to hurt him. Now they'll both hate me."

"So you're leaving, you're running away."

Sniffling, Alyssa said, "Not for good. Just for a little while. I need space to breathe, I need to get up the courage to apologize, and I need to harden my heart to the fact that Brett and I are over. I guess to make peace with the fact that we never started. A relationship was only something I wanted. I just need a couple weeks, maybe a month. I don't know. It doesn't matter."

"What about Hunter? Are you going to board him that whole time? He'll miss you."

Alyssa hadn't thought much past getting onto a plane and flying away from her trouble, though she couldn't do that either.

Placing a hand on her belly, she thought she would maybe have to start learning to take care of someone other than herself.

"He loves Brett, I'll bring him over there in the morning on the way to the airport."

"Brett can't have pets in his building."

Alyssa scoffed. "You think anyone in that dump is going to care? Hunter's not a barker—he's a quiet dog. No one will know. And if they do, well, it will force him to move out. He has no reason to live in that slum anymore."

"But what if you're pregnant? Will you tell him?"

Standing, Alyssa threw her damp shirt into her suitcase

and snapped it closed. If she forgot anything, it was a good bet her mother wouldn't mind doing some shopping.

"I'm not getting rid of it, no matter what he says. I don't have to name him on the birth certificate—that will save him child support. He wants out, I can keep him out. No big deal."

Nikki sighed. "You've thought of everything, haven't you? Can I at least take you to the airport?"

"No, that's fine. I'll drop Hunter off at Brett's and leave my car in long-term parking. Maybe in a couple days you and Dane can pick it up for me. If you do, text me so I can tell you when I'll need a ride home."

"Okay. Are you sure this is what you want to do?"

"I messed up, Nik. I messed up good. I need time to lick my wounds, okay?"

"I understand. You'll call if you need help?"

Alyssa promised. But she knew no one would be able to help her. Not with this.

---

ALYSSA GATHERED HUNTER'S toys, food bag, and water and food bowls. On the way out the door, she grabbed the dog's leash and the plastic bags she took with her to clean up after him on their walks.

On the drive, Hunter whined knowing something wasn't right, but the dog would be thrilled to see Brett. She swore the dog remembered the way Brett had carried him to his car in the park.

He had a gentleness about him, a part of him he didn't recognize or wouldn't admit to, that was open to caring for someone.

Maybe forcing him to take Hunter would give him the

strength he needed to care about someone. Maybe he and Marta would get back together while she was gone. She hated the thought, but eventually she'd have to get used to seeing him with someone else.

"Come on, babe," she said to Hunter as she pulled up to Brett's building.

His car was parked in the parking lot; that was a good thing. She didn't know what she would have done had Brett not been home. She hadn't made Hunter a reservation at the vet to board him as a Plan B.

Hunter looked around, stopping every five seconds to sniff at something.

His curiosity relieved and aggravated her. She wanted to get this over with, but she also didn't want to face Brett. What she'd said to him had been vile, evil, and she deserved whatever he gave her in return.

A little girl with big sad brown eyes sat on the bottom stair of the apartment building's interior playing with a grubby doll, and her eyes brightened when Hunter approached her for a rub.

Alyssa felt sorry for any child growing up in a place like this, and she fought the urge to gather the girl in her arms and run away. Just because she was living here didn't mean her parents didn't love her.

Alyssa's own mother had done the best she could after her father left them. She'd never felt unloved—not by her mother.

She led Hunter down the hallway to Brett's room. She couldn't accurately call where he lived an apartment. Wrangling the leash and the bag of Hunter's things hanging from her arm, she knocked on the door.

When he didn't answer, her heart slammed in panic.

She needed to drop Hunter off—she didn't have time to make other arrangements.

Taking a chance, Alyssa tried the door and found Brett staring listlessly at his TV as he lay on his futon.

His eyes flickered to her, then away.

He didn't want to see her. She couldn't blame him any. After spilling Marta's secret, she had a difficult time looking herself in the face, too.

Swallowing painfully, she tugged on Hunter's leash. It didn't take much to prompt the dog into the studio apartment after he caught Brett's scent.

Hunter's presence jerked Brett out of his indifference, and he sat up, frowning.

He looked like he hadn't slept in a while, his hair was mussed, and dark circles rested under his eyes. His clothes were wrinkled, but at least he was dressed. Alyssa didn't need another repeat performance of when she came here to check on him after his parents died.

"What are you doing here?" he asked, petting Hunter's head.

With a clatter, she dumped Hunter's things onto the floor. She let her eyes roam around the room, so she wouldn't have to make eye contact with him. "I'm leaving, so I'm giving Hunter to you." She tried to smile, but it was lost in grief. "He always did prefer you."

"What do you mean, you're leaving?"

"I, ah, I'm sorry for what I said to you on our run the other day. About Marta. It was wrong, and I'm sorry. What happened all those years ago had nothing to do with me. I'm sorry if I've caused problems between you two. Maybe, I mean, I hope, you can fix things."

She cleared her throat to try to rid it of the dryness.

Uncomfortable, she shuffled her feet, her dress's hem whispering above her knees.

"But why are you leaving?"

"My mom's been after me to visit—I haven't seen her since Christmas, so I said I would go. I can't take Hunter, so I'm giving him to you."

This wasn't going like she planned, and she didn't like the flat look in Brett's eyes.

"I can't take your dog, Alyssa."

*And you don't want me either, I get it.*

"I'm not giving you much of a choice."

She knelt and met Hunter's liquid brown eyes. "Take good care of him, okay?" she whispered, touching noses with him, earning her a lick to the cheek.

Brett stood. "I can't take care of a dog—I can barely take care of myself."

"I wasn't talking to you."

She turned back to Hunter and rubbed his soft ears. He was almost a hundred percent, but he'd probably always remember what it felt like to be separated from his family, how it felt to be lost, alone. She knew how it felt when she ran away from Brett on the trail, watched as her father walked out the door.

But she hoped Hunter would remember how it felt to be rescued, to have Brett's arms around him. She would always remember that, too.

"Take care of him, because I love him." She pushed a kiss to Hunter's nose.

"You don't have to leave, Alyssa," Brett said, taking a step toward her.

"Yes, I do. I have to get away. You don't need me. You don't want me. The hideous things I said to you yesterday made sure of that. I only wanted to hurt you as much as you hurt me."

Meeting his eyes, Alyssa knew she'd done a good job. She didn't deserve him, even if he would've wanted her. "And I'm sorry. Take care of Hunter, okay?"

Without waiting for a response, she started for the door. She had to leave as quickly as possible.

Alyssa sped up as she realized Brett was following her. "I can't have a dog in here. And what about you? Will you tell me if you're . . .?"

*Pregnant.* He couldn't even say the word.

"Then you should move," she said, not taking her eyes from her escape. "You don't need to live here anymore. Start taking care of yourself. You matter. You mean something to a lot of people."

Sighing, she turned around. She needed to see his face when she said the next part, needed to know how he really felt. "But I'm not going to tell you if I'm pregnant or not. You washed your hands of that yesterday, and with good reason. But it wasn't betrayal, no matter what you think." She lifted her chin. "I love you, and my intentions were sincere. I wanted to give you a family who would love you, too."

His face didn't soften which toughened her resolve to finish saying what she needed to say.

"You turned me away, shut me out, which is your right, so no, I won't be telling you anything. Just know that if I am, I'll be the best mother I can be. That I'll try to give our child a life that was better than either of ours."

His face remained impassive which told her more than anything he could have said aloud.

With a swoosh of her breath, she let herself out of his

apartment. In a bundle of nerves, she sagged against the dirty wall outside his door.

She'd done it.

She'd said goodbye to Brett, cut him the rest of the way out of her life.

When she let herself out of the building, the little girl was gone, and as she stepped into the sunshine, she vowed to let the little girl inside herself go. S

he was a woman, a grown-up woman, and she needed to start acting like one instead of the scared little child her father left behind all those years ago.

---

"So, she's gone."

It was hotter than hell outside, and the trees they were running under offered little relief.

When Dane suggested a run, Brett jumped on it.

Hunter needed the exercise, and in all honesty, so did he.

Moping wasn't going to do any good, and why was he anyway? Alyssa gave him what he wanted. He was alone, and she'd taken any responsibility.

"Yeah."

"When's she coming back?"

"She didn't tell me. It doesn't matter."

"Alyssa's probably the best thing that's ever happened to you. Why are you letting her walk away?"

"Let's not talk about it, okay? She's gone, and it's what we both want. What's going on with wedding stuff?"

Brett zoned into the run as Dane described the reception venue they'd chosen. He'd agreed to a fifteen-miler, which had been stupid of him, but he also realized it was to punish himself for being such a dumbass. A fifteen-mile run would numb him from the inside out, so he wouldn't think about Alyssa. He didn't need Dane to tell him she was a good thing, and he was stupid for letting her walk.

But nothing had changed for him. He still wasn't ready for a relationship, he still didn't want children. He still didn't want to get married even though the thought of never seeing Alyssa again shoved a ball of lead the size of the Grand Canyon into the pit of his stomach.

It would be worse to see her, though.

What would he do if he ran into her at Dane's and Nikki's, or at an expo, and she had a child with her? A child who would have his hair and her eyes. He wouldn't have any claim on either one of them, and by then, they wouldn't have room in their lives for him.

How long would Alyssa give him to get his shit together before his time ran out? Not very long. And how fair was that to anyone—especially his kid?

That sent chills down his spine despite the heat.

"Marta decided to move into my place," Dane said.

He'd apparently exhausted his speech about wedding reception venues and moved on to something else.

Brett wished he wouldn't have. His relationship with Nikki had made him a chatty guy, and Brett preferred the old Dane, the Dane who could run twenty miles without saying a single fucking word.

When he didn't answer, Dane asked, "When are you moving out of your pit? Your studio is barely big enough for you, let alone you and a dog."

Brett puffed. His legs burned, and his lungs were on fire. He could barely make the words come out. "I should have moved a long time ago, but what did I care? I still don't. Not really."

"We'll help you move."

*Move where?* Brett thought. People were asking him to do a lot of moving these days. Move on. Move forward. Move out. What if he didn't want to move? What if he was happy where he was? He pictured Alyssa rolling her eyes at that.

It was obvious to everyone he wasn't happy where he was—where he'd been stuck for the past several years.

Unwilling to talk any more about it, Brett let his mind blank along with his legs and the rest of his body.

He wouldn't be able to walk tomorrow.

He'd have to train Hunter to bring him beer.

***

ALYSSA'S MOTHER, PATRICE, stood in the busy baggage claim in the Orlando International Airport. Alyssa had no trouble spotting the dark-haired woman who looked just like her plus twenty-five years.

"Oh, my God," Patrice yelled, turning heads, when she spotted Alyssa making her way through the throng of people to wait for her suitcase. "Look at you! You look fabulous!"

She didn't feel fabulous, but Alyssa had to admit, traveling was easier slimmer. Fitting in the airplane's seat, using the small bathroom. To her surprise, she'd even enjoyed chatting with the man seated next to her about the latest bestsellers, and normally she avoided human contact at all costs. The flight had been pleasant, and seeing her mother was welcome, too.

"Hey, Mom," Alyssa said, stepping into the woman's embrace.

"What happened?" Patrice asked, gesturing wildly, almost taking out a small child walking by.

"I've started running," Alyssa said, leading her mother to the carousel that would hopefully spit out her suitcase.

"Nikki finally won you over, huh?" her mom asked, running her fingers through Alyssa's hair.

"No," Alyssa said. "Not Nikki."

"Oh, my God," her mother exploded, slapping a hand over her mouth, oblivious to all the stares she garnered. "You've met a man."

How her mom figured it out so fast was a mystery to her. Maybe she'd have that kind of intuition about her own children. She adjusted the huge black purse hanging from her shoulder and rubbed her belly.

"And you're pregnant!" Patrice announced to the entire airport.

Alyssa winced.

It was going to be a long vacation.

---

BRETT IGNORED A movie playing on his older than shit TV. He missed Alyssa with a fierceness he couldn't describe, an ache he buried at the bottom of his heart.

She'd been gone two weeks, three days, and fourteen hours.

But he wasn't counting. The day after she left, she emailed him the book saying she'd finished as much as she could without his final input and added an attachment of agents who represented that kind of nonfiction. "Start emailing them" was the only thing she'd ended the message with, and Brett caught the not-so-subtly implied hint she would not be helping him beg for someone to publish their book.

He didn't have it in him to work on it without her. Maybe he could hire Nikki to do it, like a personal assistant.

The project had lost all its appeal since Alyssa left, which only brought Dane's accusation to the forefront of his mind. He'd wanted to write it to help beginning runners. That part was real. But if he was honest with himself, well, if Alyssa would have turned him down, he wouldn't have written it at all.

He rested his head against the bar of the worn futon and pet Hunter, whose head was in his lap.

As the empty days went by, Brett began to spend more time at marathon headquarters.

There were things he needed to plan, like the logo that would be pressed into medals for the finishers of next year's race. The pamphlets that would be shoved into Nikki's women's race swag bags in the fall would also be stamped with the new logo.

He didn't have much of a break from planning, and Brett found the simplicity and emptiness of spending time in his office doing the same tasks he did every year disconcerting.

The routine, the feelings, were comfortable, but he drew no comfort from them. He was easing back into a life that held little appeal, but it was safe because it was all he'd known.

Later than he usually stayed, it was there at headquarters where Marta found him tinkering with the colors of the logo.

"I went by your apartment," Marta said, dropping into a chair in front of Brett's desk. Hunter was lying on the floor, and he greeted her with a whine.

"I wasn't there," Brett tried to joke, but he wasn't in the mood. "When did you get back?"

"Yesterday. Dane told me Alyssa's gone. Brett, why did you let her go?"

Marta wasn't one to waste time.

Brett lifted his gaze from the computer screen and met Marta's eyes. Her shaggy hair was wild, and she wore a green tank top and light blue denim shorts. She even had sandals on her feet. He wasn't used to seeing her look like a person, as opposed to a runner, and a smile twisted his mouth.

She frowned. "I'm being serious."

"Why do we have to talk about it? Let's talk about you. Who have you been dating? Why haven't you married and popped out a couple kids?"

Brett was proud of himself for thinking of it. All the questions she had for him went for her, too.

She was stalling in life just as much as he was.

Marta paced by Brett's desk. "I kind of feel like since I gave up our baby, I had to make that sacrifice worth it and focus on the reasons why I did it. I have a very successful career. I couldn't have done a family justice all these years. It wouldn't have been fair to my husband or kids."

"Alyssa told me you would have kept our child if I would have asked. Is that true? Did I make you get an abortion, Marta? Because all those years ago, you made it sound like you wanted to get rid of it just as much as I did."

The words felt mealy in his mouth—grainy and dirty like eating mud pies.

"Brett, I was only twenty-two, almost twenty-three. I had no business having a baby." She ran her palms over her shorts.

"And I was the same age—not that it made much of a

difference—but that's not what I asked. Would you have kept that baby if I would've backed you? Just a simple yes or no is all I need."

His voice shook, and he was more upset than he thought he'd be, talking about this.

"Yes! Yes, I would have," Marta cried. "I would have, if you could have made that commitment, and Alyssa had no business telling you that. But I was also studying, running, and trying to build a career. Where would we be if we would have kept it, Brett? Where would we be now?"

"Why does our fate always turn out badly?" Brett rose from the computer chair and leaned his hands against the cool metal of his desk. "Why couldn't we have worked out?"

Marta threw her hands in the air. "Because you wouldn't have been able to handle being married and being a dad. There was no way in hell you would've stayed with me. I would have kept that baby, yeah, and when I was nine months pregnant, or when that baby was born, you would have high-tailed it out of there, and I would have been *fucked*. I did what was best for you."

"You think so little of me." Brett's lips twisted in disgust.

"You deserve it. Where's Alyssa? You're doing the same thing to her as you did to me, so yeah, I don't think very much of you right now."

Brett sagged and fell into his chair. "I didn't make her do anything. She's visiting her parents. She's coming back."

"And then what?" Marta demanded.

Brett's eyes slid away. "Then nothing."

The fight left Marta then, and she dragged her chair in front of Brett's. She took his hands in hers, rubbed his knuckles with the pads of her thumbs.

"You love her, don't you?"

Gripping her hands, Brett whispered, "Yeah, I do."

There was no reason to lie; there was no censure in her eyes, only compassion and understanding.

"Then what are you doing?"

"I'm not good enough for her. I wasn't good enough for you, either." He resisted pulling his hands from her grasp. She would only do something worse, like hug him.

"That's not true. Your parents made you feel that way, but it's not true." She tried to smile. "When we were in school, I loved you. I loved you *so fucking much*. But I loved running, too. I knew you weren't ready for anything real. Brett," she breathed his name in a shuddery gasp, "even if I wouldn't have gotten pregnant, we wouldn't have made it."

Brett wanted to tell her yes, they would have, even opened his mouth to say so, but Marta knew him too well and lightly placed a finger over his lips. "Don't lie to me."

"No. No, we wouldn't have."

Marta nodded. "We did the right thing, but we aren't the same people now. You love her, and she loves you. It's time to leave the past behind."

"Do you hate me, Marta?" he asked, rubbing his face.

She sat on his lap and cuddled him to her. "Of course not. And neither does Alyssa. We both understand, but stop using the way your parents treated you as a shield to protect yourself because it's not working. You hurt yourself every day, every minute."

"Alyssa's in Florida."

Marta framed his face in her hands and smiled indulgently as she would a child making a momentous discovery.

"Then go get her."

CHAPTER TWELVE

Maintenance is harder than starting—Alyssa

But if you have the right partner, you can do anything—Brett

It might take a lot of convincing, though—Alyssa

You're always right, now shut up and kiss me—Brett

---

A LYSSA SIGHED AT the blood soaked into the toilet paper.

She'd gotten her period.

It was a good thing, really. She didn't need to be tied to a man who didn't want her.

Bit by bit, she was discovering her worth. She was lovable, she had something to offer a man, she could be a part of a healthy relationship.

She hadn't needed to lose weight to figure that out—she'd only needed someone, a decent man like Brett, to see through the pounds and the hurt. She'd never dated a nice man before. Funny that was all it had taken to prove her own self-worth.

"Alyssa, are we going to the beach or not?"

"Yeah, Mom. I'll be right there."

She wasn't particularly close to her mother, or to her stepfather, but this vacation felt different from the ones she'd taken in the past.

She'd done a lot of shopping with her mom, lunches, the beach. She even visited the health club, running on the treadmill, unwilling to give up her routine, while Patrice participated in her water aerobics class.

At the country club, Alyssa played tennis for the first time, taking lessons and being drawn into a doubles match with one of her mother's friends and her daughter. Five weeks in Florida and she was fitting in, building a life.

But she missed Brett so much at night she'd lay awake holding her stomach as if it were some cavernous hole threatening to consume her.

More than once she'd reached for her phone to text him, but at the last minute she always resisted hitting Send.

"You're quiet," her mother said, patting her leg as she drove them to the beach.

"Just thinking about when I should go home. I miss Nikki."

"Oh," Patrice said, crestfallen. "I've gotten so used to having you here. You're having a good time, aren't you?"

"Yeah, I am," Alyssa said, climbing out of the car.

As she waited for her mother to swipe her debit card to pay for parking, Alyssa looked around the beach. A seafood restaurant was located at the end of the long pier, and they planned to eat a late lunch there after walking along the beach.

"But my life is in Tower City."

"I don't miss that place," Patrice muttered, pulling her sandals off and testing the sand's temperature with her toes. Deeming it cool enough to walk across, Patrice made her way to the water and Alyssa followed.

"I drove by the old building a few weeks ago," Alyssa said, weaving around families setting up camp with their towels, chairs, coolers, and umbrellas, picking up shells, or making sandcastles near the water. People crowded the beach playing ball or sunbathing.

Stopping at the beach almost every day, Alyssa had gotten quite tan.

Living in the Sunshine State agreed with her.

Patrice's lip curled in distaste. "What did you do that for?"

"I was visiting someone in the area."

Seagulls flew overhead, brilliant white dots gliding against the pristine blue. The wind smelled of salt and grease, the scents of fried food from her mother's favorite restaurant floating to them.

Alyssa could live here. Rent a place on the beach. Hemingway wrote on the beach, lived on one of the Keys, if she remembered correctly. The choice would be a no-brainer if it weren't for the bugs she detested. Cockroaches grossed her out.

Her mother didn't reply, and they walked in silence to the water—close enough that the ocean kissed their toes when bigger waves greeted the shore.

A huge tanker ship was but a grey speck in the watery

horizon, and Alyssa squinted to focus on it. She liked guessing as to whether it was moving or not.

Her cramps reminded her of her period, and she wished she would've taken some ibuprofen to forget. Even though she knew it was wrong, losing her only link to Brett made her sad.

Only, people left kids behind all the time, so it wasn't much of a link, and it was better for both of them this happened.

"Mom, how did it feel to be a single mother?"

"It was tough, but I didn't go through anything other women didn't go through. Actually, I was one of the lucky ones. I had a decent job, and a neighbor in the building watched you after school when you started Kindergarten. Do you remember?"

She did, kind of, but she remembered more clearly how that enormous yellow bus terrified her, and she'd kept her eyes glued to the window so she wouldn't miss her stop. She'd known, even then, that if she were to get lost, there wouldn't be anyone to look for her, at least, not until her mother came home from work.

"Do you ever hear from him?" Alyssa crouched down to examine a shell. Though its edges were rough, she still picked it up. When she looked up from the sand, she was shocked to see tears glinting in her mother's eyes.

"No. The day he walked out the door was the last day I saw him. We spoke through lawyers after that." Her mother studied the waves rolling toward them, the tops frothy with white foam.

"I heard what he said," Alyssa murmured, her words layered under the roar of the wind, the shrieking of children nearby, and the strains of a sad song someone played on an old boombox.

She'd never told her mother this before, but somehow it felt right talking about it now. She'd urged Brett to face up to his past, to forget what his parents had done, and she needed to do the same.

Speaking with her mother about her father would help her put it away once and for all.

"What do you mean?" Patrice squinted into the light.

"When he left, I heard him. He said, 'I don't want you.' He was looking right at me."

"That's not all he said, Alyssa. I'll remember it until I die. He said, 'I don't want you to see me this way.' He was a coward, that's all. It didn't have anything to do with you, baby. Most divorces don't have anything to do with the kids. Your father met someone else, and he left me."

Sighing, she sank into the sand.

She sat by her mother, and Alyssa rested her head on Patrice's bony shoulder. Her mother never had a weight problem. Quite the opposite, in fact. When her father left, Patrice was too busy working and taking care of Alyssa to pay attention to herself. Only after she met Stan did her mother begin to enjoy life again, but by then, her father's defection had done its damage and her mother's figure had never been the same.

"For a little while he tried to stay in touch, but you'd already been hurt, and I was too busy making ends meet to care what he wanted. He sent money, but the checks were sporadic and I learned quickly I couldn't depend on him. It was a few years later I heard the woman he ran off with had children of her own and needed his salary."

Patrice took Alyssa's hand. "Don't tell me you've blamed yourself all this time? Because you misheard him?"

Tears clogged her throat, and she rested her chin on her knees and stared across the ocean. "Yeah, I have. I thought it was because he didn't want to be my daddy anymore."

"I hated him for a long time, but these things happen, and it's no one's fault. If your father wouldn't have left me, I would never have met Stan. Things happen for a reason. I've been happy all these years, and Stan was good to you while you were growing up. You have to take the good with the bad." She wiped her eyes. "Now tell me about this young man; you've been quiet about him."

Alyssa sifted through a handful of smooth white sand, smiling at the smallest of shells. "He's kind of like Dad. He didn't want me enough to work through things. Cut and run."

Patrice slipped an arm around her shoulders and Alyssa leaned in, grateful for the support. "There's someone out there who will—don't let him turn you off to those possibilities. I loved your father, just like I see you love this man. But don't let him ruin your faith. Think about staying here. I miss you." She rubbed Alyssa's cheek with her nose, the way she used to do when Alyssa was small.

"I will," Alyssa promised.

---

ALYSSA GAVE A lot of thought to what her mother said. She supposed now it was silly to shoulder all the blame for her father's abandonment, but as the years went by and as the men she dated treated her with the same disregard and disdain as what she'd seen in her father's eyes, it was an easy assumption.

Her mother called her father a coward, but she was being one, too.

She needed to go home. She'd missed the other engagement party that Nikki's and Dane's mothers threw for them. Alyssa didn't know if Brett helped or not. Whenever they spoke, Nikki didn't mention Brett, always steering the conversation toward wedding things like bridesmaid dresses, wedding gowns, and the bouquets they would carry down the aisle.

Though the break had been nice, not writing made her antsy, and she missed sitting in her loft, spending hours spinning her next story.

She wondered how Hunter was doing without her. She hoped Brett was taking care of the dog, but she wouldn't have left Hunter with him if she hadn't thought he would do the right thing.

She believed with all her heart he was capable of doing the right thing.

After booking the flight for her return home, she drove her mother's car to the beach. She needed one last afternoon there. Returning to Tower City after such a long time away, she didn't know what she would be walking into. She didn't know if Brett would be with Marta now; she didn't know if Brett would bother to talk to her again.

As she walked across the sand toward the pier, a new book idea started threading through her mind. By the time she reached the end of the wooden, weathered structure, she had a full book planned and the dedication to Brett already written.

Because she owed him for many things.

Though he'd broken her heart, he'd shown her what it was to be loved, even if just for a moment, and that was something she could never repay.

Brett walked across the sand searching for Alyssa.

Her mother said she was at the beach, and never having been to a Florida beach, he'd thought it would be easy enough to find her. But now he scanned the white sand and blue water, and he realized it would be like searching for a needle in a haystack.

People were everywhere. The shore went for miles—Alyssa could be anywhere. He could take a chance she had her phone with her, but he didn't want her to find out he was in Florida that way.

Holding his shoes, his socks stuffed into them, he walked the beach, dodging little kids running from the waves, chuckled at the birds doing the same.

Two hours had gone by when he decided to look on the pier. He was never going to find her. She had to go back to her mother's at some point, and he thought of going there to wait.

Patrice hadn't been happy to meet him, and she'd let him know it.

Her accusations of him abandoning her daughter at a time when she needed him shamed him. And when Patrice told him Alyssa was thinking about living there, no doubt enjoying turning the screws, his heart turned to a block of ice. He'd pushed her away so completely that she didn't want to live in Minnesota anymore.

He was about to give up and retrace his steps to his rental car when he spotted her. She'd let her hair grow out, and it fluttered around her head in the salty wind coming off the water.

Her sundress blew against her legs, and her skin shimmered a deep brown. She'd lost more weight, and he was proud of her for continuing her workouts when someone less strong would have buckled under the pressure of doing it alone.

Brett walked up beside her and leaned against the rail. "I've never seen the ocean before."

That she stiffened was the only reaction he could see—she didn't even turn her head toward him.

His heart sank.

She'd been gone two months now.

Sunglasses covered her eyes, her chin a sharp angle pointing away from him. "What are you doing here?"

Brett tried to swallow, but the harshness of her voice dried his mouth. "I wanted to see you."

"I'm not pregnant, if that's what you wanted to know."

He hadn't expected her to fall into his arms, not with the way he'd treated her, but she was so cold, and her news sent shivers down his spine.

He hadn't realized how much he'd been hoping she was.

Now there was nothing to keep them together. There was no reason for him to insist on being in her life other than one thing.

"Oh."

She looked at him then, lifting her sunglasses and perching them on the top of her head. "Is that all you have to say? I'm surprised there's no sigh of relief, no fist pump. You wouldn't have wanted that baby, and you don't want me."

She looked away, but not before he caught the glint of tears in her eyes. They gave him hope. If she still cared enough to cry, they might still have a chance.

"Your mother said you're thinking about staying here, in Florida, I mean."

"You talked to my mother?"

Brett dropped his shoes onto the battered wood of the

pier and looked down at the water. They were quite high, and his stomach shifted. He didn't know how to swim well, and he'd heard terrible things about an ocean's undertow. And there were probably sharks.

"How do you think I found you? Nikki gave me her address. Thank God for GPS. This is my first trip out of Minnesota. My first time on a plane."

"I'm sorry you wasted it on me," Alyssa said, staring into the infinite blue horizon. "Go home, Brett."

"See, that's the thing," he said, brushing her hair away from her face, though it did little good against the wind. "I don't have one. My parents didn't give me a home. My shitty little studio has never been home, just a place to hide. I've never had one, not until you. Not until we started spending time together, and I started looking forward to seeing you. I know we've gotten off to a bumpy start, but I'm asking for another chance. One last chance to be with you. Is there any way I can make it up to you?" He took her shaking hand and brought it to his lips. "Please?"

Alyssa seethed. Brett had come all the way from Minnesota for her and for what? Because he missed her a little bit? Maybe because he still needed help with the book. Well, too bad.

"We don't have anything," she snapped, yanking her hand from his grasp. "All we do is fight and have sex. And what about Marta?"

Brett leaned against the rail, picked at the splintered wood with this fingernail.

She knew that look, his posture. She'd hurt him yelling

at him, but he couldn't have expected her to fall into his arms and let him keep hurting her.

"Marta called me out on a lot of things," he murmured, and she had to lean closer to hear. She hoped he wouldn't get any ideas she wanted to be near him, even though he smelled like heaven.

This wasn't a good place to talk, not about something like this, but she couldn't go anywhere with him. She was too weak to defend herself and not give him what he wanted.

"I wasn't ready to be a dad, even if she would have kept our baby had I asked. She recognized that in me. She also realized she couldn't raise a child by herself, not at that age, not back then, and she did what she had to do, for both of us."

"Well, that was a long time ago," she said. As far as she was concerned, this conversation was a dead end. "You haven't made any progress, Brett. I thought maybe you could, for me, because God, sometimes it really seemed like you loved me, you know? But every time things got serious, or too sticky, you ran away."

He opened his mouth to interrupt her, but she shook her head. "I know what I did wasn't right, trying to get pregnant to keep you with me was a stupid thing to do. But it showed me that we don't have anything else that *would* keep us together. I love you, but you don't love me, you used me for the book. I can find someone who will treat me better, who wants to share a good life with me. Really. Go home."

Before Alyssa realized what happened, Brett pushed her against the rail, the wood biting into her back. Startled and frightened, she met his furious eyes.

"Are you seeing someone? Are you still seeing Tom?"

"What? No, you're crazy. I'm not seeing anyone." Deflated, she looked away. "I've only wanted you, Brett. I've only wanted you."

Brett sank to his knees and took her hands.

"Alyssa, these past weeks have been hellish for me. I woke up wanting you, I went to bed aching for you. It's difficult to give love when you've rarely received it, but I love you. I may never have shown you in the right way, or even at all, but I have, and I do. I want to build a life with you, one day I would like to have a family. I'm not perfect, and I'm going to need help being who you need me to be. But I promise I will always do my best to give you a home."

Tipping her face to the sky, Alyssa tried to think of what to say. "Are you asking me to marry you?"

Brett laughed. "Yeah, I guess I am. But can we wait until Nikki and Dane do their thing?"

"Sure. I've always wanted a huge wedding. Those take time to plan," she said, running her fingers through his hair.

Wincing, Brett rose to his feet and gathered her into his arms. "How about we get married here, on the beach, and Hunter can be our ring bearer?" he asked, resting his chin on the top of her head.

As she laid her cheek against his chest and listened to his heart beat, Alyssa considered his suggestion. "My mother would be thrilled if we did that."

Brett kissed her nose. "I'm getting more than just you in this bargain, aren't I?"

Rising to the tips of her toes, Alyssa wrapped her arms around his shoulders. "Do you mind?"

A laugh rumbled through his body, and she relaxed, finally secure in his love for her.

"I wouldn't have it any other way. You know I need all the family I can get."

Alyssa kissed him.

She would be his family.

After all the years of giving her characters their happily ever afters, she was finally getting hers. She'd been brave enough, strong enough, to fight for what she wanted. Alyssa wrote her own story, but it wasn't the end.

They were just beginning.

RUNNING SCARED

Chapter One

"I was so embarrassed," Marta Braddock murmured, cupping the icy mug between her palms.

Ian Butler laughed, drying a glass with a white terrycloth towel.

To see Marta sitting in his bar sipping a frosted mug of beer made him believe miracles could happen after all.

He'd have bet the bar, hell the whole building, it would never have happened in a million years. Marta being in Minnesota was a dream—and a second chance.

The bar was empty as usual, not even his friends Dane and Brett stopped by on a regular basis anymore. But he'd rather spend time with Marta any day of the week, and he winked at her, enjoying her story.

"Then what happened?"

"Luckily, she wasn't angry. I mean, how many redheaded Hollys work at the university? It was easy to stick my foot in my mouth bringing up Dane, but she was gracious about it."

"What did she say?"

He hadn't been this content in a long time. When Brett told him Marta was moving back to Minnesota, it was like a wish he'd never dare say aloud was granted, and suddenly, his whole world was open to him again.

Casually, he leaned a hip against the bar, resting his elbow on the polished wood, propping his chin on his fist.

Her eyes danced in the lights that showcased the bottles in front of the mirrored wall.

She looked as he remembered her: brown shaggy hair, usually pulled back with a running headband, brown eyes, plump lips.

Marta rarely fussed with makeup, complaining she would only sweat it off, and she usually did.

Tonight, she wore a nylon running skirt with a Tower City Marathon tank top. A Tower City Marathon running jacket hung from the back of her stool.

She looked like the life-long runner she was, her face showing the wear and tear of what she did for a living, lined from strain and sun exposure, her eyes hardened from the vicious training schedule she endured to keep in shape.

Or had that been Brett and what he'd done to her?

Ian rolled his shoulders in an attempt to ease his stress. He didn't like thinking about Marta's history with Brett, but he could never seem to help himself.

"She invited me for coffee later this week. I'll probably go because it'll be nice to know people on campus. I'm going to be spending a lot of time there."

"It's great you're making friends right out of the gate."

"She's not usually there after spring semester, but she

needed to offer a summer course. How about you? Any plans for this summer?"

Ian never made plans.

Stacking glasses under the bar, he shook his head.

"Nothing. I'll help you move into your apartment. That's the most exciting thing I've got going on right now."

He tried to play it cool, but he was looking forward to spending time with her a lot more than he should. And it wasn't entirely true, there were things that needed his attention, but he didn't want to load her down with his problems.

Like the twenty-one-year-old delinquent slamming her way into the bar.

"Hey, where've you been?"

"Leave me alone!"

Sadie, Ian's little sister by thirteen years, crashed through a door that opened to a stairway leading to their living quarters on the second floor.

"What was that about?" Marta asked, eyebrows raised as a door upstairs crashed.

Normally they wouldn't have been able to hear Sadie's display of temper, but tonight the jukebox had run out of quarters, and neither he nor Marta had fed the machine to keep it going.

The silence was welcome, and often when the bar was empty, he cleaned in the quiet, or used the time to catch up on his reading.

It wasn't good for business, but he preferred it when no one was around.

"My sister, Sadie. She's bitter our parents aren't coming back from their permanent vacation. They prefer their house in Georgia to the apartment upstairs, and they have no interest in moving back—it's too cold."

Marta took another sip of her beer.

"How do you think you're going to fare this winter?"

Marta shifted on her stool and stuck her tongue out at him. "I used to live here, remember?"

Yeah, Ian remembered.

He could recall every second of their time at the university.

Every study group, every pizza run, every drunken sleepover.

Dane and Liz, Dane's girlfriend back then, and Brett and Marta. Ian and whatever chick he'd been hanging with at the time.

His years at the university had been bittersweet because every moment he spent with Marta was another second he knew she would never be his.

---

*Running Scared* is available in paperback, Kindle, and Kindle Unlimited. You don't have to wait to read Ian and Marta's story.

---

Read it today!

# ABOUT THE AUTHOR

Vania Rheault has lived in Minnesota all her life. In 2003, she graduated with a BA in English with a concentration in creative writing from Minnesota State University, Moorhead. When she's not writing, she's reading, playing with one of her three cats, or going to movie night with her sister.

Find Vania on www.vaniamargene.com and these social media platforms:

www.ingramcontent.com/pod-product-compliance
Lightning Source LLC
Chambersburg PA
CBHW021001120726

47905CB00009B/2805